LOVE YOU TO DEATH

BOOKS BY ANYA MORA

Good Bad Mother

LOVE YOU TO DEATH

ANYA MORA

bookouture

Published by Bookouture in 2025

An imprint of Storyfire Ltd.
Carmelite House
50 Victoria Embankment
London EC4Y 0DZ

www.bookouture.com

The authorised representative in the EEA is Hachette Ireland
8 Castlecourt Centre
Dublin 15 D15 XTP3
Ireland
(email: info@hbgi.ie)

ISBN: 978-1-83618-467-6
eBook ISBN: 978-1-83618-466-9

PROLOGUE

Something is wrong.

My old wedding album is on the coffee table, pristine and out of place, its glossy cover reflecting the dim light. I haven't opened it in years. It should be in the storage unit with the rest of my late husband's things.

"I didn't put that there..." I whisper to myself, the words thin and brittle.

But that's not what makes my stomach drop.

A loose photograph rests on top. My fingers go cold as I reach for it. The moment my eyes register what I'm looking at, a jagged exhale slices through the silence.

Sadie.

My daughter's bright, innocent face—obliterated. Deep, violent scratches carve through her features, crude gouges cutting her out of the memory. Someone did this with something sharp. Someone wanted to erase her.

A strangled sound escapes me. "*No.*"

My pulse thrashes in my throat. My fingers tremble as I run them over the torn paper, feeling the grooves where something cruel dug into my little girl's face.

The air feels too heavy as panic builds in my chest like a scream I can't release.

Who did this?

ONE

THREE MONTHS EARLIER

My daughter isn't here.

I stand up from the picnic blanket, scanning the waterfront park, looking for Sadie. The sun is still high in the sky. It is a rare and welcome sight after months of dreary rain. In Silverport, a small inlet town in Washington, gray skies are the norm—the light is a gift as we usher in summer.

Where would she have gone? I bite my bottom lip, trying to gauge how panicked I should be. Looking at my phone, I realize I dozed off for a while. Maybe thirty minutes. Lots of terrible things can happen in that length of time. And none of them is worth the short-lived glory of a midafternoon nap.

Sadie isn't a toddler who would have wandered off and gotten lost. But at eleven years old, it's not like her to go off without telling me. I swallow, not seeing anyone anywhere. It's a secluded park, one we like to frequent for that reason. I'm not a social butterfly. I'm a bit of a hermit, if I'm being honest. A quiet park on the last day of school seemed ideal, but now I wonder if being here alone was a dangerous idea.

My heart pounds as panic begins to rise. I cup my hands around my mouth, calling for her.

"Sadie!"

My voice is loud, much louder than normal. I'm not the kind of person who often raises her voice or gets angry. I am calm and steady—which is a nice way of saying I suppress nearly all my emotions.

"Sadie!" I call again.

My pulse starts to hammer against my throat, each beat louder than the last. On the picnic blanket there is an abandoned coloring book and a set of new markers—gifts I got her for the last day of fifth grade.

With shaking hands, I grab my phone from the blanket, shoving it in my back pocket before walking quickly toward the bathrooms. Maybe she wandered off without me noticing and got locked in a stall or something? Unlikely, but possible.

At the restrooms, I yank open the women's door. "Sadie?" I call. No one answers. I peer under all the stalls. They're empty. No one's here. The walls blur at the edges as I turn to exit the bathroom.

I gasp. As I step back outside, I walk right into a man, nearly nose-to-nose.

"Oh my God." I press a hand to my chest, not having expected to quite literally run into a stranger.

He's handsome. I clock that, but I can't focus on his startlingly clear blue eyes right now. I have to find my daughter.

"What's wrong?" he asks, his light brown brows knit together in worry. His blonde hair falls across his forehead, wavy and sun-drenched. "I heard you calling, shouting for someone. Do you need help?"

Tears well in my eyes, and I shake my head. "This can't be happening," I whisper, ready to burst into tears. I cannot lose my daughter. Fear spreads through my body, my blood running cold at the thought.

"What can't be happening?" he asks kindly.

My priority is finding Sadie. I step past him, walking back

toward my picnic blanket. "I can't find my daughter," I tell him, my voice tight and tearful.

He's tall, broad-shouldered, handsome, and he follows me. I run a hand through my long black hair. "She was here, but I dozed off," I say, my voice quiet, nearly a whisper. "We'd been here for a few hours. She was coloring, and then..." I swallow. "I can't believe I fell asleep. What kind of mother am I?"

He frowns. "One who is rightfully worried," he says, "but come on, we can find her. You don't have to do this alone."

"Thank you," I say, as a cold sweat breaks out on my brow line. Together we run down to the tree line. "Maybe she went in the water?" My voice is cracked with fear. "She's not a good swimmer..." Beyond us is the rocky shore of Puget Sound.

He leans down, his hand running through the salt water. "It's icy."

In the distance, there are some kayakers, but they're far away and certainly not an eleven-year-old girl. Terrifying thoughts crash into one another as I imagine not finding Sadie.

"Maybe she went back to your car?" he suggests, scanning the waterfront. "If she isn't there, we can look on the trails."

"She's all I have in the world. I can't lose her," I say, panic coiling through my rib cage.

"You *didn't* lose her. We're going to find her," he says. He's calm and steady, and the fact that he knows how to comfort a worried mom means something. It touches me.

"Thank you..." I search for his name. "Sorry, I'm Anna. What was your name?"

"Parker," he tells me with a gentle smile. "Come on. Where's your car?"

"It's the silver SUV up ahead," I say, pointing over the hill to the small parking lot.

Running, we quickly reach my car. But she's not there. "Maybe I should call the police?"

But just then, Parker turns and points. "Is that her?"

I turn back toward where our picnic blanket is spread out, and there she is: Sadie, sitting cross-legged with her marker in hand. Her curly black hair frames the gentle expression on her face.

"Oh *thank God.*" Warmth spreads through my body, melting the icy grip of fear. I run toward her, the knot in my stomach loosening with each stride.

We get to the blanket, and I kneel down, panting. "Sadie," I ask, "where did you go?"

"What do you mean?" Sadie frowns. "You fell asleep, so I walked to the water." She points to a pile of rocks she's collected, some broken clamshells. "I was over at the beach, looking for treasures. I took the long way back, through the woods."

There is a clamshell in her hand, and she's using a marker to draw a heart on it. She's creative, and I appreciate her spirit. I shake my head. "I was so scared something had happened," I mutter.

"Sorry," she says, then looking up at the man, "Hi," she says. "I'm Sadie."

"I'm Parker," he says, crouching down, offering her his hand. She shakes it.

I turn to Parker, a strange mixture of gratitude and vulnerability settling within me. "Thank you again," I say, wishing I could fully express how much his presence has been an unexpected blessing.

He stands, his warm gaze meeting mine, and offers a small, reassuring smile. "No problem at all. Turns out I wasn't much help, but I'm glad she's safe." He takes a few steps backward toward the trails. "See you around, Anna. Sadie."

"Yeah," I murmur, watching him go. I have an overwhelming urge to say more. I want to thank him properly, but the words get caught in my throat as he disappears down the trail. Instead, I turn back to Sadie, relief washing over me like a flood.

I pull her close, kissing the top of her head. "I thought I'd lost you," I whisper, unable to keep the tremor from my voice.

Sadie looks up at me, her eyes wide and sincere. "Mom, I'm not going anywhere. Promise."

Her words hit me like a jolt, and I cling to her, feeling the ache of everything I have lost. It's as if life is testing me, waiting to see how much more I can bear. There is a sting behind my eyes, but I force myself to blink the tears away. I have to be strong for my daughter.

I think of Parker again, wishing I'd managed to say more. His kindness steadied me in a moment when I was slipping. I try to gather myself, but the thought lingers. There is a hollow ache within me. A fear that I can't protect the people I love from life's cruel turns.

"Come on, honey," I say, standing and brushing off my knees. "Let's go home."

Taking a tight hold of her hand, we walk back to the car. She says she is too old to hold hands, but I'm not letting go until we're safely inside. My mind is still replaying the moment I thought she was missing.

I've already lost my husband. I can't lose my daughter too.

TWO

Two days later, I'm with Sadie at the Silverport Co-op, getting a few groceries. Just as I've added a bag of Pink Lady apples to my cart, she nudges me with her elbow.

"Mom," Sadie whispers, "look, it's that man from the park."

I turn, looking up, and see Parker on the other side of the produce aisle. He's picking out avocados. In his cart, I see cilantro, limes and tomatoes. He looks even more handsome than I remember. He's tall and broad, built like he was carved from something strong. His shoulders were made for gripping, with arms that stretch the fabric of his sleeves just enough to make you stare.

Quickly, I give myself a mental inventory. My dress is soft and worn-in, like a favorite memory, its earthy tone blending in quietly. My long dark hair falls over one shoulder in a loose braid, though a few pieces have slipped free, brushing against my cheeks. I tuck them back behind my ears, glancing down at my leather sandals, scuffed and familiar. I tighten my hold on my woven tote, the coarse handle pressing into my palm. I half wish I could disappear into the background.

I smile in his direction, feeling a warm heat creeping in, hoping no one else has noticed.

"Mom, why are you *blushing*?" Sadie asks, her brows knit together.

I realize my daughter is less of a little girl every day. At this moment, she seems like the middle schooler she is about to be at the end of summer.

Ignoring Sadie's comment, I push my cart toward him. "Hey," I say. "Parker, right?"

He looks up, two avocados in hand, and grins. Parker has the kind of face that makes people stop mid-sentence—strong jaw, high cheekbones and blue eyes that make me melt. "Hey. Anna and Sadie, the girls who got away."

His voice is a problem. Low and smooth, with just enough rasp to make your pulse trip over itself. I smile in a way I haven't smiled in months—in at least six months, to be precise. For a moment, guilt tugs at me for smiling, for finding joy in another man. But then it passes. I'm thinking about Parker, the man in front of me, who's asking Sadie what she's up to. I focus on the present moment, knowing that, really, that's all we have.

My daughter twists her lips together, as if proving her disinterest. I nudge her, not wanting her to be rude. She sighs loudly. "I'm going to my friend Tabby's house tonight for a sleepover. Mom said I can pick out some junk food to take," Sadie says.

Parker nods, then looks at the cart. "Apples count as junk food in your house?"

Sadie smirks at that. "No, my mom isn't that crazy. We were grocery shopping too."

He smiles warmly. "In that case, there's a tough decision you've got to make. Sweet or savory?"

Sadie shrugs, not giving him an inch. Inwardly I wonder why I want my daughter to be polite to this stranger. But then I look up at him, his kind eyes softening my edges.

Finally she answers him, "I've already decided. I'm bringing a giant bag of caramel corn." She cocks her head. "What are you doing tonight? Looking for single moms in the produce aisle?"

In many ways I appreciate how forthright my daughter is. Sadie is so outgoing, speaks her mind—the true opposite of me. I've never been like her. Even when I was young, I was reserved and withdrawn. Of course, I had been shuffled from home to home as a foster child, never having a family of my own to depend on. I never felt secure enough to be myself entirely.

But Sadie is safe. And she's like her father was—a big personality.

Parker takes Sadie's snark in stride, and without missing a beat, he laughs. It's rough-edged and warm, a sound that lands in your stomach and lingers there. "I was planning on making some guacamole. I have carne asada marinating at home."

"Fancy." She walks away, looking over her shoulder. "I'm gonna go get some bananas, okay, Mom?"

"Okay," I say softly, feeling like parenting a preteen is getting more difficult each day. I turn to Parker. "Sorry about that. She's had a hard year."

Parker smiles easily. "No worries." I see his eyes flicker down to my left hand. There's no ring. And then my eyes look to his hand. No ring there either.

I press my lips together. "Well," I say. "It was nice seeing you again."

"It was," he says.

There's a pause. His blue eyes don't stop looking at me.

"I know this is forward, but do you want to come over for tacos tonight?"

My eyes widen, then dart over to Sadie who is now at the deli counter, completely uninterested in Parker. But me, I find myself inexplicably drawn to him. I can't explain it, but I am. "Do you live around here?" I ask him.

"Not always," he clarifies. "I have a little beach cabin on this side of the water. My condo is over in Seattle. I'm a professor at the University of Washington. On sabbatical for the upcoming year."

"I see. So, you come out to Silverport when you want a getaway?"

He nods. "Yeah, especially in the summer months. It's so beautiful. Seattle's great, but it's busy, loud."

"I get it," I say. "I hardly ever go to the city. I prefer the peace and quiet."

"Well, if you want to come over for tacos, the deck is open. With a gorgeous view of the water."

I press my lips together, already knowing what I want to do. "All right," I say, unexpectedly excited at the prospect of a date. It's been only six months, yet I feel a small flicker of hope blossoming in my chest. "That sounds nice."

"Perfect," he says. "Do you like margaritas?"

"I love them," I tell him honestly, with a rush of excitement.

"Great. Come over after you drop Sadie off. I'll text you my address."

We pull out our phones and exchange information. I create a contact for him, already knowing I don't want to lose this connection.

A few moments later, I push my cart toward Sadie. I debate telling her my plans for the evening, and I almost do. But I hold back. There is no need to involve my eleven-year-old in my dating life.

I haven't dated anyone since... I swallow hard, the weight of the past months settling heavily on me. I haven't dated anyone since my husband.

Theo.

Even just thinking about him makes my chest hurt and my throat burn. I blink hard, pushing down the rising swell of emotion.

After six months I still catch myself looking for his car in the driveway, half expecting him to walk through the door at the end of the day.

But now he's gone, and here I am, making plans to meet someone new. The thought exposes me and makes me vulnerable. It feels wrong somehow.

Am I ready for this?

"Should we find the caramel corn?" I ask brightly, focusing on my daughter instead.

Later, as we load our groceries into the car, my phone vibrates with a text. I glance down, seeing Parker's name. My heart skips as I open it.

Can't wait to see you tonight. Feels like fate to run into you again.

His excitement is palpable, and a wave of guilt washes over me. Sadie chatters away about her sleepover as I drive, blissfully unaware of my swirling thoughts.

Theo's memory hangs in the car like a weight, pressing down on us. And suddenly, without warning, I'm not wondering how my date with Parker will go tonight. Instead, I am wondering whether it is even safe to let another man near me.

Because everyone believes Theo's death was an accident. But I'm not so sure.

He had secrets, and so do I.

THREE

Six weeks later, I'm twisting my brand-new diamond engagement ring around my finger. Sadie and I are both sitting on her bed, cross-legged on top of the quilt I made for her when she transitioned from a toddler bed to a twin-sized bed all those years ago.

Looking at her now, she seems more grown up than ever. She's not a teenager, but when I look at her, it's as if her childhood has already slipped away.

"It's just... all happening so *fast*, Mom."

I reach for her hand. Thankfully my daughter doesn't resist. "Six weeks *is* fast," I say gently, "but Parker and I are in love."

Maybe she's right, I admit to myself. Maybe it is too soon. But when Parker pulls me close, when he kisses me like he's been waiting his whole life to do so, I don't care about timelines. I care about him. About our family.

"I want you to be happy," Sadie says softly. "Don't think I'm trying to be, like, a problem. It's..." She pauses, choosing her words carefully. "It's just a *lot*, Mom." She shakes her head. "I still miss Dad."

"Sweetheart," I tell her, "You'll always miss Dad. *I'll* always miss Dad. He loved you so much. But no one's replacing him."

"Do you think you'll get married soon?" she asks anxiously.

I shake my head quickly. "No, there is no rush."

She rolls her eyes. "Then why did you get engaged so fast?"

I bite my bottom lip, knowing her question is valid. "It was spontaneous," I answer honestly. "I didn't expect it."

"Everything is going to be different now." Sadie curls up on her bed, turning her head to face the window, the moon swollen in the night sky.

I look around her bedroom. The walls are pink, the trim is white, and a chandelier hangs from the center of the ceiling, glass beads sparkling. I decorated this room for her when she was four. It was a lifetime ago. Now she seems much too old for this space. Where did the time go?

Her bookshelf is shaped like a dollhouse, something I lovingly picked out, considering my own fixation with creating miniature objects. Her actual dollhouse was moved to the attic a few years ago, when she decided it was too babyish and was embarrassed with the idea of girls from school seeing it. Theo moved it to the attic, and I packed away all the tiny pieces of handmade furniture I had spent hours crafting.

Everything is different now. The family that once existed has been packed away too, but instead of simply tucking it away in the back of the attic, it's stored as a living memory in the corners of my heart.

I squeeze Sadie's hand.

"Are you upset," I ask her softly, "that Parker and I didn't talk to you first, or...?"

She doesn't answer. Instead she asks, "Is he moving in?"

I bite my bottom lip. "We haven't figured that all out yet, sweetheart. I want him to live here so we can share more of our life with him before we get married."

"I'm leaving for Grandma and Grandpa's in two days," she says quietly. "That's not changing, is it?"

I shake my head. "Of course not. They're so excited to have you this summer. That's not going to change at all." She's going to her father's parents' house in the countryside for a month—it's been the routine for the last five years, and she adores it.

"Good," she says, "because Grandma got eight new chickens, and I was planning on naming them all."

I smile and reach for her, wrapping my arms around her and kissing her head. "You'll name them all," I say. "And I was thinking, maybe when you get home, before school starts, we can redecorate your bedroom."

She beams up at me then. "*Really?*"

"I know you've been saying it's too 'little kid' for ages. So, yeah, after your time at Grandma and Grandpa's farm, we can do that project together. Maybe even get you a vanity so you can put out all your makeup and hair stuff."

She grins, and I know I've said the right thing. I'm not trying to buy my daughter's love, but giving her this olive branch seems to make it easier for her to swallow all this change. The timing seems to be lining up well for me too. Not that I need her gone while Parker moves in, but it might be nice for us to adjust at a slower pace, one step at a time.

"So how did he ask you?" Sadie says, leaning back on her pillow. I lie down beside her, my arm wrapped around her.

"We were out at his cabin on the waterfront, sitting on the deck. We had tacos like we did on our first date. And he asked if I would be his wife. He said he wanted to spend his life with me —with *us*."

"You really love him?" she asks after a moment.

"Yeah," I say. "I really do."

"Was it love at first sight?"

"Not exactly," I say with a small laugh. "But maybe love at third date?"

She groans. "Okay. That's still pretty fast, right?"

"I don't know. Love is a tricky thing, Sadie. And it's different for everyone, for every relationship."

I don't tell her more; I don't tell her that I've been in love exactly two other times in my life. Instead, I kiss her on the forehead.

"Tomorrow will be busy," I say. "We've got to do laundry and pack up all your things."

"Will I see Parker before I go?" she asks.

"He'll be here tomorrow morning," I say. "He says he's going to bring donuts and coffee."

She sticks out her tongue playfully. "I guess he does sound like a pretty good guy."

I smile, standing from the bed. "I love you, Sadie."

"I love you more, Mama."

I close her door, hoping she can sleep soundly with my life-changing news. Sadie wanted to know if I loved Parker. Of course I do. There is no way she could understand how sometimes, when he held me, there was a feeling I couldn't place—like comfort tinged with déjà vu. It is the warmth of moving forward, I suppose.

When I get to my bedroom, I pull out my phone before I even take off my shoes and socks. I text Parker. *I told her. She seems okay about it.*

He replies right away. *Oh, baby, I'm so glad. I wish I were there with you right now to hold you tight.*

Soon enough, I tell him. *I'll see you in the morning.*

Yep, he answers. *With your iced vanilla latte and Sadie's hot chocolate.*

I love you so much, Parker Madison.

And I love you so much, soon-to-be Mrs. Madison.

I set my phone down, my cheeks hurting from smiling so much.

I never imagined in a million years that I would be engaged

less than a year after my husband died. But here I am, a large diamond ring on my finger and a grin on my face. I lie back in my bed, wanting to hold on to this moment as long as possible. There's been enough pain, enough suffering in the last few years—not only with Theo's death, but with all the secrets and lies that came before it.

Now, though, that can all be put behind me. I can look toward the future with bright eyes, with hope. Because all that pain from my past isn't going to be a part of my future.

And as for Parker—he must never find out. About any of it.

FOUR

Client Notes: Initial Observations

Session: Intake

Summary:

The subject's grief appears calculated—crafted, even. Beneath the surface of their carefully chosen words lies something unspoken, something far heavier than sorrow. Their partner's name was barely mentioned, yet the weight of their absence filled the room like static in the air.

Key Observations:

- **Control:** Their language felt rehearsed, their emotions boxed neatly away.
- **Distance:** When asked about their partner, they deflected with practicalities. But the moments of silence that followed felt louder than their words.

Note: They twisted their wedding band throughout the session. When the partner's name was mentioned, their grip tightened.

Therapist Reflection:

Their narrative is like a puzzle, one where the missing pieces could change everything. As they left the room, I couldn't shake the feeling that I was looking at the calm before the storm.

Conclusion:

This is not simply grief. There's a game at play here—one I might not fully understand yet.

FIVE

"I love you so much," I tell Sadie, not wanting to say goodbye quite yet. A chill settles over me, though the sun is warm on my back. I blame it on nerves and try to shake it off, reminding myself this is just another summer goodbye. Sadie is exactly where she should be for the next month.

Her grandparents, Theo's parents, Marsha and Conrad, are standing a few feet away on the front porch of their big white farmhouse. They have a beautiful home and property, and I'm thankful that my daughter gets to spend a whole month of her summer here. If she were home, she'd be growing up way too fast. When she's out here in the wide-open spaces of the twenty-acre farm, she can let the rest of the world fade away for a little while.

"Can we speak for a moment before I go?" I ask Marsha and Conrad. Sadie runs off with the dog, leaving me alone with her grandparents.

"Everything all right?" Marsha asks, her brows creasing.

"Sure," I begin. "I just wanted to fill you in on our life a bit." I pause, my heart pounding all of a sudden. I had been mentally preparing myself for this conversation while driving over, but now it's here. "The thing is, I got engaged this week."

Silence.

"To be *married*?" Marsha asks, her voice sharp with alarm.

I swallow. "I know it's a surprise," I say. "His name is Parker Madison. Sadie knows, of course. But it's a bit of a shock. Being here with you is good timing, I think."

Marsha stares at me, lips pressed so tightly together they disappear.

"Is there a wedding date?" Conrad asks finally, his voice unreadable.

I shake my head. "Nothing is set yet. It's all very new."

Marsha exhales. "Six months," she murmurs, mostly to herself.

My stomach tightens.

"Well, I suppose congratulations are in order," she says, but there's no warmth in her voice. She wipes at the corner of her eye, then steps forward, giving me a quick, tight hug. Her hand lingers on my arm, but when she pulls back, I see something in her eyes—something heavier than grief. It's disappointment.

Not just disappointment. *Disbelief.*

She pauses. "Are you okay, Anna?"

The question lands differently this time, like she's asking if I've *lost my mind.*

I nod quickly, pushing down an unexpected surge of emotion. "I worry about Sadie, but I think everything will be fine," I say lightly, hoping my weariness doesn't show.

Marsha shakes her head. "I hope so..."

She looks over at Conrad as if prompting him to say something. He crosses his arms instead.

"You're moving on... *fast*," he says finally, voice low.

I blink, my face heating. "I—"

Marsha turns away, rubbing her forehead, before facing me again. "It's just... Theo's barely gone, Anna. And you're getting *married?*" She shakes her head. "What are we supposed to tell Sadie about that? About what it means to love someone?"

"This has nothing to do with my love for Theo."

"Doesn't it?" Her voice is soft, but the words cut.

Conrad looks past me, his eyes settling on Sadie. "She's just a little girl. She's already lost her father. And now, what? She's getting a replacement?"

"That's not fair," I say, my voice unsteady.

"Neither is burying your son," Marsha whispers.

The words hit me like a slap. A hot flush of shame creeps up my neck. I open my mouth, but I don't know what to say.

Marsha glances toward Sadie, her expression unreadable. Then she nods once, like she's made some sort of decision. "We will take good care of her."

She says it with such finality, it makes my chest tighten.

Marsha looks at Conrad again, prompting him to move. A quick side hug from him suffices.

"I hope you have a great month," Marsha says finally. "We'll be in touch. FaceTime whenever you want."

Sadie runs over, and I kneel down to hug her, holding on for a beat longer than usual. Her hair is warm from the sun, and for a second, I don't want to let go.

"Call and text me," I whisper.

"Okay, Mama. Talk soon."

As she runs toward the chickens, a pang of nostalgia washes over me, elusive and fleeting, like an old song I can't recall.

I swallow hard and get in the car.

I don't look back.

The mountain road stretches ahead in a blur of green and gold, sunlight flickering through the trees. I merge onto the highway, turning off the radio, letting the silence settle around me. It feels right—*me, alone with my thoughts.* And right now, I have plenty.

Am I really doing this?

I grip the wheel tighter.

Yes. Yes, I am. Of course I am.

Marsha and Conrad don't get to decide this for me. They don't get to dictate how long grief should last, how soon is too soon to build a life again.

Parker loves me. He loves Sadie. And yet—

She's already lost her father. And now, what? She's getting a replacement?

I exhale sharply, shaking it off. *They're wrong.*

Three hours later, I call Parker on speakerphone as I near my house. "I'm almost home, only a few minutes away," I say, forcing a smile into my voice.

"Great," he says, his voice warm. "I'll probably get there around the same time as you. It's crazy, isn't it? Already moving in together," he chuckles.

"Yes," I reply, my voice steady. "But if you'd rather, we could always spend some time at your beach house too. We don't have to rush into moving everything here."

"Oh, didn't I mention? I've rented it out for the month."

"You didn't mention that," I say, a note of surprise creeping in. "Is it someone you know?"

"No," he explains casually. "I list it now and then, during months I won't be there."

"That makes sense," I say, noting my husband-to-be's practicality.

"Extra money for our wedding."

"Our *wedding*," I echo as I drive. "What did your sister say about the engagement?" I ask, eager to keep the conversation light. I've heard lots about his sister, Helen, though we haven't met yet. She lives in Seattle, and has been out of town traveling since Parker and I started dating.

"She was speechless," he admits.

I laugh lightly. "So were my in-laws. Well, *ex*-in-laws. Or old in-laws? I don't really know what to call them."

"How about Marsha and Conrad?" he suggests.

"That works." I force a smile. "Well, they were... surprised, to say the least."

His tone shifts. "Did they take it all right?"

I hesitate, then nod to myself. "I think so." The words feel thin, unconvincing. "Sadie seems okay with it, as far as I can tell."

My gaze drifts to the horizon, the weight of the conversation pressing against my chest.

"I think it's going to be great," he assures me. "Now, get home so I can drag you into bed."

I laugh, ending the call and feeling the quiet settle around me again.

I pull up to the house and unlock the front door, stepping inside the home that's been mine for a little over a decade. Theo and I bought this place right after Sadie was born. It was a big step, scraping together a down payment and making an offer on a cozy Victorian that needed tender loving care, tucked a few blocks from downtown Silverport.

We never outgrew it, even though I had hoped we would. Little by little, we renovated each room, making it our own. "Home" has always felt like a place where I could heal, a place to put down roots. It's no wonder my work revolves around crafting dollhouses and tiny furnishings. I've spent years creating little scenes of lives I never had as a child.

When Theo died, I couldn't imagine living anywhere else. This house wasn't just a place—it was our life. The creak in the third stair, the paint splatter on the kitchen floor from when we tried to DIY the cabinets, even the lingering smell of the lavender candles he hated but humored me with—all of it held pieces of him. Moving would have disrupted too much, for both Sadie and me. And maybe, deep down, I felt like leaving would confirm what I was terrified to admit: that I didn't deserve to move on.

While memories of Theo linger in the house, his belongings have been packed away. A month ago, I rented a storage unit and moved all his things there.

Some things felt impossible to box up—his old leather wallet, still scuffed at the edges, the worn flannel shirts he always reached for, even in the summer heat. I considered donating everything to charity, but I thought of Sadie, of what she might like to have as she gets older. So everything was packed away in the unit.

Now, as I enter my home, preparing for a new man to move in, I try to push the past away.

But it clings to me.

SIX

SEVEN MONTHS EARLIER

I wake to the sound of Theo moving through the house. The morning light is soft and gray. The house is quiet. For a moment, I lie there, cocooned in warmth, willing it to be enough.

By the time I reach the kitchen, my husband is ready to leave. His hiking bag is slung over one shoulder, a thermos of coffee is waiting on the counter. He already smells like pine needles and fresh air, like movement and distance.

"You're leaving early," I murmur, pouring my own coffee.

"Wanted a head start." He zips up his jacket without looking at me. "Should be back midafternoon."

I nod, watching him with an odd detachment. He is steady and practical, always following through on his plans. Unease stirs within me. "Be careful."

"I always am." He steps closer, pressing a kiss to my forehead. The gesture is perfunctory, but I close my eyes and lean into it.

It's been months since he kissed me properly. Longer, maybe.

I can pinpoint when the shift happened—when his hands

stopped lingering, when my body became something he moved around instead of toward.

Now, all that's left are these careful gestures. A forehead kiss. A passing touch that barely registers. Small mercies to keep us from acknowledging the growing space between us.

And yet, I still lean into him.

Because even now, I don't know how to reach across the gap.

And then he's gone, the door clicking shut behind him, the sound lingering louder than it should in the silent house.

The morning drags on. I try to fill it—cleaning, laundry, anything to quiet the thoughts swirling in my mind. Sadie is in the living room drawing, her small body hunched over in concentration.

"Hey, kiddo," I say. She looks up, smiling, and the sight immediately grounds me.

Sadie is warmth. Sadie is light. Where Theo has drifted further away, she has only pulled me closer.

I watch as she carefully selects a color, filling in the sky with streaks of blue, completely absorbed in the tiny world she is creating. There is nothing hesitant about her. No uncertainty in the way she exists.

I wish I could give her more. She deserves a home that doesn't feel like it's shifting beneath her feet. A mother who isn't always carrying something unspoken. A father who doesn't vanish into the wilderness and come back quieter than before.

I kneel beside her, brushing her hair back from her face. "What are you drawing?"

She grins, holding it up. "A house. But it's different. The roof is pink."

I swallow, the ache deep but familiar.

"I love it," I whisper.

And for now, that has to be enough.

Later, we make hot cocoa, piled high with whipped cream, laughter spilling between us like sunlight into a dark room.

"Let's go sledding tomorrow," I say.

Sadie's eyes brighten. "Really?"

"*Really.*" And for the first time in weeks, a flicker of hope within me. Maybe this is how it starts—choosing happiness, one moment at a time.

But then the phone rings, slicing through the quiet. My heart leaps at the sound. For a split second, I can't help but wonder if it will be the one person I told never to call here again. The one person I can't help but hope rings every time I hear the phone.

I answer without thinking. "Hello?"

"Mrs. Caldwell?"

It isn't him.

The voice is clipped, unfamiliar. "This is Officer Carter with the State Park Service. I'm afraid there's been an incident involving your husband."

Something cold creeps up my spine. "What kind of... incident?"

"He was found at the base of a ravine." A pause. "I'm afraid... he didn't survive the fall."

The phone slips from my hand.

The world tilts.

"Mom?" Sadie's voice, high-pitched and frightened. She tugs at my arm, her small hands clutching my sweater. "What's wrong? What happened?"

I kneel, pulling her close, my voice breaking. "It's Dad. He's... he's gone."

Her wail cuts through me, raw and primal. I hold her tightly, trying to absorb her grief, trying to keep us both from falling apart. I see Theo's hiking boots by the front door, wondering why he didn't wear them. It was icy out. He knew better than that. I know he did.

My best friend Jillian arrives hours later, her coat dusted with snow. She pulls me into her arms, says nothing, just holds me as I break down all over again.

"It's going to be okay," she whispers into my hair, though we both know it won't.

That night, Sadie is curled on one side of me, Jillian on the other. The house is silent, but my mind is anything but. I replay the morning over and over, searching for something I missed.

A sign. A warning. *Something.*

But there's nothing.

And yet, one thought keeps creeping in, relentless.

Was my husband's death really an accident?

SEVEN

PRESENT DAY

Back home, I slip off my shoes and pour a glass of lemonade, savoring the quiet. Knowing soon enough, everything will change.

I'm only a few sips in before there's a knock at the door.

I walk to answer it, finding Parker on the porch, holding a bouquet of pink roses.

His arms wrap around me—strong, steady, familiar—pulling me close. The tension in my shoulders unravels as I sink against him. He always feels like certainty, like solid ground beneath my feet.

"Welcome home," he murmurs, his words warm against my skin. He kisses me, his scent wrapping around me—clean, fresh, laced with something unmistakably him.

I exhale, pressing my face into the roses. Soft petals, sharp thorns, a contradiction—like love itself.

"Gosh, I adore them," I say softly, inhaling their fragrance.

After setting the roses in a vase on the kitchen counter, we head to his car to bring in the few suitcases he brought. Together, we carry them up to the bedroom. Yesterday morning, along with the donuts, Parker had brought some boxes of his belongings. After he left, I finished unpacking them, realizing just how different my life would now be. Parker moving in was altering the course of my life forever. The weight of the change was not lost on me.

Today, though, has already stretched on for so long, with the lengthy round trip to the farm. Now, the edges of this new reality begin to settle over me, and I realize I need a moment alone.

"I'm going to take a quick shower," I tell Parker. "It got so hot on the drive." Sadie's grandparents live over in Eastern Washington, a full three hours away. The moment you cross the mountain range, the heat swells, dry and desertlike.

"All right, baby," he says, giving me a quick kiss. "I'll unpack these." As I walk to the stairs, I notice Parker's keys are already on the hook by the front door.

He lives here now.

The thought follows me into the bathroom. Steam curls around me as I step into the shower, the heat swallowing me whole. I tilt my head back, letting the water rush over me, trying to let it loosen the tightness in my chest.

I should be happy. This is a fresh start, isn't it?

A new life. A new husband.

And yet—

My fingers press against the cool tile as a wave of unease settles over me.

Six months ago, Theo stood here. His razor by the sink. His aftershave lingering in the air. His side of the bed still warm.

Now, Parker's shirts are in the closet. His shoes next to the bed. His toothbrush next to mine, standing in the exact same spot Theo's used to be.

I tell myself this is normal. People move on, they rebuild.

Then why does it feel like I'm walking through a house haunted by a life that isn't mine anymore?

I squeeze my eyes shut, trying to drown out the whispers of guilt.

I love Parker. I *do.* He is good and kind and steady, and I want this—want *him.* But I can't shake the feeling that I'm standing in a place that still remembers someone else.

He will sleep on what used to be Theo's side of the bed.

His voice will echo in the kitchen where Theo's once did.

His hands will touch me, trace the same paths, whisper the same promises in the dark.

And when Sadie calls for her father in the middle of the night, will she expect Theo's voice? Or will Parker's be enough?

I press my forehead to the tile, water dripping down my spine like fingers tracing an outline of something already fading.

Theo is gone.

Parker is here.

And I—

I'm somewhere in between.

By the time I step out of the shower, my skin is flushed from the heat, my emotions raw. I wrap myself in a towel and run a comb through my hair, shaking off the last threads of doubt. Stepping out of the bathroom, I walk into the bedroom. It's empty, and I assume Parker went downstairs.

"Parker?"

Silence.

My stomach tightens.

"Parker?"

Still nothing.

I move toward the door, listening for movement. The house feels different now—too quiet, too still. Unease slithers up my spine.

I glance out the bedroom window. His car is gone.

My pulse spikes, my fingers tightening around the towel. My mind moves too fast, too far, a flood of thoughts crashing into me before I can stop them.

What if something happened?

What if he left and never came back?

What if—

I reach for my phone on the bedside table with unsteady hands. A text is waiting.

Just ran out to get us some dinner. Love you, baby.

I exhale sharply, my shoulders dropping, but the panic still lingers beneath my skin, buzzing like static. The way it always does when someone I love disappears. Theo left one morning and never walked through the door again. One second he was here, the next he was gone, and nothing—not the police, not the prayers, not the desperate screaming pleas inside my head— could bring him back.

And now, my body doesn't know how to separate absence from abandonment.

I squeeze my eyes shut, pressing a hand to my chest. Parker is coming back. He's fine. I am fine.

As I turn, my gaze catches on the dresser—Theo's old dresser—and the object resting on top of it. A bottle of cologne.

My heart stops.

I would recognize that bottle anywhere. I pick it up, my hand shaking. It's half-empty. I recognize the scent of leather mixed with sandalwood as well—it's Theo through and through. It is the cologne my husband always wore, every day. My dead husband.

Parker has never worn cologne at all. He says he doesn't like it. He smells like the shower, like fresh air, like sunshine.

I stare at the bottle in my trembling hand, feeling a chill run down my spine. It shouldn't be here—I packed everything away and took it to the storage unit myself. But the scent lingers, rich and familiar, as if Theo had just been standing right next to me. As if someone just sprayed it into the room.

A shadow seems to stretch across the bedroom, darkening the walls. I catch the faintest whiff of sandalwood, as if the scent itself is settling into the space, clinging to the air around me.

I close my eyes, suddenly uneasy. When I open them, the bottle is cold, damp in my hand. I set it down slowly, my heart racing and palms sweating as I glance around the empty bedroom. The quiet presses in.

A dark, quiet certainty settles over me.

This is just the beginning.

EIGHT

When Parker gets back to the house, he finds me sitting on the bed.

"Did you get some takeout?" I ask.

He smiles. "Yeah, I put it on the kitchen counter. I got Thai food. Peanut satay sound good?"

I nod. "That's great," I tell him, swallowing hard. My eyes dart over to the dresser, where the cologne is sitting.

His eyes follow mine, and he frowns. "What's that?"

I shake my head, unsure what to say.

He steps toward the dresser and picks up the bottle. "Is this a gift?" Parker's voice is deep and smooth, the kind that makes people lean in just to hear it better. He looks closer, realizing it's half-empty. "What's this for?" he asks, glancing at me.

"I was going to ask you the same thing," I say bleakly. "Is it yours?"

He sets the bottle down. "You know I don't wear cologne," he says steadily.

Confusion clouds my thoughts, and my throat is dry. This... was *Theo's* cologne. The one he wore. I don't know if this is his personal bottle, but—

"Did you put it there?" I find I have to ask the question. "Are you pranking me or something?"

Parker stares at me, confusion clouding his face.

There's a beat of silence.

"It's Theo's cologne." I finally choke out.

"Why would I do something so cruel?" Parker asks, quickly crossing the room and sitting beside me. He reaches for my hand. "Why would anyone?"

"Well, I don't understand," I reply, casting my eyes to the ceiling. "*Someone* put it there."

"Well, I didn't." He squeezes my hand, and his warm grip comforts me. "Are you suggesting some ghost of husbands past came into the house and put this bottle of cologne here while I was out getting Thai food?" He smiles gently.

"I don't know what I'm saying," I admit, laughing nervously. It's the kind of laugh that threatens to choke me. "Never mind," I say, brushing it off. "It must just have been some weird coincidence or accident or—"

Parker moves closer, looking at me. His blue eyes soften, like he's memorizing every part of my face in an effort to understand me. "Is everything all right?" he asks softly.

"Yes," I say quickly. "We're in love. We're getting married. This is the next right thing. It's just—"

He nods slowly, and my stomach growls.

"Let's get you some food," he says, wrapping an arm around my back, and pulling me in for a quick hug.

"Okay," I agree, but before heading to the kitchen, I pick up the bottle of cologne. "Why don't I just put this away real fast?"

He nods. "That sounds like a good idea."

Not wanting to make the drive all the way to the storage unit, I walk instead to the end of the hallway and open the small door leading to the attic. The narrow, steep flight of stairs creaks under my weight as I climb it quickly.

It's the place where my secrets have been hidden.

Once upstairs, I pull the cord to turn on the light. The plywood floorboards groan with each step. Sunlight streams through the circular window in the rafters, casting long shadows. The attic feels so empty now that Theo's belongings have been moved to storage. Kneeling in front of a box of old art supplies, I pull it open.

The cologne in my hand feels heavy and weighted with the past. A past that someone is trying to bring into my present.

I open the cap of the cologne, pressing down to dispense a whiff. The familiar scent of sandalwood fills the attic, wrapping around me in its nostalgic warmth.

I place the cap back on and set the bottle on top of the art journals, wanting it out of sight. Folding the tabs of the box back down, I step away, brushing dust off my knees.

I take one last look at the boxes before clicking off the light and heading downstairs.

By the time I reach the kitchen, I have put the memories aside for now. Instead, I greet Parker with a smile.

"Thank you for this," I say, wanting to put the cologne situation behind us. "I bet it was Sadie," I tell him after a moment. "Maybe she thought it was a sweet gesture. It just didn't land right."

He nods. "Actually, that makes the most sense in the world, doesn't it? She probably was trying to be thoughtful, unaware of how... uncomfortable it felt. Don't think about it again," Parker says tenderly, handing me a plate.

"This food smells delicious," I tell him, stepping close and offering a kiss. "Thank you."

We eat, gazing into each other's eyes. Maybe my happily-ever-after is just a long time coming. Maybe I have nothing to worry about. Maybe it's all going to end up better than I ever imagined.

But maybe not.

After all, the attic holds secrets. And so do I.

NINE

SIX MONTHS EARLIER

The cemetery is colder than it should be. The kind of cold that lingers and seeps into your bones. Wind cuts through my coat, but I barely register it. My eyes are locked on the dark casket being lowered into the frozen ground.

Theo's casket.

Sadie clings to my hand, her fingers trembling. At ten, she's too young to understand the permanence of what is happening, but the tears in her wide eyes tell me she understands enough.

The minister's voice drifts over the small gathering—hollow words: "beloved husband and father," "devoted friend," "gone too soon." They mean nothing. They don't touch the gaping void inside me.

Jillian stands beside me, her arm looped through mine tightly, supporting me in a way nothing else can. My friend has been my rock these past few days, the one person who hasn't tried to smooth over the jagged edges of my grief. Marsha and Conrad stand nearby, their sadness etched in quiet lines. Earlier, Sadie had clung to them for comfort. Now, she's pressed tightly against me, her trembling unmistakable.

When the minister invites final goodbyes, Jillian squeezes

my arm. "I'll be right back." She steps forward, placing a single white rose on the casket, her face tight with suppressed emotion.

Sadie looks up at me. "Mom? Do we have to?"

I kneel, brushing a strand of hair from her face. "Only if you want to. You don't have to do anything you're not ready for."

She bites her lip, glancing at the grave. "I want to go home."

I wrap my arms around her. "Okay. We'll go home."

The drive is silent. Clutching her stuffed toy, Buttercup, Sadie stares out the window but sees nothing. Jillian grips the wheel, her presence steady. When we pull into the driveway, Marsha and Conrad follow us inside, ushering Sadie away with murmured reassurances.

I linger by the car, staring at the house. It looks the same—same shutters, same porch light casting a dim glow against the evening.

But it's different now. As if Theo's absence has seeped into the siding, pressing down on the foundation, warping the shape of it. I tighten my grip on the car door.

The wake is inside. People are inside. Voices waiting, murmuring condolences over plates of catered food. But once I cross that threshold, I will be alone.

I squeeze my eyes shut.

Theo left this house alive. The last time I saw him here, he kissed my forehead, zipped up his jacket and walked out the door. I hadn't known it was a final goodbye.

Now I have to step into the aftermath.

A fresh wave of exhaustion crashes over me. I don't want to go inside. I don't want to see his boots by the door, his coffee mug still on the shelf, waiting for hands that will never reach for it again. But I have no choice.

I exhale slowly, force my feet to move.

The door swings open before I reach it. Someone—I don't

even register who—ushers me in, the warmth of the house swallowing me whole.

Inside, the house is filled with hushed voices, casseroles no one will eat, condolences that mean nothing. Jillian remains close beside me, steering me through the motions. Our housekeeper, Marla, stays, wiping counters and doing dishes, until the last guest leaves.

Jillian finds me at the kitchen table, staring at a half-empty mug of tea. "Anna," she says gently, sitting across from me. "You need to eat something."

"I'm not hungry."

She covers my hand with hers. "You don't have to do this alone. Please, let me help you."

I nod, though I don't know what help even looks like.

The days blur after that.

Marsha and Conrad stay, taking care of Sadie, handling the practicalities I can't face. Sadie clings to them, her grief spilling out in waves of tears and silence. I try to be present, to be the mother she needs. But I'm failing.

The nights are the worst. I lie in bed staring at the ceiling, replaying the moment the phone rang, the words that shattered everything. But it's not just the call that replays in my mind.

It's the last time I saw Theo. The way he stood by the door, zipping his winter coat, his expression unreadable. The way he kissed my forehead, brief and distant, like a man already halfway gone.

"Should be back midafternoon," he had said.

And I had nodded, like it was any other day. Like there hadn't been months of silence between us. Like I hadn't watched him retreat, one step at a time, without ever stopping him. Like I wasn't the reason for it.

I roll onto my side, pressing my fingers against my lips, willing the words back.

"I'm sorry."

But I never said that to him. And now, I never can.

I close my eyes, willing sleep to come. But it never does.

One night, Jillian sits beside me on the couch, a glass of wine in hand. "You can't keep everything bottled up."

"I don't know how to let it out."

"You don't have to know," she says. "Just start somewhere."

But where do you start when everything is broken?

I spend hours in my studio, trying to find solace in creating.

My hands move mechanically—tiny pieces of furniture, miniature curtains, delicate dishes. But the magic is gone. Everything I make is hollow, a pale imitation of what once brought me joy.

A creak echoes from the hallway. I freeze, as my heartbeat swallows the air. But it's nothing. The house settling. Pipes shifting. The same noises I've lived with for years. But now, they feel different. Closer.

I force my focus back to the tiny armchair in my hands, running my fingers along the delicate fabric, trying to anchor myself.

Another sound. My heart lurches, and I turn sharply, expecting... Theo?

I swallow hard. No one is there. Of course no one is there.

I press my palms against the worktable, exhaling slowly. I can't concentrate. I can't create. And worst of all, I can't tell if the fear that keeps rising in me is real... or just something I've brought upon myself.

Weeks pass. The house becomes less of a shrine to Theo, more a place where life must continue. Marla keeps coming to help. Marsha and Conrad leave, promising visits. Jillian stays a little longer, but eventually, she has to go back to L.A.

The first day I am truly alone, the silence is deafening. I wander through the house, touching walls, furniture, remnants of a life that no longer exists. Theo's hiking boots still sit by the door. I can't bring myself to move them.

The ache of his absence is unrelenting.

Grief moves in strange ways—it rearranges time, stretches the nights too long and the days too thin. Some moments, I forget he's gone. I reach for my phone to text him, glance at the door expecting him to walk in, feel the space in bed beside me and convince myself he's just on a trip, just out running errands, just—

But then reality crashes back in, sharp and merciless.

I sit on the floor, staring at a photo of Theo and Sadie. They're laughing, full of life. I want to cry. But I can't.

All I feel is emptiness. But beneath it is something else.

Fear.

TEN

A few days later, I step out of the shower. The air is thick, heavy with humidity, steam curling against the mirror like breath on glass. I drag my hand across it, leaving streaks of clarity, but the fog still lingers—on the glass, on my skin, in my thoughts.

I wrap a towel around myself and step into the bedroom. My eyes flick to the dresser before I can stop myself. But there's nothing there. The cologne bottle is gone.

And yet, for a brief, ridiculous second, I had expected to see it again, standing upright as if it never left. As if it wasn't a mistake. As if it didn't send a shiver down my spine the moment I saw it.

I exhale, shaking off the thought. Parker wouldn't lie to me.

He glances up from the bed, his gaze warm, easy. I smile, reminded of the last few nights—slow, unhurried, stretched out like honey over the long summer hours.

Without Sadie here, we've had the kind of time we never do. Mornings spent tangled in sheets, afternoons drifting without urgency, evenings melting into dusk.

I'm finally starting to relax.

Parker has been gentle, patient, steady, as if he senses that something about the cologne unsettled me—even if I haven't fully admitted it. He didn't push when I hesitated, didn't make me feel ridiculous for questioning it. And somehow, in the last few days, that quiet understanding has unraveled the knot in my chest, one thread at a time.

But still, something lingers. And it's not just the absence of Sadie. It's something else.

I step closer to my fiancé, who sits on the edge of the bed. He is tying a pair of tennis shoes. His movements are precise, practiced, and there's something about his posture—his shoulders a little too rigid, his head tilted slightly downward—that feels different. It makes me pause for half a second.

"Is everything okay?" I ask him.

"I'm just heading out for a jog," he says, not looking up at first. Then his eyes meet mine, his expression warm, but guarded. It feels different than the last few days, when he has been so relaxed.

"Perfect sunny morning for it," I reply, choosing to trust him. "I'm just going to have some coffee, and then I'm going to head up to my studio. I'm feeling really inspired right now."

"That's good," he says, nodding.

He knows how hard it's been—how impossible it has felt to pour myself back into my work since losing Theo. How every time I sit down to create, my mind blanks, my hands stall, as if grief has stripped away the part of me that once knew how.

Parker has never pushed, never made me feel like I *should* be further along. Instead, he's been gentle in his encouragement, offering quiet suggestions, leaving space for me to rediscover my own momentum. He sets my sketchbook on the table without a word, brushes a hand over my shoulder when he sees me staring at an empty page for too long. Once, he came home with a gift card to the local art supply store.

"You'll get there," he told me. "In your own time."

And maybe, for the first time, I believe that's true.

"There's actually something I wanted to talk to you about," Parker says now, his tone shifting slightly. It's casual, but there's an undertone of unease. He doesn't stand, his hands resting on his knees as though he's considering whether to say more.

"What is it?" I ask, moving to the dresser and pulling open the top drawer. I rummage through it without really looking, my hands brushing against cotton and lace. The height of summer has made everything sticky and oppressive, even here in the air-conditioned house. I decide to skip the shorts and T-shirts and look for a sundress instead.

I step into the closet, my fingers skimming the rows of hangers until I find my favorite light blue linen dress. The fabric is soft and familiar, and holding it reminds me of simpler days—days when Theo and I would sit out on the porch, sipping iced tea and watching Sadie play in the yard. My chest tightens for a moment, a pang of guilt threatening to bubble up, but I shove it down quickly.

I carry the dress back into the bedroom and begin pulling it over my head. Parker is still sitting there, his gaze following my movements. Not with scrutiny, but with quiet attention, like he's simply taking me in.

"What did you want to talk about?" I ask, hoping to distract myself from the strange tightness in my chest. I smooth the fabric of the dress and glance at him.

He hesitates, just for a second, before answering. "The thing is... it's my sister, Helen," he begins.

My eyes perk up. "Do I finally get to meet the infamous sister?"

"Actually, yes." He pauses. "She needs somewhere to stay for a few weeks. Typically, I would have had her stay at my beach house. It would be the perfect spot. She's been there plenty of times. But, trouble is, I've leased it out for the summer. Remember?"

"I see," I say slowly. "And your condo in the city?"

He frowns. "I told you, the bathroom is being remodeled right now."

"Oh, right." He mentioned there had been an issue with the bathroom sink and that he wanted to remodel before putting it on the market when we got married. "Has the construction already begun?"

"Thankfully, yes," he says, rubbing his face. "The contractor was available, so he's getting started right away. I'm actually heading over there this afternoon to go through the logistics. You're welcome to come if you'd like?"

I hesitate. "Oh... I actually can't. I'm meeting my friend Jillian for dinner."

"Jillian?"

"I've mentioned her lots of times," I say with a laugh. "She's *Aunt* Jillian to Sadie. We've been best friends since college, and she was a lifesaver when Theo died." I pause, remembering the way she helped care for me and Sadie. Her friendship means the world to me. "She's in town visiting her parents, so we're meeting for happy hour. And then hopefully you can meet her tomorrow? It's strange enough to be engaged without her approval." I say this jokingly, but Parker doesn't register the humor.

I step back into the bathroom now that I'm dressed and run a comb through my wet hair. Glancing over my shoulder, I see him standing in the bedroom, still looking conflicted.

"Can she stay here?" he asks bluntly. "It would only be for a few weeks," he adds quickly.

"That's fine. I'm only hesitant because I don't know her, but I'm not trying to be difficult," I tell him honestly.

"Thank you," he says, but his tone is still uncertain. "It would be strange to tell her no."

I nod, agreeing. "Besides Sadie's grandparents and my best friend Jillian, I don't have any family," I admit, my tone softening. "But if Jillian needed a place to stay, I can't imagine telling her no."

"I was hoping you would see it like that. I know you don't have experience with siblings, but Helen and I are close. She's only a few years younger than me, and I've always looked out for her. Since our parents passed, it's just her and me against the world."

I think about being an only child and how Theo, my late husband, was an only child too. I don't know much about sibling dynamics, but I appreciate his desire to protect her. And this is what I wanted when I asked Parker to move in with us, isn't it? Our lives to become entwined, and to create a new, bigger family?

"Well, I think it's sweet that you look out for her. I don't want to be the person who comes between you both."

Parker nods. "She needs family right now. Her boyfriend just broke up with her, and I think she thought they were going to get married. They'd been together awhile, so it's all so very sudden."

"I see," I say. "When was she thinking of coming over?"

"I told her I could pick her up in Seattle tonight, after I check in with the contractor."

I stare at him. "So you already told her this was okay?"

"...Tentatively," he admits sheepishly, stepping toward me in the bathroom. He wraps his arms around me, and I meet his gaze in the mirror.

I smile back at him, wanting to be amiable. "If Helen is anything like you, I'm sure it'll be great."

Parker pats me gently and affectionately on the butt as he heads out, leaving for his jog.

Dressed, I walk down the stairs, through the living room and toward the kitchen.

Then I freeze.

There's a photo on the coffee table, unframed, on top of a pile of books. I'm sure it wasn't there last night.

I bend down, pick it up, my hands shaking as I do.

The photo is familiar. It was taken fourteen years ago, on my wedding day.

My throat tightens.

In it, Theo and I stare at each other adoringly. I'm in a big white dress, my veil pulled back, and he's in a tuxedo. We're smiling, flowers surrounding us. It's one of the dreamiest photos I own.

Breath tangles in my throat. It shouldn't be here. This photo was tucked away in a box at the storage unit. There's no reason it should be out.

My body stiffens. I look around the living room, my heart thudding in my chest. But there's no one else here. I'm alone.

So why do I feel like someone is watching me?

ELEVEN

I don't know what to do with my wedding photo, except tuck it into my back pocket.

I walk to the kitchen, carrying on as normal. I can't over-think the situation. I can't wonder if Parker saw it before he left for his run, if he put it there, or if I'm losing my mind entirely.

It *had* to be Sadie who set this out, I tell myself. Sadie trying to start something before she left. She wasn't excited about how much things would change with Parker in our home. And I know children process grief in all sorts of ways... maybe this is her way of trying to make sense of her father really being gone.

The last few days Parker and I have spent outside, or in the bedroom—we haven't sat in the living room, so it could have been there for days. As I heat the water for my coffee, I hope my fiancé didn't see the photograph.

But still, there's a thrum in my heart I can't ignore.

I pour myself a cup of coffee, adding a dash of oat milk, and scan the fridge for something to eat. The morning air is warm, the scent of salt water drifting in through the open windows. Outside, the inlet is still, the water barely moving.

Before I can grab anything, the front door opens.

Parker steps inside, fresh from his morning jog, his T-shirt damp with sweat. He grabs a water bottle from the fridge, twisting off the cap as he exhales.

"Good run?" I ask, leaning against the counter, aware of the photo in my back pocket.

He nods, taking a long sip. "Yeah. Humid, though." He wipes his forehead with the back of his hand.

Before I can say anything else, the back door swings open, and our housekeeper, Marla, follows him inside.

She lets herself in like she always has, moving with the ease of someone who belongs here. Marla has been our housekeeper for years. She's in her sixties, tall and lean, with sharp eyes that miss nothing. Her graying hair is always pulled into a tight bun. Her movements are efficient. There's a quiet watchfulness about her, a protectiveness I appreciate.

"Morning," she says, setting her tote bag down by the laundry room. Her voice is brisk, unreadable. Out of courtesy I had texted her about my engagement, knowing not only that she would be doing more cleaning with another member of the household, but also how dearly she had loved Theo. This is the first time she is coming face-to-face with the man who has replaced him.

Parker straightens, glancing at me. "Oh— Hi," he says, offering a friendly nod. "You must be Marla?"

She barely looks at him. "And you must be Parker."

The air feels thick between them, an unspoken assessment happening right in front of me.

I clear my throat. "Marla's been with us forever," I say, forcing lightness into my tone.

"Right," Parker says, glancing at me before turning back to her. "Well, it's very nice to meet you." He flashes her one of his warm smiles, the kind that usually makes people melt.

She nods curtly, but her eyes flick to me instead. "I'll start in the dining room."

Then she's gone, disappearing down the hall before I can say anything else.

Parker leans against the counter, watching her leave. "She doesn't like me." He whispers.

I exhale, rolling my shoulders back. "She just... she held a special place in her heart for Theo. And Sadie. And now, well, everything is different."

Parker's quiet for a moment, then sets down his empty bottle. "Guess I'll have to win her over."

I don't say anything, because I don't know if that's possible.

Parker heads upstairs for a shower, and I reach for a banana to have with my coffee before walking to my studio.

With my hand on the doorknob, I pause, feeling as though someone is watching me... "Is that you, Theo?" I whisper, the words making me feel a bit crazy.

My husband is dead, I tell myself. He's not here. I shake my head.

But if he were, what would he think right now? Parker has moved in, and he's sleeping on the same side of the bed Theo did.

"I'm not betraying you, I promise. I'm just trying to be happy," I whisper, to nothing, to the house, to no one.

There's no ghost here. No lingering shadow of the man I once loved like nothing else. But I can't help but wonder... *Is there a ghost of Theo lingering in this house?*

Because even though the coroner said his death was a tragic accident—a slip and fall on a hike down a ravine—it's impossible for me to push my doubts aside entirely.

Theo *wouldn't* have slipped and fallen. He wasn't that kind of man. I said as much to the police after I read the coroner's report. They said it was an accident, but *was* it? Could it have been something else?

Theo was meticulous. Theo spent his whole life outdoors. There's no way someone as adventurous as him would have just slipped and fallen to his death. He was much too sure-footed for that. Too solid. He wasn't the kind of man who had accidents. He was the kind of man who was precise—annoyingly so.

Except that day he wasn't wearing his hiking boots. A day when it was snowing. Everything was black and white with him. *Exact.* There is no way he would have started a hike unprepared, especially in those conditions. It just doesn't add up.

And that's why I've never been able to forgive myself.

TWELVE

I unlock the door to my studio and push it open.

I shut the door behind me. I lock it too, just like I always do.

Alone, I consider the morning. The wedding photo.

Even without slipping it from my pocket, I can see it in my mind—the way it sat perfectly centered on the coffee table, waiting for me. The photo had been packed away with Theo's things, tucked deep in the storage unit where it belonged. And yet, somehow, it ended up back in the house.

Marla had been here since then, but would she have gone through my things? A shiver runs through me. It wasn't just the photo itself—it was the feeling of it. The way it seemed deliberately placed. Not tossed. Not forgotten. *Arranged.*

As if someone wanted me to see it. In the moment, I let myself believe it was a mistake. But was it?

I close my eyes and exhale slowly. Confrontation has never been my strong suit. Theo and I would fight about it. I kept everything in, and then when it spilled out, he couldn't handle it. It was too much at once. Maybe our life, our marriage, would've been different if there had been a steady river of feelings, not a dam that might break at any moment. I'm a private person, and it's been my downfall in many ways. I lock myself up tight. It's the only way I can keep a little bit of control over the world around me. A little bit of control over my life.

So much of my life growing up was out of my control—shuffled from foster home to foster home after my mom died. Never having anything, truly. Never anything that was *just mine.*

A bedroom. A bathroom. A journal.

Everything was either a hand-me-down or something I wasn't allowed to call my own.

When I moved into this house with Theo, I insisted on having a space just for me. Virginia Woolf once said every woman needs a room of her own. And I agree.

This place has been my safe haven. My sanctuary. I look around now, knowing I've abandoned it since Theo's death.

I set my coffee down on my work desk and unpeel the banana. I take a bite, looking around the room curiously, as if I'm stepping into it for the first time.

I'm not, of course.

I've been working in this nine-by-ten space for eleven years, looking out the window at the pine tree in the front yard—its needles endlessly covering the driveway, the squirrels happily scurrying up and down its branches year-round.

Beyond the tree is the front yard, the neighborhood street. It's a quiet place, and honestly, I rarely spend much time looking out the window. I'm usually more focused on what's happening inside this room. My projects.

Right now, I stare at my dusty workstation. It has been untouched for months. Once Theo was gone, I was too consumed by my grief, too focused on protecting Sadie, too determined to just get through each day. I didn't have time to create artistically. It felt like channeling my emotions in an unhealthy way, and that's not what I wanted to do.

I want to be better this time. Smarter. Wiser.

A better widow.

A better fiancée.

A better mom.

I sit down on my stool. It has a high back and is made of metal. It isn't exactly comfortable, but I like it that way. I don't want to get too relaxed when I'm in here. I want to work. To get lost in what I'm doing.

My desk is covered in tools—my magnifying glass, my tweezers, piles of thin wood, paints in every shade imaginable, tiny paintbrushes, larger brushes and an X-Acto knife.

So many types of glue: wood glue, craft glue, carpenter's glue, rubber cement. Every adhesive you could think of. Each chosen intentionally, depending on the piece I was building.

In the corner to my left is my 3D printer and desktop computer. Theo bought them for me as a gift five years ago. It was a great idea, something I've used regularly when creating my miniatures. I design pieces on the computer and print them, keeping my inventory fresh and up to date.

If I were on top of my online business right now, I'd probably be 3D-printing miniature Stanley tumblers, I think wryly. They'd probably sell out as quickly as the real-life versions do.

But I'm not motivated to sell anything. Thankfully, I have enough money from the life insurance to cover my needs for the foreseeable future. For now, I have the luxury of working on a project purely for creative reasons.

When I woke up, I had this vision of what I wanted to make. I wanted to recreate the highchair Sadie used as an infant. One of my happiest memories is when Sadie was nine months old in that highchair. Theo was there, taking photographs on his phone. And I was holding a tiny bowl of avocado puree I'd made for her. I had been obsessed with home-made baby food.

"Do you think she'll like it?" I had asked Theo as I did the airplane motion with the spoon, swooping it toward Sadie's open mouth.

She had clapped her hands, then smashed her fists on the highchair tray, laughing as she greedily took a bite.

Her "mmm" had sounded like the word *more*, and I had laughed.

I remember looking over at Theo. He was laughing too. It was one of those moments—the kind you wait your whole life for.

I kept feeding her spoonful after spoonful of avocado, knowing this was it. This was the moment. It was simple. It was perfect. It was my family—all in one space. I wish we had stayed such a perfect family.

My daughter was beautiful. My husband was kind. And I had made the baby food by hand. That's something I wished my mom would've done for me.

My mom... My mom was never the one to feed me. She wasn't there to make airplane sounds with baby food, making sure I was well-fed.

I blink back tears now as I reach for pieces of balsam wood to create a highchair.

Sadie's highchair.

My fingers tremble slightly as I run them along the smooth grain of the wood. Memories press down on me, thick and heavy, like the air before a storm.

I try to focus on the project. I try to lose myself in the details —the precise cuts, the delicate assembly, the paint strokes that will bring the piece to life.

But my thoughts keep pulling me back to Theo.

Theo...

To his laugh that filled this house. To the photo I tucked into my pocket. To the cologne that shouldn't have been there. To the faint sense that none of this—none of it—is a coincidence.

It has to have been Sadie.

My chest tightens, and I set the wood down, pressing my palms flat against the desk to steady myself.

This house is mine, but it doesn't seem like it. Not anymore. Two strange objects have appeared in the last few days. And tonight, Helen will be here.

The air shifts, cool and charged, brushing against the back of my neck. I whip my head around. The room is empty. Of course it is. But still... I *feel* it. Someone lingering. *Watching*.

My eyes drift to the locked door, the only barrier between me and the rest of the house.

And for the first time since Theo's death, I wonder if locking it is enough.

THIRTEEN

A few hours later, I am thankful I had set an alarm to remind myself about drinks with Jillian. The sound startles me, and I jump up from my progress at my workstation.

The highchair is done, along with the tiny bowl and silver spoon for the avocado puree. It has been a delight. Rejuvenating in ways I hoped it would be, the work has reminded me how much fun it is to be lost in the creative process.

When I step away from my worktable, I exhale, enjoying a sense of accomplishment. I stretch my hands over my head, my back stiff from hunching for hours. A smile spreads across my face at the pleasure of my body being used in a familiar way.

I pocket my phone, pick up my coffee cup and banana peel, and head out. My stomach growls. I've barely eaten today, and it's already four o'clock.

I open the door and step into the hallway, remembering that Parker has headed into the city.

After locking the studio door behind me, I walk downstairs to deposit my dishes. On the counter, I spot a note from my fiancé:

Anna,

*I didn't want to bug you. I'm so proud of you for pushing
through and finding your way. I love you so much, and I can't
wait to introduce you to Helen tonight. You're going to love her.
Thank you for your graciousness and constant generosity.*

Love, Parker

I pick up the note, smiling as I fold it carefully before
carrying it upstairs to my bedroom. I slip it into my top dresser
drawer alongside some personal items—jewelry and scarves.

I lie back on the bed, letting the stillness cradle me while I
gather my breath between one moment and the next. I know I
need to change and put on something decent for meeting Jillian,
but first, I want to FaceTime Sadie.

I hold the phone in my hand, pressing her grandparents'
number. A moment later, Marsha's face appears on the screen,
her fine lines and wavy gray hair sparkling in the afternoon sun.

"Hey, Anna," she says. Her tone is tight, as if she doesn't
want to talk with me. "Let me guess—you're looking for your
sweet pea."

I nod. "Yeah. Is she around?"

"Just a sec, let me see." The phone shifts in Marsha's hand,
unintentionally giving me a view of the farm. It looks as idyllic
as always—a rolling green lawn and a horse in the distance.

My daughter is so lucky to have grandparents who welcome
her this way each summer. It gives me a sense of peace, knowing
that no matter what's happening in my world, that right now
she's safe and protected.

A minute later, Sadie's face lights up the phone screen.
"Hey, Mama!" she says. "Guess what I named the tiniest
chicken?"

I grin. "Peanut?"

She laughs. "No, close. I named her Snickerdoodle."

I snort. "Right, so similar—peanuts and snickerdoodles, they go hand in hand."

"Well, they're both *food*," Sadie says, giggling.

"Okay, fair point," I say, laughing.

"Did you know Grandma and Grandpa have forty-eight chickens right now?"

"I did not know that."

"Grandpa has this whole electrical setup now. There's a conveyor belt, a camera, incubators... it's a whole thing. But basically, I only have to collect eggs every day because I want to. Technically, you wouldn't even have to for like a *week*."

"Wow," I say. "I didn't realize they had such a fancy operation going on."

"It's super fancy," Sadie says. "The neighbors even come by to buy eggs from them. It's like a whole enterprise."

"Sounds like it," I say, smiling. "You look so happy."

Sadie pinches her freckled cheeks dramatically. "So, you're saying I'm cute?"

I laugh. "Yes, Sadie, I'm saying you're the cutest thing I've ever seen in my whole dang life."

"Well, I named one of the chickens Charlotte because Grandma and I watched *Charlotte's Web* last night. Did you know that's basically the saddest movie of all time?"

"I did," I say. "Don't even get me started on *Babe*."

Sadie laughs. "So, what are you up to?"

She sits in the grass, picking at blades between her fingers, and I'm mesmerized by her. She is the epitome of perfection, and sometimes I can't believe she came from me.

"I'm going to meet Aunt Jillian for dinner tonight," I tell her.

"I'm jealous," Sadie says. "I miss her. I haven't seen her since... well, since Dad..."

There's a pause.

I nod, remembering. "I know, sweetheart. But the plan is to spend Thanksgiving with her this year, so you will see her soon enough."

"It will be so fun. Aunt Jillian told me we can go to Disneyland one day."

I laugh. "Wow, I hadn't heard that. What a nice auntie."

"The very best."

I smile brightly. "So, did you do anything else today?" I ask.

She twists her lips. "Well, I made a birdfeeder with Grandpa today in his workshop."

"Have Grandpa text me a photo. I wanna see."

"Okay." She smiles, then adds, "Are you making anything right now?"

"Actually," I say, "I was making a memory of you today."

Sadie scrunches up her face. "What does that mean?"

I explain the kitchen scene I was recreating, and she grins.

"You miss me, don't you?" She laughs.

"I do," I say. "I miss you so much."

"Okay, well, I love you, Mom. But I gotta go because Grandma needs help."

"With what?"

"We're picking blueberries. I'm making a blueberry pie!"

"Okay," I say. "Don't keep her waiting. I love you, Sadie."

"I love you too, Mama. Talk soon!"

I end the call, my whole heart tightening. I love her so much. She is my sunshine, my true north, my everything good. But something isn't right.

A cold unease settles in, curling around the edges of my joy. Sadie never went into the attic.

A terrifying thought runs through me.

If it wasn't Sadie... who was it?

FOURTEEN

I exhale slowly, trying to shake my thoughts off, trying to move forward.

With a more measured step, I change for drinks with Jillian. I step out of my old blue linen dress and into a black slip dress with open-toed heels. I brush my hair and twist it into a low bun, securing it with a tortoiseshell clip. A swipe of soft red lipstick and a touch of mascara complete the look.

In the mirror, I look composed—polished, even. My diamond engagement ring catches the light, a shimmer of something solid, certain. But beneath the surface, a weight lingers, pressing just out of sight. I feel lighter than I've felt in ages, yet not entirely free.

I text Parker quickly before heading to my car:

I got your note. I love you so much, baby, and I can't wait to meet Helen tonight. Yours always.

As I drive, I move through the motions, but the unease lingers, pressing in like a shadow just out of reach. As I park in front of the wine bar, I see Jillian walking down the sidewalk to the bar.

"Hey," she says, waving. "I just got here."

"Oh, good. I didn't keep you waiting."

"Not at all. Look at you—you look *amazing*," she says, and I roll my eyes.

"Well, I thought I'd get dressed up just for you."

"Wow," Jillian says, eyeing me with a smirk. "I don't know if it's me coming to town or Parker, but whatever it is—you're *glowing*."

I laugh, shaking my head. "Oh, please. Have you seen yourself? You're the one who looks amazing. What's your secret?"

She shrugs. "A little of this, a little of that. Mostly drinking green juice every morning after Pilates, and trying not to be a total lunatic over the divorce proceedings."

"Ugh," I say, wincing. "How's that going?"

Jillian and her husband of two years filed for divorce a few months ago.

"Honestly? It's just a weird kind of stress. It's amicable—I mean, now that I think about it, Todd and I were never going to be that kind of 'forever' couple—but it's still emotional. And now I'm going to have to date again or something. I don't know. My therapist said I should just take a year for me."

I nod, but my mind drifts to Sadie. She still asks about Todd sometimes. He was never *Uncle Todd*, nothing quite like that, but there was a familiarity, a comfort. He was there for birthdays, for summer barbecues, for holidays when they were in town. A presence that, however brief, is now another absence.

"Does Sadie miss him?" Jillian asks, reading my thoughts.

"She hasn't said much," I admit. "But I think so. Kids don't always know how to say they miss someone."

Jillian sighs. "Yeah. That's the worst part, honestly. Untangling a life, figuring out what's left over."

I swallow, wondering if I should have done the same.

She looks at me, reading my face as if realizing something. "Okay, I'm sorry. That came out wrong. I'm supposed to start this whole thing with, 'Oh my God, I can't believe you're actually *engaged!*'"

I laugh, but it feels brittle. "I know. It's wild, right?"

"When I got the text from you, I was literally *dumbfounded*. I was like, 'Are you *kidding* me? Out of all people, *Anna* is engaged.'"

I laugh again as we step into the bar, the scent of oak and ripe fruit curling in the air.

Soft lighting glows from hanging Edison bulbs, casting a warm, amber haze over the dark wood tables. Shelves of wine bottles line the exposed brick walls, each label promising something bold, something decadent. A low hum of conversation fills the space, punctuated by the occasional clink of glasses, the quiet pop of a fresh cork.

We weave through the intimate clusters of people until we find a high-top table near the window. Outside, the city moves on, indifferent to the shifting pieces of my life.

I settle onto the stool, exhaling. "I know. I was as surprised as anyone. When I dropped Sadie off at her grandparents the other day, I thought Marsha was just going to fall over in shock."

"Well, you've always been so quiet and shy. The idea of you dating seems wild, let alone getting *engaged*. I mean, I have to meet the guy."

"You will," I say.

"I'll be in town, staying at my parents' for my cousin's wedding, so we can hang out anytime you're free."

Jillian has a stylish haircut—a sleek black bob that falls just below her ears, like she lives in Parisian society. She's the reason I put on red lipstick today. She always looks so good, and today is no different. She's wearing a cream-colored linen suit with a sheer blouse underneath the blazer.

When the waiter comes over, she orders for us both: two gin martinis with a twist, the cheeseboard and the duck pâté.

"So," she says, turning back to me. "You're engaged. Tell me —is the sex *incredible*?"

I groan the way you can with an old friend. "Oh my God. I should have known—"

"What? I've known you since college. I've known you since you and Theo *did it* for the first time. Remember how exciting that was? I remember you came back to our dorm, just beaming, freaking out, shocked."

"Well, I didn't have a lot of experience," I say, cringing at the memory.

"I know, but now look at you!" She shakes her head. "It wasn't that many months ago you were unable to get out of bed after Theo... It has all happened so fast. You barely told me you were dating."

"I wasn't meaning to date," I tell her honestly.

"So you didn't date anyone before Parker? Like you skipped your *ho phase*?" The way she says it, in an exaggerated whisper, makes me roll my eyes.

Jillian is the kind of friend who brings out something in me that not many people do. She's similar to Sadie in a lot of ways— a big personality, unafraid to say what's on her mind. The literal opposite of me. I think that is why we get on so well. Opposites attract.

I cringe. "Honestly, there wasn't. I never even imagined dating again. It just... came together so effortlessly. It made sense." I hold back, though, from telling her the rest, telling her the concerns I have. Telling her the entirety of my plans.

"So, you're happy?" she asks, raising a perfectly arched eyebrow.

"I'm so happy." I pause. Maybe too long of a pause. Or maybe Jillian's just known me too long and too well.

"What?" she asks.

I shrug, but the movement feels tight. "I don't know. Some-times, I get this feeling—like Theo's there. *Watching* me." The scent of his aftershave flashes through my mind, sharp and sudden, like he just walked past. Tears sting my eyes. "I know it sounds crazy. He's gone. We put him in the ground. You were there, holding my hand at his funeral."

But still, the photograph. The cologne. The secret in the attic...

I swallow hard. "I just keep wondering... what would he think about all of this?"

"I bet he'd be happy for you, Anna," Jillian says, reaching for my hand. She squeezes it gently. "He loved you as best he could."

I lick my bottom lip, understanding exactly what she means by that. The last year of our marriage was especially rough.

"Do you ever see him?" she asks gently.

There's a beat of silence.

"Who?"

"You know who—Grant."

Another beat.

I bristle. "No," I say firmly. "Of course not."

Her eyes search mine, expecting more. I can't tell if she believes me.

"What?" I say. "He and his wife moved away. I don't even know where."

"Hmm," Jillian murmurs as the waiter brings our second round of martinis. She picks hers up, offering a change of subject. "To new love," she says as she raises her glass.

"To new love," I repeat, clinking my glass with hers.

"Look," she says, swirling her drink. "I'm proud of you."

I laugh. "Proud of *me*? For what?"

"I don't know. When we were freshmen in college, you were a virgin, and you were afraid you'd never pop your cherry."

"Jillian, for God's sake." My cheeks burn at her forthright nature as I make sure no one overheard her.

"What?" she laughs, taking another sip. "You're all grown up. Grown up in ways I'm not even. But still, Parker is a stranger, Anna. How well do you really know him?"

I freeze, my drink halfway to my lips. Jillian doesn't break eye contact, and her words hang in the air between us, direct and undeniable.

Jillian knows some of my darkest secrets. For a moment, I want to defend myself, but instead, I take a long sip of my martini and set it down with a deliberate clink.

"Parker isn't a stranger," I say quietly, but even to my own ears, the words don't sound as steady as I want them to.

Jillian grins, leaning back in her chair. "If you say so, Anna. If you say so."

I swallow. She's wrong.

Because if she's not... I don't know if I want to know the truth.

FIFTEEN

Client Notes: Initial Observations

Session: First Session

Summary:

The subject presents with a carefully controlled demeanor, though moments of vulnerability slip through like cracks in a polished surface. Their words circle something significant, yet they avoid naming it outright. When the conversation turns to their partner, an air of ambiguity lingers. It hints at unresolved tensions and deeper conflicts.

Key Observations:

- **Emotional Undercurrents:** The subject describes their relationship as "solid, for the most part," but their delivery carries an edge—a flicker of something unsaid. When recounting moments of strain, their tone tightens, hinting at frustration or betrayal.
- **Contradiction:** They portray themselves as a caregiver, yet their phrasing is clinical, even transactional.

Descriptions of "what they gave" to the relationship are recounted with precision, as though balancing an unseen ledger.

- **Shifting Blame:** Their account of pivotal events paints their own role sympathetically, but their partner's role remains cloaked in shadow. The omissions appear deliberate, leaving questions about where accountability truly lies.

Notable Insight:

The subject shared a recent memory:

"I found something. It was tucked away where it shouldn't have been—like a secret I wasn't supposed to uncover. It wasn't mine, but it wasn't theirs either. I didn't know what to do with it, so I left it there. I still don't know if that was the right choice."

The words felt heavy with meaning, though they dismissed the moment with a laugh that didn't reach their eyes.

Therapist Reflection:

The session ended on a charged note. As they leaned forward, their voice softened to a near-whisper: *"You can love someone and still not trust them. Sometimes, I think the not trusting is what keeps you tethered."*

Conclusion:

The narrative is layered, with truths deliberately left unsaid. What lies beneath the surface remains elusive, but it is clear this is more than unresolved grief. The dynamic they describe suggests a push-and-pull of control, trust and secrets yet to be fully uncovered.

SIXTEEN

After I leave the wine bar, Jillian's words keep rolling around in my head.

Jillian's wrong, I tell myself firmly. She said Parker is a stranger, but he isn't.

I send him a quick text: *Headed home now. See you soon. XOXO*

He hearts the message immediately, just like I knew he would. Parker is the kind of man who always does the right thing, says the right thing, wears the right thing. He doesn't get upset. He doesn't get angry. He doesn't ruffle feathers. He's even-keeled in the way I appreciate, and he's also emotionally available—something Theo never was.

For a fleeting second, I think about someone else. Someone who *did* ruffle feathers. Who did say the wrong thing at the wrong time. Who wasn't even-keeled or careful or measured— but who knew me in a way no one else ever has...

Grant.

I tighten my grip on the steering wheel, push the thought away. *Not tonight.*

When I pull up to my house, I allow a hush to bloom in my

chest, preparing myself to meet Helen. I was certainly not antic-ipating a houseguest, I didn't even make sure the guest room was clean. Parker did kind of throw that on me at the last minute, and I was so wrapped up in myself today that I didn't even give Helen much thought.

But as I walk up to the house, pushing open my front door, I realize my pretend honeymoon this month—just a cocoon of Parker and me—is being invaded much sooner than I imagined. I'd wanted this time for us to be alone, to get to know each other in an even deeper way without Sadie around. Not that I don't want Sadie here with us, but it just seemed serendipitous the way it was unfolding. We'd have a month without her so that we could find our own rhythm as a couple.

Now Helen's here, cutting all of that short.

"Hello?" I call out, walking down the hallway toward the kitchen. I pass the living room and dining room, noting there aren't any random photographs set out unexpectedly. *Thank God.*

No one's in the kitchen, but I see the sliding door is open. On the back patio, I see Parker laughing with a woman my age. There's an open bottle of rosé on the table and a box of cookies from a Seattle bakery.

I step outside. "Hello," I say.

Parker jumps up, reaching out for me. "You're home, baby," he says. He gives me a quick kiss. "You look beautiful, all dressed up."

I shrug. "I was meeting Jillian. She's sophisticated, so I always try to put on a good show for her."

"I like it," Parker says with a broad smile.

I realize he's probably never seen me this dressed up. I don't usually put on much makeup, and we've only known each other in the summer, which means I'm usually in a sundress or cutoff shorts. Suddenly self-conscious, I reach my hand out to Helen.

"Hello," I say. "Welcome to my—*our*—home."

"Hello to you," Helen trills. "Look at *you*! Parker's so modest. He said you're beautiful, but my God, you're *gorgeous*."

I look at Helen properly then, taking her in. She's blonde and blue-eyed, with tan skin. She's wearing athleisure—a pair of yoga shorts and a sports bra—with her hair tied up in a bun on the top of her head.

"Oh gosh," I say, shaking my head a bit at the compliment and tucking a loose strand of hair behind my ear. I sit down at the patio table, kicking off my heels. "My feet are aching," I say, rubbing my feet. "I'm usually in a pair of Birkenstocks this time of year."

"Parker," Helen says, "get your fiancée a glass of wine."

"I don't know if I should," I say. "I just had two martinis."

Helen laughs. "Two martinis? You're just as repressed as my brother."

I press my lips together. "What do you mean?"

She laughs again, harder this time. "Oh, you know, he's always so *restrained*, held back."

I look at Parker then. "I never think of him like that," I say with a smile.

She shrugs. "Well, he's just a little high-strung." She scrunches up her nose, as if I would understand exactly what she means, but I don't. The Parker I know has been easygoing, amicable, generous, available. I can't imagine him any other way.

I lean back in my chair. "I guess people change depending on who they're with in a relationship."

Helen smiles. "Oh my God. Let's *not* talk about relationships." She covers her face with her hands, shaking her head.

"Oh sorry," I say quickly. "I didn't mean to bring up anything—"

"No," she groans. "It's fine." She drops her hands and reaches for her wine. "Please, seriously, have a glass. Don't let me drink alone."

Parker gives a little laugh and pours a glass for me. "Here you go, my love."

"Thank you," I say, moving the rosé toward myself and taking a sip. It's cold and crisp.

"Anyways," Helen continues, without missing a beat, "Steve was a piece of work. We all knew that. It's just... the breakup came out of *nowhere*." She looks over at Parker at this, and I see a flicker of understanding pass between them. "I thought he was good for me. Thought I was good for him."

"What happened?" I ask.

She sighs. "I don't want to talk about it."

"All right," I say. I almost laugh, considering she's the one who brought it up. But I swallow it down with another sip of wine.

As I watch her drink, I try to get a read on her. She's younger than me—five years maybe—and I'm thirty-five. Maybe she's just a late bloomer. I try to push away my negative thoughts, but one keeps pushing itself back up: *immature*.

"Anyways, it's so kind of you to have me," she says, leaning over the glass-topped patio table and reaching for my hands. "Like, seriously, a godsend. I *had* to be here."

"Well, I'm glad it worked out," I say. "Parker says you're a consultant?"

"Sort of," she says. "I do social media for brands, kind of, like, graphic design."

"Okay," I say slowly, letting the vague answer settle. "What kind of clients do you work with?"

"That's the thing. I'm sort of in between clients."

I glance at Parker, trying not to tense. She's clearly avoiding details—about her job, about her ex. I don't know if it's just discomfort or something more, but it sits wrong.

Helen takes another sip of wine. Her second glass since I've been home. I glance at the clock in the living room. Only fifteen minutes.

"Anyway, that's the thing," she continues now. "Work has been so hard, and it was easier when I was with Scott. He was steady, and he supported me." She frowns. "Until he didn't."

I want to like her. I really do. Parker speaks so highly of her, but there's something off-putting about her. She keeps staring at him—not just looking but *watching*. Like she's studying him, waiting for something. It's subtle, but it's enough to make my skin prickle. What is she looking for?

"Anyway, enough about me. What were you up to today?" Helen asks. She leans back, swirling the wine in her glass. Parker sits there completely silent. I look over at him, trying to read the situation. Is his sister always like this?

I choose my words carefully, which is something I usually do, but I'm especially careful tonight. "I worked a bit in my studio—I'm an artist—and then I FaceTimed my daughter this afternoon, before I met my best friend Jillian for drinks."

Helen pounces. "How do you know Jillian?"

"Well, we met in college. We were roommates freshman year, so I've known her a long time."

"Oh wow. So, she knew your husband?"

The question lands like a slap, and there's an uncomfortable pause.

For a second, I just blink at her, my brain scrambling to process the abrupt shift. The way she says it—too casual, too direct—as if she's determined to peel back layers I wasn't offering up.

Parker's eyes twitch. "Helen," he says gently. "That's not appropriate."

"What do you mean?" she says, raising her hand and pointing to me. "Anna was married for a long time and has a daughter. Sadie looks beautiful, by the way. I saw her pictures in the living room. And I'm sorry, Parker, but are we not supposed to act like she's had a life before you?" Helen shakes her head. "That's weird. Sorry if I'm being rude. It's just... isn't Parker being odd?"

I look at my fiancé. "He just means... well, he wants to respect me." I say it honestly, and I appreciate his kindness. "But Parker, it's all right for her to ask questions. Theo and I were married a long time. Jillian was actually the maid of honor at our wedding. So, yeah, she knew him well. She was there for me when we lost him, and it's nice that she's in town right for a few weeks. Now she can get to know you, Parker. She's dying to meet you."

He smiles, reaching his hand out for mine and squeezing it. "I wasn't trying to be intense," he says. "Siblings can just be a little much sometimes."

Helen rolls her eyes. It's a quick gesture, but I catch it out of the corner of my eye.

"Do you have a big family?" she asks suddenly.

I shake my head. "No, none. No siblings. My mom died, and I never knew my dad."

She frowns. "You should do a DNA test. We could get a kit tomorrow—see if you have long-lost siblings, aunts, maybe even your dad. I mean, what if he lives in Silverport? Wouldn't that be *wild*?"

"Jesus Christ," Parker mutters. "Helen."

She shoots him a look. "What? It's fascinating."

My skin prickles. "I appreciate the excitement, but I actually don't want to take one of those tests."

"Are you scared?"

I shake my head. "It's not fear. It's just... my plate is full. Sadie's still grieving, and I'm starting a life with your brother. I don't have the space to dig up my past when I don't even know where I'd put the pieces."

Helen nods slowly, a smile spreading across her face. "Okay. You are so smart, and kind, and thoughtful. How in the world did my brother land you, exactly?" She shakes her head, incredulous. "I mean, Anna, you are *stunning*. Not just gorgeous, but inside too. You're thoughtful and so grounded. Have you always been like this?"

I laugh. "Oh my gosh, Helen, you are quite the personality yourself," I say, a little undone at her generous compliments.

She's not rude, I realize then, but she's also not kind. She's unfiltered in the way I adore. She reminds me of Jillian, if I am being honest.

I look at her, trying to keep my tone light. "I happened to meet your brother at the park. I thought Sadie was lost, and he helped me find her. Turns out she was down by the water, collecting rocks and clamshells. Then she painted them," I say, smiling at the memory.

Helen nods slowly. "She's a sensitive girl, like you."

I nod. "You could say that."

She looks over at Parker, tilting her head slightly, as if appraising him. "And how are you getting on with these *sensitive* women?" she asks him with a grin. "He has a lot of exes, you know."

"Helen," Parker says, chuckling uncomfortably. "Please, enough for one night."

"Oh, I don't mind," I say, curiosity creeping into my tone.

Parker had spoken about his past relationships, but none of them seemed particularly significant or long-lasting.

"Oh, according to Parker, his last girlfriend was evil. Literally *evil*," Helen says, lowering her voice but not her enthusiasm. "This was the girl right before you," she says, pointing at me. Her gaze is locked on me, unblinking.

"Okay," I say slowly, trying to diffuse the tension. "And who was she?"

"Blue," Helen says, her tone dripping with disdain.

"*Blue?*" I repeat.

Helen nods, taking a sip of her wine. "Yep. But Parker says her heart—it was all black."

"And what happened to Blue?" I ask, my curiosity fully piqued now.

Helen looks at Parker for a moment, then throws her head back and laughs. "Oh, that's too dark of a story for wine night."

"You don't say," I add dryly, taking a sip from my own glass. She's done it again—brought up something, then refused to discuss it.

She smirks at me, leaning closer. "Blue got what she deserved. But honestly? I think most women in Parker's life do."

Her words linger in the air, heavy and charged. I glance at Parker, who is staring into his wineglass, his expression unreadable. No one speaks.

The tension at the table is palpable, and for a moment, I wonder if I should excuse myself and leave them to their sibling dynamic. But before I can move, Parker takes my hand.

"Helen has had too much wine," he says softly, his thumb brushing over my knuckles.

I decide to let the moment pass. "Well, it's been a long day," I say, standing and slipping my feet back into my heels.

I step into the house, leaving the patio behind. As I walk down the hallway, there is a prickle at the base of my neck, like someone's watching me. I glance back toward the sliding door, but all I see is Helen laughing at something Parker has said, her head tilted under the glow of the patio lights.

I shake off the feeling and head upstairs. As I close the bedroom door behind me, a small knot of unease settles in my chest.

Who was Blue?

And why did Helen's words sound like they held a warning?

SEVENTEEN

The next day I'm in my studio. The late afternoon light casts long shadows on the walls. My hands move carefully over the tiny map I've spent the last hour creating.

Theo had been so excited the night he had spread his map across the dining room table. The eve of the trip he'd been planning for him and Sadie, just the two of them. Their first overnight camping trip.

I run my fingers along the edges of the miniature map. The tiny trails, the delicate switchbacks—exact replicas of the ones Theo had traced on his real map. I can still picture him at the table, Sadie perched on his lap, her little hands smudged with marker as she "helped" draw their route.

He'd been smiling, so patient with her. He was always so good with her.

I try to shake the memories loose. The scene in my mind holds so many little details: the table, the markers scattered on the floor, his blue scarf draped over the chair, the red hiking backpack in the corner that I had given Theo as a Christmas gift that year.

I exhale slowly, considering the map one last time. Deciding it is perfect, I lift it to take it outside to dry in the summer sun.

I walk to the door and unlock it, and just as I step into the hallway, I hear Parker's voice.

"What have you been doing locked away in there?"

His question startles me. I rarely shared my art with Theo. I steady myself and turn toward him. He's standing at the bottom of the stairs, looking up at me, smiling, his head tilted with kind curiosity.

"Oh," I say, trying to sound casual. "Just a project."

"For what?"

"I'm working on my miniatures." I keep my creative work close to my chest, the same way I don't intrude on Parker's work.

He goes to Seattle every so often to check on the condo, but since he is on sabbatical from his tenured position at the university, he has a flexible routine. In my other life, Theo would complain I was too private, so I appreciate that Parker has never been intrusive about what I do in my studio. Or asked questions about why I always lock the door behind me.

Now, though, his eyes narrow slightly, and he steps closer. "Is that... a *map?*"

"Yes," I say, shrugging. "It's a memory I'm working with. It centers around a camping trip Theo planned with Sadie."

I immediately regret the words as soon as they're out.

Parker's jaw tightens, and his voice is careful. "Anna."

"What?" I say defensively.

"Why do you keep doing this?"

"Doing what?"

"Bringing up the past." His tone isn't angry, but it's firm. Controlled. "I get it. You have memories. You and Theo had a life. But at times it's like..." He trails off, rubbing the back of his neck. I'm startled to see he looks hurt. "Like you're still... *there.*"

I blink, the sting of his words hitting me harder than I expect. "That's not fair," I say, my voice soft but clear.

"I'm not trying to be unfair," he says, stepping closer, and I see a sadness in his eyes. "But, Anna, every time I think we're moving forward, something like this happens. It's like there's no room for us." He pauses. "For *me*."

I walk past him, toward the kitchen, trying to find the right words. "That's not true," I whisper.

He studies me for a moment, his expression softening. "Isn't it?"

I shake my head, swallowing the lump in my throat. "Theo was Sadie's dad, Parker. He was part of my life. I'm allowed to remember him."

"I know," he says, his voice quiet. "But at some point, don't you think it's time to let go?"

My chest tightens, and tears prick the corners of my eyes. "You don't understand."

"Maybe not," he admits. "But I'm trying to."

I want to reach for him, to close the distance between us, but my hands stay frozen with the map.

Before I can say anything more, Helen's voice cuts through the tension like a knife.

"*Wow*," she says, leaning against the kitchen doorway, her ever-present wineglass in hand. Her gaze flicks between us, sharp, assessing. "Trouble in paradise?"

I glare at her. "Not now, Helen." She's enjoying this too much.

She smirks, raising her glass in mock surrender. "Okay, okay. Just saying... you two might want to figure this out before the wedding. Unless, of course, you like living in a soap opera."

Parker shoots her a look. "Helen."

She shrugs, unbothered, but there's something else—a flicker of something in her expression, something too controlled.

Before I can read it properly, she rearranges her face into a smile. "Hey, I'm just here for the entertainment."

She takes a sip of her wine, but her eyes linger on me a second too long before she disappears into the living room, humming to herself.

Later, after getting ready for bed, I come downstairs to get a glass of water. The house is quiet, with only the drip of a faucet breaking the silence. As I pass the kitchen, something catches my eye.

I stop, my heartbeat swallowing the air.

Theo's scarf.

The navy one he always wore in the winter. The one he wore on his first camping trip with Sadie. I can still see it in the photos—wrapped around his neck as he crouched beside her at the fire, teaching her how to roast marshmallows just right.

And now, it's draped over the back of a kitchen chair, like someone left it here on purpose.

I can't move. I stare at it, my pulse racing.

"Anna?"

I jump, spinning around to see Parker standing near me in the foyer, a book in his hand. He'd been reading in the living room. His eyes flick to the scarf, then back to me.

"What's that?" he asks, his voice calm but confused.

"I... I don't know," I whisper. "It was Theo's," I admit.

He steps closer, his expression gentle but probing. "Did you put it there?"

"What?" I ask, my voice rising. "No! I didn't touch it!"

His brows knit together, but his tone stays even. "Okay. I'm just... trying to figure out what's happening here."

I inhale sharply, my mind scrambling for an explanation. Maybe I pulled it from the closet without thinking? Maybe it was tucked in with Parker's things, and I didn't notice? Maybe it's been on a chair this whole time?

But I know none of those things is true. It is the middle of summer, and I took Theo's things to the storage unit myself.

"Well, it wasn't me," I murmur. My hands are trembling.

Helen's voice floats in from the living room. "Oh, this is getting *good*," she says, laughing. "Better than anything on Netflix."

"Go to bed, Helen," Parker says, his tone clipped.

I quickly push past them both, heading upstairs, my heart pounding.

As I shut the bedroom door behind me, I lean against it. My mind spins, my chest tight.

The cologne. The photo. Now the scarf.

Sadie couldn't have put the scarf there. She is three hours across the state. And no matter what Marsha and Conrad truly think of me and my engagement, there's no way they could be behind any of this.

What about Helen? I realize I'm not entirely sure why she's here. Is she trying to mess with me, unhappy about my engagement to her brother?

Then my train of thought turns even darker. Marla, our housekeeper, is the only other person who has been in our home. She's been with us for years, and I trust her implicitly. But could she be behind these objects, angry that I've moved on from her beloved Theo so quickly?

I think of Parker, and I tightly squeeze my eyes shut. I know it can't be him, not when these objects are causing him so much hurt. He's only trying to help.

Nothing is right. The home that has always been my sanctuary suddenly feels like a trap.

It's like the past won't let me go. And deep down, I know why.

And it's worse than anything Parker could ever imagine.

EIGHTEEN

The next morning, I try to push the scarf out of my mind. After seeing it, I carried it upstairs to the attic, placing it in the far corner with the cologne, like a thought I didn't want to revisit. A light had been left on, making it obvious someone had been up there. Did I leave it on when I packed away the cologne? I truly can't remember.

I try to suppress a yawn, exhausted. Parker finally let the scarf go last night. Instead of fighting with me, he had simply joined me in bed and took my hand in his, as if promising that we could get through anything together.

Now, Parker kisses my temple, his lips warm against my skin as we sit on the couch with the wedding planner's binder open between us. I'm trying to focus on cake flavors, seating arrangements and the font for invitations, but his touch distracts me.

"I can't believe we're actually doing this," he says softly, his voice low and full of warmth.

"Me either," I admit, leaning into him. "A winter wedding is romantic though. And there will be enough time so we aren't rushed with planning."

His arm wraps around my shoulders, pulling me closer. "You know, you're making me the happiest man alive."

I smile, even as my stomach churns. He looks so sincere, so deeply in love. "Well, you're not too bad yourself," I tease, nudging him gently.

"Not too bad?" he echoes, mock-offended.

"Okay, maybe better than 'not too bad.' You're..." I trail off, my gaze meeting his.

"I'm what?" he presses, a small grin tugging at his lips.

"You're my *everything*," I say quietly, my voice barely above a whisper.

His expression softens, and he cups my cheek with one hand. "And you're mine."

The kiss is slow, tender, his lips brushing against mine as if we're the only two people in the world. For a moment, I let myself fall into it—his warmth, his steadiness, the way his hand lingers on the small of my back as if he's afraid to let me go.

But he doesn't let go.

Instead, his grip tightens, pulling me closer until I'm straddling his lap, my knees pressing into the couch cushions. His fingers slide up beneath my shirt, tracing the dip of my spine.

"We're alone," he murmurs against my lips, his voice low, filled with something I feel curling deep in my stomach. "Helen's out at the store. There's no one here but us."

I exhale, my head tipping back as his mouth trails along my jaw, down my throat. His hands move with intention, peeling away fabric, leaving heat in their wake.

I don't think. I don't question.

I just let myself want.

And when we come together, it's slow and unhurried, a quiet kind of urgency, his body moving against mine as if he's memorizing me. As if this moment is something he wants to keep.

After, his fingers trace lazy circles against my hip. The house is still quiet, the world beyond us blurred and distant.

I press a kiss against his shoulder, letting myself believe—just for now—that this is enough.

After we dress again, we smile at the intimacy we indulged in. My eyes move, resting on the binder filled with wedding plans. "Okay," I say, "Back to business. What's next on the list?"

Parker chuckles, flipping the page in the binder. "Flowers. Do you have a favorite?"

"Peonies," I say without hesitation. "Though they might be hard to find in winter."

He nods, making a note. "We will find these prized peonies, whatever the cost."

I hear the back door open, breaking the moment.

"That must be Marla," I say, standing and checking my blouse is buttoned properly.

She finds us in the living room, and I am glad she arrived now, not ten minutes earlier when Parker and I were naked. Her hair is neatly pinned back, her cleaning supplies in hand.

"Good afternoon, Anna," she says politely.

"Hi, Marla. I didn't remember you were coming back today."

She frowns. "I thought we discussed I would be coming twice a week from now on."

I nod slowly, realizing I have been so all over the place lately. Sadie is gone, Parker has moved in, and now so has Helen, and Jillian is in town too. And not only do I feel inspired to work again, but I am also now planning a wedding. Maybe it is a godsend to have Marla here more often to keep the house in order so I can focus on everything else.

"We should head out," I suggest to Parker. "Give her space to work."

"Good idea," he agrees, standing and grabbing his keys.

Marla's eyes don't leave Parker as we leave the house, and

there's something in her expression that sends a shiver down my spine.

As we walk to the car, Parker slips his hand into mine. It is easy, natural, the way he touches me. Like he's meant to.

"So," I say as he starts the engine, "how long is Helen staying, exactly?"

Parker glances at me, his brow furrowing slightly. "Why?"

"I'm just curious," I say quickly. "I mean, she's great and all, but... she doesn't seem to have much of a *plan*."

He sighs, gripping the steering wheel. "She's going through a lot, Anna. The breakup shook her. I don't think she knows what she wants right now."

I nod, biting my lip. "I get that. I do. But..."

"But what?" he asks, his tone gentle but firm.

I hesitate, not wanting to come across as unsupportive. "It's just... this is *our* home, Parker. I thought this time would be just for us, you know? Especially with Sadie away."

He glances at me again, his expression softening. "I know. And I promise, it's temporary. She just needs a little time."

"Okay," I say, forcing a smile. "I trust you."

Later, Parker holds the door open for me as we step back into the house, our arms loaded with samples and brochures from the florist and bakery. I drop my bag onto the counter, releasing a quiet breath. It's been a long day, but productive. The wedding planning is less daunting now, like we're actually making progress.

Parker presses a kiss to my temple. "I'm going to throw on some workout clothes. I want to get a jog in before it gets too dark."

"Good idea," I say. "I'll meet you outside on the patio later for a drink."

He heads upstairs, and I hear the faint creak of the floorboards overhead as I rummage through the kitchen. I pour myself a glass of sparkling water with a splash of lime and head toward the patio, pushing open the sliding door to let in the warm evening breeze.

The sound of Parker's footsteps on the stairs makes me glance back toward the house. He's coming down, but his jog has clearly been forgotten. His expression is tight, his brows furrowed as he holds something in his hand. There's a weight to the way he moves, a hesitation that sends a cold prickle up my spine.

"What's wrong?" I ask, my stomach tightening.

He steps onto the patio, his gaze locked on me, as if trying to gauge my reaction before he even speaks. Slowly, he lifts his hand, revealing a glint of gold between his fingers.

Theo's wedding ring.

The world narrows in on that small, familiar band—the one I haven't seen since the day I tucked it away in a box, buried with everything else I couldn't bear to look at.

"This," Parker says, his voice quiet but heavy. "It was sitting on the bathroom sink."

I blink, my chest tightening. *No.*

My mind races, grasping for logic, for a reason—anything that makes sense. But there is none.

Parker steps closer, his eyes searching mine. "Did you put this in the bathroom?"

I shake my head, feeling angry at being blamed for something so atrocious, "How can you even ask me that?"

He looks down at the ring, turning it over in his fingers like it might hold some kind of answer. "Are you sure you didn't...?" His voice trails off, gentle but probing.

"Are you serious right now?" I snap, my defenses kicking in. "Of course I didn't put it out. Why would I do that?"

"I'm not accusing you," he says quickly, holding up his hands. "I'm just... trying to understand why it's here."

I swallow hard, my mind racing for a plausible explanation. Could I have knocked it over in the attic when I replaced the cologne? Even if I had... it doesn't explain why it ended up on Parker's sink.

"Marla was here today," I say suddenly, clinging desperately to the best idea that comes to mind. "Maybe she found it while cleaning and thought it should be out?"

"You think she may have found it and assumed it was one of ours?" he asks, trying to make sense of it.

"Maybe?" It sounds plausible as he says it, and I want to cling to that hope. But I know Marla doesn't touch personal items. She's very particular about that.

He shakes his head, clearly skeptical. "Do you think Marla is interested in... sabotaging us? I know it sounds paranoid but... you did say how much she loved Theo."

"I don't know," I say, throwing my hands up in exasperation. "Maybe it was Helen."

"*Helen?*" Parker's voice is laced with disbelief. "Why would my sister do that?"

"She's... unpredictable," I say weakly, the words falling flat even as I say them. "She probably thought it was funny or something."

Parker's expression shifts, concern flickering across his face. "Anna..."

"What?" I ask critically.

He hesitates, then steps closer, his voice soft. "Are you sure you're okay? Lately, it's like you've been clinging onto the past. Like maybe you'd rather be in your memories instead of here, in the present."

I stare at him, my chest tightening. "You think *I'm* doing this? That I put the ring there and somehow forgot about it?"

"No," he says quickly, but there's a flicker of uncertainty in his eyes. "I just think... maybe this house, these memories— they're weighing on you more than you realize."

The sound of Helen's harsh yet amused voice cuts through the tension. "What's going on now?" she asks, wandering onto the patio with a glass of wine in her hand.

"Nothing," Parker says firmly, slipping the ring into his pocket. His tone leaves no room for argument, but Helen's smirk says she doesn't believe him.

"Doesn't sound like nothing," she says, her bright eyes darting between us.

I force a smile. "Just a misunderstanding."

Helen raises an eyebrow but doesn't push. Instead, she takes a sip of her wine and saunters toward the roses in the backyard, humming to herself.

Parker turns back to me, his expression a mix of frustration and worry. "I'm going to head out for that jog now," he says quietly.

"Fine," I say, my voice tight.

He leaves the yard, and Helen gives me a long look, as if trying to read me. The tension in the air thickens, pressing in, but I can't let it show.

The weight of it all lingers—the cologne, the photograph, the scarf, the wedding ring. Someone is placing them deliberately in my house. Someone wants them found.

But why?

And worse... who?

NINETEEN

I should be happy. I should be whole.

I've met Parker—the man I'm going to marry, the new love of my life. We're planning a wedding, laying the foundation for a future that's safe, secure and steady. It's everything I thought I wanted.

So then why do I feel hollow, like I'm living someone else's life?

The thought sticks with me as I walk through town. The late afternoon sun paints the streets in gold. But the sunlight casts shadows that are too long and too dark. After Parker left for his jog, I decided I needed some air, some time to think.

I stop at the corner of a quiet street, staring blankly toward the all-too-familiar coffee shop. The faint scent of espresso drifts through the air. It doesn't calm me. It flings me back to memories too precious to ignore.

And that's when I see him.

Grant.

He's leaning against a car parked a few feet away, his hands tucked into his jacket pockets, his head tilted slightly as he watches me. The sight of him pulls the air from my lungs, leaving me unsteady.

Grant looks the same, yet somehow more defined. His dark hair is longer now, curling at the nape of his neck. He's wearing a white collared shirt, the sleeves pushed up just enough to reveal the leather band of his watch. His jeans are worn but tailored. His scuffed boots are planted firmly, centering him in an unshakable way.

He's always looked like he walked out of a story—effortlessly thoughtful. Strong jaw, high cheekbones, a mouth that always seems on the verge of something—wry or knowing, like he already sees where the conversation is going. His gaze cuts right through the surface and into the marrow of who you are. And those eyes—deep-set, watchful—like he's memorizing you without ever having to try.

"Anna," he says, his voice low and familiar, carrying months of unspoken words.

I freeze, unable to move.

"What... what are you doing here?" I manage to stutter, my voice barely audible.

He steps closer, the tension between us palpable. "I just moved back. We never sold the house, so I'm living there now," he says softly. "My marriage... it's over."

His words hit me like a tidal wave. I'm suddenly drowning in everything I thought I'd buried.

"You *left* her?" I whisper, more to myself than to him.

He nods. "I did. It wasn't working. It hadn't been for a long time. You know that better than anyone."

My eyes drop to the pavement, the weight of his presence pressing down on me. Grant wasn't just anyone. He was a writer—a novelist who could strip down the human soul in a way that felt both tender and excruciating. He had a way of seeing people. Of seeing me. In ways I didn't always want to be seen.

And now, here he is, looking at me like I'm a puzzle he's still trying to solve.

"I didn't know you moved back," I say, finally lifting my gaze.

"I didn't think you'd care to," he replies, his voice soft but steady.

Care to? The words sting, though I know they shouldn't.

"What do you want, Grant?"

He hesitates, his jaw tightening as if he's weighing his next words carefully. "Can we talk? Just for a minute?"

I should say no. I should walk away. But my feet don't move, and I suddenly hear my own mouth betray me. "Okay."

He nods toward his car, and before I can think better of it, I follow. The leather seats are warm from the sun, and the faint scent of him—cedar and ink, the same as always—wraps around me.

We drive in silence to the edge of town, stopping at a lookout point where the water crashes against the rocks below. The horizon is painted in hues of gold and lavender, too majestic for a moment that has suddenly turned so dangerous.

"I haven't seen you since... since Theo," Grant says finally, his hands tightening on the steering wheel.

The sound of Theo's name makes my chest tighten. I stare out at the waves, willing myself to stay composed.

"I'm sorry," Grant continues, his voice low. "For everything. For him. For us."

I bite the inside of my cheek, refusing to look at him. "You never even called to ask if I was all right."

"Would you have wanted me to?"

I shrug. Tears sting in my eyes. "It was awful. Losing that life."

"How have you managed?"

Still not daring myself to look at him, I answer. "Having Sadie kept me grounded. Kept me moving forward. And in so many ways, I had lost Theo long before he died." I shake my head. "You know that."

There's a pause.

"I've been writing about you," he says suddenly, his words slicing through the air.

My head snaps toward him. "What?"

"You've been in every story I've written since I left," he admits, his gaze fixed on the water. "I've tried to stop, but I can't. You're in everything, Anna."

I don't know what to say to that. I don't know if I want to know. My heart is pounding.

"Why are you here?" I ask again, my voice trembling.

He finally looks at me, and the intensity in his eyes is unbearable. "I've come by the house a few times, but no one was home, or at least no one answered. I've needed to see you."

"I'm engaged," I blurt out, the words tumbling from my lips like a shield.

"I figured," he says, his voice soft but unyielding. He looks at my hand. "I saw the ring."

"Does that upset you? That I've moved on?"

He sighs. "I just want to know that you're happy. Are you happy, Anna?" he asks simply.

The question lands like a stone in my gut. *Am I happy?* Parker is everything I thought I wanted—kind, stable, loving. But happiness? I don't know if I've ever felt that. Not for a long time...

"You shouldn't be here," I say, my voice barely above a whisper.

He leans closer, the space between us shrinking until his warmth brushes against me.

"I loved you, Anna," he says, his voice breaking. "I still do."

"Don't," I whisper, shaking my head. "You can't say that."

"It's the truth," he says. "And I think... I think Theo knew."

The words hit me like a punch, leaving me gasping for air.

"What?"

"I think he knew about us," Grant repeats quietly. "He never said anything, but there were moments... the way he looked at me. I could sense it."

My mind races, my chest tightening. *Did* Theo know? Is that why he pulled away from me in those final months? Is that why...

No. I can't think like that. I refuse to.

"Anna," Grant says, his voice gentle but insistent. "I'm sorry. I shouldn't have—"

"Stop," I interrupt, my voice more pointed than I intended. "Just stop."

His eyes soften, and he reaches out, his fingers brushing against mine. The contact sends a jolt through me, electric and impossible to ignore.

"You're right, I shouldn't have come," he says, pulling back. "I just... I needed to see you."

The silence between us is deafening, and for a moment, I think I might let it break me.

"You need to drive me home," I tell him. Not trusting myself. "Now, please."

He nods and silently turns the car around. We don't speak. How can we? What do you say to the man who changed your world, and then left it? What do you say to the man who was the worst and best thing that ever happened to you? What do you say to the past when it has already been buried?

I'm engaged to Parker. I am not with Grant. And to be brutally honest with myself, I never was. Our relationship was nothing more than an affair. We were both married. Both lost. Both longing for more than we had.

When he stops his car at my house, I push my emotions away, knowing they have no place in my present reality.

"Goodbye, Grant," I finally say, my voice barely audible.

He nods, his expression a mix of pain and understanding. "Goodbye, Anna."

As I step out of the car and into the fading light, his gaze lingers on me, the weight of everything left unsaid pressing down like a storm.

Inside, the house is dark and quiet. I walk toward the kitchen, needing water for my parched throat. My mind is still spinning from everything that just happened.

Parker's voice suddenly pulls me back to reality. "Anna?"

He's standing in the living room, his face pale, holding something in his hand. My heart lurches as I move closer, trying to make sense of what I'm seeing.

It's a photograph.

Theo and me on our wedding day. The photo I had found on the coffee table. I thought I had buried it in my dresser drawer after finding it.

"What's this doing here?" he asks, his voice strained.

My stomach drops. "What is it?" I whisper, playing for time as I step closer.

"This was in your dresser drawer," he says, holding it up. "I was looking for a phone charger, and I found it."

I freeze, my mind racing. Why was he looking in my dresser for a phone charger? Am I out of bounds for wondering? But I know I can't ask that now. Not when he's holding that.

"I don't... I don't know how it got there," I say, my voice shaky.

Parker's brow furrows, his confusion quickly turning to something darker. "Anna," he says gently, "are you sure you didn't put it there? As a memory you want to keep close?"

The heavy words hang in the air.

"I didn't," I snap, my tone defensive.

He exhales, rubbing the back of his neck. "It's just... this isn't the first time something like this has happened. First the cologne, the scarf, then the ring, now this. Are you... are you okay?"

His question hits me like a slap. "What is that supposed to mean?"

"It's not supposed to mean anything," he says, his voice calm but edged with worry. "I'm just... I'm worried about you."

"Worried about *me*?" I repeat, my voice rising. "Maybe Marla found it and thought it should be out," I say quickly, trying to sound logical.

His expression tightens. "Anna, that doesn't make any sense."

"Why not?" I snap, my desperation creeping into my voice. "I told you Marla had a soft spot for Theo."

He takes a step closer, his eyes searching mine. "You think the housekeeper stole a key to your storage unit and rummaged through it to find old photos? And then brought them back here to make you feel guilty for moving on?"

Before I can respond, Helen's voice cuts through the tension. "You two bickering again? God, it's like I'm living in a telenovela."

I whip my head around to see her leaning against the doorway, her eyes sparkling with mischief.

"Not now, Helen," Parker says, his tone more severe than I've ever heard it.

"What?" she says, feigning innocence. "I'm just saying, you two need to lighten up. Life's too short for all this drama."

Parker pinches the bridge of his nose, clearly at the end of his rope.

I can't take it anymore. "Helen, maybe you should... I don't know, go out for the evening?" I say, my voice trembling with barely contained anger.

She raises an eyebrow, smirking. "Sure thing, Anna. Anything to keep the peace in paradise." She saunters out of the room, leaving me and Parker standing in the silence.

"Anna," he says finally, his voice soft but firm. "I love you. But this... whatever's going on here... well, it's starting to concern me."

The words cut deep, but I can't let him see how much they hurt.

"I don't know what you want me to say," I whisper.

He shakes his head, looking down at the photograph one last time before placing it carefully on the coffee table. "Maybe you can say you are sorry."

Sorry.

For what? For questioning things that don't make sense? For not letting this go? For keeping secrets?

Parker watches me for a second longer, like he's waiting for me to say that word. When I say nothing, he exhales and walks away. I stay frozen, my fingers curled into fists, my pulse thrumming in my throat.

My thoughts drift to the attic, and a sharp chill runs through me.

Because if he ever goes up there—if he ever finds what I've hidden— there will be no turning back.

TWENTY

Client Notes: Fourth Session

Summary:
The client described an evening of quiet unease in their relationship. A specific memory surfaced: returning home to find their partner absent. Maybe they were never there at all.

Key Observations:

- **Fascination:** The client's descriptions of their partner border on poetic. There's an undeniable pull, as if the partner is more an idea than a person—an ideal they could never quite meet.
- **Gaps in the Story:** The narrative around the partner is evasive, as though the client is wanting to keep them protected, safe.
- **Intensity:** The client's attachment to their partner is both tender and tense, as though holding on too tightly might cause the thing they fear: collapse.

Therapist Reflection:

I find myself unsettled by the way the client speaks of their partner. Their words draw a vivid, cinematic portrait, and I can't help but wonder: who is this person? What lies beneath the surface they so carefully construct? My curiosity may be inappropriate, and yet it lingers. This is not about voyeurism. It's about understanding the dynamics that fuel this connection.

Note to File:

The client's partner looms over these sessions like a shadow. Each new detail is a thread in a web I find myself unwillingly drawn into.

The next morning starts tenderly, with sunlight streaming through the windows as Parker sets a tray on the bed. A plate of fluffy pancakes with strawberries and whipped cream is next to a vase holding a single rose. He leans over and kisses my forehead, the argument from last night forgotten.

"Happy birthday, my love," he says, his voice low and warm.

I sit up, the sight of him and the effort he's made bringing a smile to my face. "You didn't have to do all this."

He laughs softly. "It's your birthday. Of course I did."

We eat together, sharing bites and sipping coffee. Parker insists on feeding me forkfuls of pancake, and I playfully swat his hand away, laughing. For a moment, everything is perfect again—calm, steady, normal.

"Another year older," I say quietly, swirling my coffee. My life has changed so much in twelve months. I can't hash it out right now, with Parker here beside me, but I think of how just one year ago I was sneaking around with Grant. Six months later Theo died... and now this.

Parker sets his mug down and looks at me. "Another year, but many more to come."

He pulls out a small velvet box, and my heart skips a beat. Inside is a delicate necklace, a small charm encrusted in diamonds sparkling in the light.

"It's beautiful," I whisper, tears pricking my eyes.

It isn't something I would have ever chosen for myself. It's flashy in a way I am not. I look at Parker, wondering what he sees when he looks at me. Does he know me? *Really* know me? In moments when we are lost in kisses, whipped cream and strawberries, I think he does. But this gaudy necklace is entirely foreign to me.

"It's probably too extravagant," he says, clasping it around my neck. "But the moment I saw the clam-shaped charm, I knew it had to be yours. It reminded me of the day we met, when Sadie was painting the shells she had collected from the beach. Where our love story began."

Tears fill my eyes as my fingers brush over the charm. I lean into him, letting the moment linger, trying to absorb the weight of his love.

"Thank you, Parker, for everything."

The day moves on, and I find myself in the kitchen, putting the final touches on the table. Parker is outside hanging string lights, and Helen is fussing over the arrangement of napkins again.

Jillian arrives, sweeping in with her usual flair, carrying flowers and a box of fancy chocolates.

"Birthday girl!" she exclaims, pulling me into a hug. "Tell me this isn't one of those quiet, introspective birthdays. You deserve a little *fun*."

"It's just dinner," I say, smiling. "Parker's here, Helen, and now you. That's plenty for me."

She eyes me knowingly. "You're always so modest. One day, we'll throw you a party so big you'll have to hire a bouncer."

I roll my eyes, then pull her over to Parker, eager for them to finally meet. "This is my fiancé," I tell her.

"Oh *my*, you said he was handsome, but Anna!" She gives Parker a warm hug, and he laughs.

"I've heard so much about you," he says with a smile.

"Only the scandalous parts, I hope," Jillian trills.

We all laugh, but before anyone can reply, the doorbell rings.

"I'll get it," Parker calls, moving toward the sliding glass door. He swings the door open, and I hear the unmistakable sound of Sadie's voice.

"*Surprise!*"

I rush to the door, and there she is—my sweet Sadie, grinning and clutching her stuffed animal. Behind her, Marsha and Conrad stand awkwardly, bags in hand.

"Sadie!" I exclaim, pulling her into my arms. "What are you doing here?"

"I wanted to surprise you for your birthday!" she says, her voice full of excitement.

I look over her shoulder at Marsha, who cringes. "She told us she had your permission, that you two had planned it. But apparently, she didn't tell us the whole truth..."

Sadie looks up at me, her face so innocent and hopeful. "I just wanted to see you, Mama."

My heart melts, and I stroke her hair. "You should've told me, sweetheart. But I'm so happy you're here."

Marsha looks apologetic. "We're so sorry—we don't want to impose. We planned on coming for only one night."

"No," I say firmly. "You'll stay. Helen can take the couch, I'm sure. It's fine."

Helen overhears this as she walks in from the patio and groans dramatically. "Oh, the sacrifices I make for this family."

Jillian snorts, and even Conrad chuckles. The tension eases as everyone starts pitching in, rearranging chairs and making room at the table. There is a massive sense of relief that even the unexpected is going okay.

As the kitchen bustles, the mood shifts to something verging on joyful. Jillian chops garlic while Helen stirs a pot of sauce, and Marsha works on a salad.

"It's like we're in one of those cheesy cooking shows," Jillian jokes. "Except none of us is winning any awards."

"Speak for yourself," Helen says, tossing a pinch of salt into the pot. "I could totally have my own show."

"Sure," Jillian quips. "It'd be called *Half-Baked Chaos*."

I snort. Clearly my best friend has gotten the measure of Helen quickly. Even Marsha laughs at that, and I find myself smiling, grateful for the moment. Sadie sits at the counter, watching everyone with wide eyes. Her presence fills the house in a way I didn't realize I needed.

Our al fresco dinner is served just as the sun begins to set. The string of outdoor lights casts a soft glow over the table. Parker uncorks a bottle of wine, pouring glasses for everyone except Sadie, who sips lemonade.

The conversation flows easily, but there's an undercurrent of something deeper. Conrad is quiet. His gaze drifts to the garden as if lost in thought. At one point, he looks at me and says, "Theo loved this time of year. He always said the light in summer evenings was magic."

The table falls silent for a moment, everyone unsure how to respond. It's Jillian who finally breaks the tension.

"Well," she says, raising her glass, "to *Anna*. For being the glue that keeps us all together. And for having excellent taste in friends and family."

Everyone laughs, clinking glasses, the heaviness dissipating.

Sadie leans against me, her small hand in mine. There is a sense of peace I haven't felt in a long time. For once, everything is as it should be.

After dinner, we head inside for cake. Jillian insists on

lighting the candles herself, and she sings loudly and off-key, making everyone laugh. Sadie claps her hands, her joy infectious.

As I blow out the candles, I close my eyes, wishing for more. Happiness? Stability? A way forward?

But just as we're about to slice the cake, the faint hum of the television breaks the moment.

A flicker of light. A voice.

A voice I know.

Theo.

The room snaps to stillness, the only sound the soft crackle of the video. The air thickens, pressing down on my chest.

On the screen, Theo is holding a toddler-aged Sadie, her giggles filling the room. I'm there too, my hair loose and wild, smiling in a way that feels foreign now. The camera pans, capturing a moment so perfect it's nearly unreal. Theo pulls me toward him, twirling me in a dance—right here in this kitchen— as Sadie spins around us.

My stomach plummets.

This isn't possible.

The wineglass in my hand slips. It shatters on the tile, shards glinting under the flickering blue glow of the screen.

I didn't do this. My phone isn't streaming an old family video.

Someone else did.

A slow pulse of panic surges through me. This is premeditated. Intentional. Someone in this room did this.

A silence grips the kitchen, so sharp it could cut. No one moves. No one speaks.

Except for Theo. His laughter—alive and present and here when he should be gone.

Parker is the first to snap. "Who put this on?" His voice bites through the silence, sharp and demanding.

No one answers.

The video continues, Theo's deep laugh infectious, inescapable.

Parker's eyes cut across the room, landing on each of us, searching for a culprit. "Seriously. Who is streaming this?"

Sadie shakes her head, wide-eyed. Helen raises her eyebrows but says nothing, sipping her wine, unreadable. Jillian looks between us all, her unease growing.

Marsha clears her throat, her voice hesitant. "Maybe it was in the player already?"

No. No, it wasn't.

Parker is already shaking his head, his voice tightening, his fingers pressing into the counter. "We don't have a DVD player. It's coming from someone's phone. It has to be."

He turns to me, suspicion flaring in his eyes. "Anna?"

A beat of silence.

I know what he sees. My wide eyes. Air sticking to my throat. The way I'm frozen, my heart slamming against my ribs.

My throat closes. I try to answer, but my voice won't come. I don't know how this is happening. I don't know who did this. But I know one thing.

This wasn't me.

Parker exhales sharply. "Show me your phones."

Helen snorts, swirling her wine. "Oh, *please.*" She lifts her glass with a smirk that doesn't reach her eyes. "Not exactly my style to dig up the dead."

I whip toward her, my voice snapping out before I can stop it. "Helen."

Sadie shifts closer to me, her small hand clutching my sleeve.

Parker isn't buying any of this. His hands press against the counter, fingers splayed, bracing himself like he's about to blow the entire room apart.

His voice drops lower, more measured. More dangerous.

"Anna," he says again, slowly this time. "Are you sure you aren't...?"

Everyone is looking at me. Everyone is waiting.

A slow, sickening realization unfurls inside me.

This is a warning.

Not from me. From someone else.

Someone wants me to see this.

Someone wants Parker to see this.

Someone knows everything.

I can feel Parker's rage coiling beside me, can sense the tension in the air about to snap.

Sadie looks up at me, her big eyes filled with confusion. "Mom?" she whispers.

"I don't know," I whisper. "I don't know."

Parker stares at me for another moment, his jaw tightening before he looks away, his shoulders stiff with disbelief. The video crackles as Theo's laughter fades into the background, replaced by the sound of Sadie's toddler giggles. The juxtaposition is like a blade slicing through the air.

Helen leans back in her chair, swirling her wine with a smirk that doesn't reach her eyes. "Well," she says, breaking the silence. "This is awkward, but are we still going to have that delicious-looking cake?"

Parker's gaze snaps to her, piercing with warning. But Helen raises her glass as if to toast the chaos.

Parker stares me down, his body rigid, his jaw tight. He doesn't believe me.

But I don't care. Because the truth is—I don't know what's coming next. And that terrifies me more than anything.

Jillian clears her throat awkwardly, standing. "What do you need, Anna?"

"I don't know what I need," I say quickly, answering Jillian, my voice too loud. "But it's fine. Everything is fine."

But it's not fine. Nothing about this moment is fine.

The video continues to play. Theo is staring at all of us from the screen, his expression touching something deep in my heart, as if he remembers everything we left unsaid.

And just like that, I'm back in the kitchen the last morning before he died.

Theo standing by the door, zipping up his coat. His hiking bag slung over one shoulder. The smell of coffee and pine clinging to him.

We thought we had all the time in the world.

And now here he is, alive on this screen, frozen in a moment I can never step into again. I blink hard, my throat tightening, because suddenly it's too much: his voice, his laugh, the way he moves—so natural, so unburdened.

He had no idea he was running out of time. And the worst part is, neither did I. As the video reaches its end, the screen goes black. It leaves only our reflections in the glass. No one speaks. No one moves.

And in that heavy, suffocating quiet, I feel it. The past isn't haunting us.

It's here.

TWENTY-TWO

Sadie's bedroom door is closed, and the faint glow from the hallway light spills across the woodgrain floor. I hesitate, hand on the knob, trying to steel myself for the conversation ahead. I know she's upset—her reaction at dinner made that clear. But I can't leave this unresolved. Not tonight.

"Sadie?" I call softly, knocking twice. "Can I come in?"

There's a pause, long enough to make me question whether she's ignoring me. But then her small voice calls back, muffled. "Yeah."

I open the door and find her sitting cross-legged on her bed. Buttercup, her floppy-eared stuffed animal, is clutched tightly in her arms. Her face is turned away, staring at the string of fairy lights she has draped across her headboard. They cast a soft, golden glow, but the shadows on her face tell a different story.

I sit on the edge of her bed, careful not to crowd her. "Hey," I say gently. "You've been quiet. Are you okay?"

She shrugs, her eyes still fixed on the lights. "I don't know."

"It's okay if you're not," I say. "Tonight was... a lot. The video, seeing Dad like that... I wasn't expecting it either."

She looks at me now, her brows furrowing. "You didn't know?"

I shake my head. "No, I was as surprised as you were."

Sadie presses her lips together, thinking. "Do you think... do you think someone played it on purpose?"

"I don't know," I admit, pushing aside my fear for a moment, determined to be present for this moment with my daughter. "Maybe someone thought we'd like seeing Dad. It was a happy memory, wasn't it?"

Her fingers tighten around Buttercup. "Yeah, but it hurt too."

My chest tightens. "I know. But it also reminded me of how much he loved us. The way he spun you around like that, holding you close—it's nice to remember the good times, even when it makes us sad."

Sadie nods slowly, her expression softening. "I miss him," she whispers.

"I do too," I say, reaching for her hand. She doesn't pull away, but she doesn't squeeze back either. "I miss him every single day."

She looks down at Buttercup, her voice small. "I wish he was still here. Why did he have to go hiking that day?"

The question twists something deep inside me, and I take a steadying breath.

I see it so clearly.

"*Should be back midafternoon,* he had said, zipping up his coat without looking at me.

I had barely reacted. Barely registered the moment for what it was.

A quick kiss to my forehead. His scent—pine needles and coffee, the sharp bite of the morning air—clinging to him.

I hadn't known it would be the last time I'd ever touch him or hear his voice, his footsteps, the way he always cleared his throat before speaking.

I swallow, blinking hard, willing myself back to the present. Sadie is still looking at me, waiting for an answer I can't possibly give.

I reach for her, brushing a curl from her cheek. "I don't know, sweetheart. It was an accident. A terrible accident. He loved being outdoors, you know that. He would've never gone if he thought it wasn't safe."

"I know," she says, her voice cracking. "But it's not fair. None of it's fair..."

"I know it's not," I say, my own voice trembling. "And I wish I could change it. I wish I could bring him back."

Sadie finally looks at me, her eyes filled with tears. "I want everything to go back to how it was."

I blink back my own tears, my heart breaking for her. "I know, sweetheart. I do too."

"No, you don't," she snaps suddenly, pulling her hand away. "You're with *Parker* now. You don't even care about Dad anymore."

"Sadie," I say crisply, the sting of her words taking me by surprise, wondering if she has picked up on conversations her grandparents may have had the last few weeks. "That's not true."

"Then why does it feel like it?" she says, her voice rising. "You're acting like Dad didn't even matter."

I reach for Sadie again, but she jerks away, standing and pacing the room.

"You moved on, like he was nothing. Like he's gone, so whatever, time to start over with someone new."

The words cut deep, but not because they're hers.

I know where they came from. Marsha and Conrad. Their grief, their anger in losing their son—poison dripping into Sadie's ears.

I can almost hear Marsha's voice now, sharp and bitter. *Your mother didn't waste any time, did she?*

Sadie hadn't reacted then. She had just hugged me and walked inside. But now, I see it—those words have been growing inside her, twisting into something ugly, something raw.

I swallow hard, steadying myself.

"That's not fair," I say, standing too. "Your dad mattered more to me than you can imagine. He always will."

"Then why do you act like this is okay?" she demands, tears streaming down her face. "It's *not* okay. It's never going to be okay."

"Sadie..." My voice breaks, and I struggle to find the right words. "I'm trying. I'm doing the best I can. But I can't give you what you want. I can't bring Dad back."

She stops pacing and stares at me, her chest heaving. "I want my family again," she whispers. "But it's gone forever, isn't it? It's *never* coming back."

I step closer, desperate to comfort her. "We're still a family, Sadie. It's... it's different now. But I promise you, I'm here for you. Always. And so are Grandma and Grandpa, and Aunt Jillian."

She shakes her head, turning away. "It doesn't seem like it. Grandma and Grandpa say it's all too fast. That you don't even *know* Parker."

"Sadie," I plead, but she climbs back onto her bed, curling up with Buttercup and shutting me out.

I stand there for a moment, helpless, my heart aching. "I love you," I say softly. "More than anything."

She doesn't respond. Her small frame shakes with quiet sobs, and all I can do is watch. I am powerless to make it better.

I finally back away, leaving the room. In the hallway, I lean against the wall, letting the tears I'd held back fall freely. I failed Sadie tonight. I failed both of us.

. . .

Downstairs, the house is still. Too still. Someone has turned the video off, but the memory of it plays in my mind, Theo's laugh echoing faintly in my ears. I don't want to focus on the past, but the joy in his voice, the way he spun Sadie around like she was the most precious thing in the world, is inescapable.

I glance at the kitchen table.

The cake sits untouched, the knife still resting beside it, waiting. The candles have long since burned out, wax pooling onto the frosting. No one had the heart to slice into it, not after what happened.

I exhale shakily, running my fingertips along the edge of the plate. It was supposed to be a simple night, a happy one. But now? Now, I don't know what happens next.

As sweet as the memory was, doubt creeps in. Dark and insistent.

Who turned that home movie on? Parker's reaction flashes in my mind, harsh and defensive. Would he do something like that? Would he try to manipulate me?

Or Helen, always one to meddle, her biting tongue never far from her twisted sense of humor. Could she have thought it was funny? Or worse—could she have thought it would hurt me?

Jillian, Marsha, and Conrad have nothing but good intentions when it comes to Sadie and me. But their words still echo, rattling around my head like loose change.

"*Six months.*" Marsha's voice had been quiet but edged with something sharp.

"*You're moving on fast.*" Conrad's arms crossed, his expression unreadable.

"*What are we supposed to tell Sadie about that? About what it means to love someone?*"

"*Neither is burying your son.*"

That last one still burns.

I swallow, pressing my fingertips to my temple as if I can physically push their voices away. They have major concerns over the impending marriage. But would they do something so hurtful to get my attention?

And then there's Grant. He obviously couldn't have played the family video tonight. But then I remember he mentioned stopping by the house... What if he came inside? What if he was motivated out of jealousy? A pang of guilt twists in my chest. But the question lingers, refusing to leave. Could his wife have discovered the truth about the affair? And if she did... how far would she go for revenge, now that her marriage is finally over?

I shake my head, pushing the thoughts away. Whoever did it must have meant well. They must have thought it would bring us comfort.

But I know that line of thinking is intentionally ignoring the truth. Someone is out to hurt me.

As I make my way back to my bedroom, the unease lingers, curling around me like fog. I glance at the shadowed corners of the house, half expecting to see Theo standing there, watching.

He's gone. I know that. I've told myself that a hundred times. But the house is different tonight. Heavy. Restless. Like it's keeping secrets of its own.

And then, a thought presses in, unshakable.

Parker is a stranger.

Sadie said it. And Jillian said it too.

I swallow, my fingers tightening around the doorknob.

I know my fiancé.

Don't I?

TWENTY-THREE

Sadie's small suitcase thuds softly as Conrad loads it into the back of their car. The morning is bright but cool, the kind of weather that belongs more to late autumn than early summer. Sadie lingers on the porch, Buttercup tucked under her arm, her face turned downward as if studying the worn wooden steps.

I kneel in front of her, brushing a strand of hair from her face. "You're going to have fun back at the farm, sweetheart," I say softly. "Two more weeks of running with the chickens and playing with the dog."

She shrugs, her lips pressed into a thin line. "I guess."

Marsha approaches, her usual briskness softened by the moment. "We'll take good care of her, Anna," she says, giving me a pointed look, as though I need convincing. She hesitates, then lowers her voice. "Listen, about last night—"

"I don't want to talk about it," I say quickly, my tone sharper than I intended.

Her eyes narrow, but she doesn't push. She doesn't have to. Because I already know what she thinks. She made it clear the last time I dropped Sadie off at the farm. The way she stood in the doorway, arms crossed, voice low but firm. *This is too fast.*

And the worst part? Sadie had looked at me then, the same way she looked at me last night. Like she wasn't sure what to believe.

I swallow hard, forcing my expression smooth.

Sadie will be fine.

Concern flickers in her eyes. She knows something's off. We all do. Marsha exhales, giving me one last searching look before turning away. The conversation is over, but the weight of it lingers.

I hesitate, my pulse flickering with something uneasy.

Marsha and Conrad showing up yesterday. The home video playing last night. Is it just a coincidence? Or is this their way of reminding me, of making sure I don't forget who Theo was? Before I can chase the thought any further, Sadie throws her arms around me suddenly, squeezing tightly. I hold her close, closing my eyes against the sting of tears.

"I love you, sweetie," I whisper. "You call me anytime, okay? No matter what."

"Okay," she murmurs, her voice muffled against my sweater.

I release her reluctantly, watching as she climbs into the car. Marsha and Conrad wave as they pull out of the driveway, the old car kicking up a small trail of dust. Sadie presses her palm to the window, and I wave back until they disappear around the bend.

The house feels too empty the moment they're gone.

I linger on the porch, pulling my cardigan tighter around me. The weight of last night— the video, Parker's tension, Sadie's pain—settles heavily on my chest. I turn to go inside, but the sound of raised voices pulls me toward the back patio instead.

I walk around the house, pausing at the back gate. I can see them: Parker and Helen, standing by the edge of the patio, their postures stiff with anger. Helen's arms are crossed, her expression keen, while Parker gestures emphatically, his face red. I can't make out what they're saying, but their tones are clipped, hostile.

I step through the gate, the hinge creaking as it swings shut behind me. "What's going on?" I ask, my voice louder than I intended.

Both heads snap toward me. Parker's face tightens, his jaw working as though trying to swallow his frustration. Helen merely raises an eyebrow, her smirk laced with disdain.

"Nothing," Helen says, her voice dripping with dismissal. "Just a sibling squabble."

"Doesn't matter," Parker snaps, but there's an edge to his voice that tells me it does.

I look between them, my patience frayed. "Doesn't *matter?* After last night, I'd like to know what's happening. Who turned on that video? Neither of you wants to admit it, and now you're arguing out here like—"

"It wasn't me," Parker cuts in, his voice jagged. "And it wasn't Helen either."

Helen tilts her head, her gaze sliding to Parker. "Interesting how you're so sure."

"Because I *know* you," Parker shoots back. "And because you found *this.*" He holds up a small object, glinting in the sunlight.

It takes me a moment to recognize it. My chest goes tight. "Is that...?"

"It's what Helen found in the couch cushions," Parker says, his voice clipped. "The same couch where she slept last night."

I step closer as the object comes into focus. It's a compass. The brass casing is worn, but I'd know it anywhere. My hands tremble as I reach for it. I turn it over, and there it is—the inscription I had engraved years ago: *For Theo, You Are My True North.*

"This... this was in the storage unit," I whisper. "I swear it was."

Parker crosses his arms, his expression unreadable. "Apparently not."

Helen snorts softly, her eyes sharp. She's watching me. Studying me.

"So it *magically* ended up downstairs?" she says, her tone thick with sarcasm. "How convenient."

I shake my head, my stomach twisting.

No. This isn't happening...

"I don't understand," I murmur, my voice shaking. "Who would even know where it was?"

"Besides *you*?" Parker exhales sharply, dragging a hand through his hair. "That's the question, isn't it?"

Helen's smirk fades, replaced by something darker. She glances at Parker, then back at me. "I don't know what's going on in this house," she says. "But it's creeping me the hell out."

I clutch the compass so tightly my knuckles turn white. I suck in a breath and hold it there. I need to think. But the walls feel like they're closing in.

The cologne. The photograph. The scarf. The wedding ring. The home video... And now this.

This isn't random. This isn't an accident. Someone is playing a game with me. My mind spins, flipping through possibilities like a deck of cards.

Did Sadie come back to make me see something I don't want to? Is Helen watching me too closely, pushing, needling—does she know what I've done? And Parker, standing stiffly beside me now, wholly unreadable—does he know more than he's saying? Then there's Marla, silent and ever-present, probably listening right now, and always loyal to Theo—would she want to remind me of what I lost? I think of Marsha and Conrad, disapproving that I am moving on from their son so fast.

Or Grant—does this have something to do with him? With *us*?

I force myself to swallow, my throat tight. The storage unit. It was locked. I packed everything away myself. No one was supposed to touch anything inside. And yet, here it is.

I want to believe it's nothing—a coincidence, an accident—but the air around me is thick, charged with confusion. "Parker," I say, my voice trembling, "I am scared someone's trying to mess with us."

He snorts, his jaw tightening. "I think this house is filled with reminders of a past life *you* can't leave behind."

I stare at him, stunned by the bitterness in his voice. "What's that supposed to mean?"

"It means," he says, his voice rising, "I'm doing everything I can to move forward, to build something new with you, and all I see are these constant reminders of Theo—of a life I'll *never* fit into."

I open my mouth to respond, but nothing comes out. Helen steps back, clearly not wanting to get caught in the middle, and I'm left staring at Parker, his shoulders tense, his face drawn.

"Do you need space?" I ask finally, my voice soft. "Is that what this is about?"

He looks at me, his eyes flashing with anger, hurt, desperation. Love. "No," he says firmly. "Space is the last thing I want. That's a step *back*, Anna, not forward."

His words hang between us, heavy and charged. The pang of guilt within me is dark and deep.

I think of Theo, of what we left unsaid, of the loss we had that we could never talk about. A loss that broke something fundamental between us. I never truly opened up to him after that. Not the way I should have. Instead, I allowed myself to disappear into another man. Into Grant.

With Theo, I let the cracks widen. I let the distance grow. Now, with Parker, I'm determined not to make the same mistakes. I *can't*.

"I want to make this work," I say, my voice steady despite the tremor in my chest. "I do."

He nods, but his expression doesn't soften. "Then we need to figure this out. All of it."

I glance down at the compass in my hand, the smooth brass cool against my skin. It feels heavier than it should. Its presence raises questions I don't have answers to.

The sound of gravel crunching pulls my attention to the driveway. A sleek black car rolls to a stop, the sun reflecting off its windshield. My lungs stutter as the driver's side door opens.

Parker looks over, frowning. "Who the hell is that?"

I don't answer. But I already know. The figure steps out, his silhouette unmistakable even from this distance.

Grant.

TWENTY-FOUR
TWO MONTHS BEFORE THEO'S DEATH

The hotel lobby is a sanctuary of indulgence. Marble floors gleam under the muted glow of crystal chandeliers, and the soft strains of piano music float through the air. The scent of lilies and polished wood creates a cocoon of luxury, a world apart from the mess that has become my life.

Grant waits near the reception desk, his hands in his pockets and his shoulders relaxed. He looks out of place here, his crisp white shirt and dark jeans hinting at simplicity, yet he belongs all the same. His hair catches the light, the subtle streaks of gray at his temples giving him an effortless sophistication that makes my heart pound.

When he sees me, his eyes light up. An unfamiliar heat rises in my cheeks. This is the first time we've met like this, in a hotel, and the thrill of it has all my senses on high alert.

"Anna," he says, his voice warm as he steps forward.

"Hi," I reply, any other words lost on me. I am mesmerized by this man.

"You look..." He trails off, his eyes lingering on mine. "Divine."

"So do you," I say, the words tumbling out unbidden.

He places his hand gently on my lower back, guiding me toward the elevators. The warmth of his touch seeps through the thin fabric, holding me and unsettling me all at once. My pulse quickens as the elevator doors slide closed, and for the first time, I'm acutely aware of the intimacy of the space. His scent—faintly woodsy, with a trace of something warm and familiar—envelops me.

Neither of us speaks as the elevator ascends, but the air between us hums with an unspoken electricity.

The room is everything I'd imagined and more. Floor-to-ceiling windows offer a panoramic view of the town, its buildings bathed in golden afternoon light. A plush king-sized bed draped in crisp white linens dominates the space, and a small sitting area with overstuffed chairs and a low table is arranged near the window.

Grant sets his bag down by the door and turns to me, his expression soft. "What do you think?"

"It's wonderful," I whisper, stepping farther into the room. The carpet is thick beneath my boots, muffling my movements as I approach the windows. Silverport stretches out before me, endless and alive.

"You deserve a wonderful life," he murmurs, his voice low as he comes to stand behind me. His hands rest lightly on my shoulders, his thumbs brushing against the bare skin above the neckline of my dress.

I close my eyes, leaning into his touch. For a moment, the weight of everything—the lies, the guilt, the impossibility of what we're doing—fades away.

The knock on the door pulls us out of the moment, and Grant steps away to answer it. A uniformed attendant wheels in a tray with silver domes concealing what I can only imagine is an indulgent brunch spread.

"Thank you," Grant says, tipping the attendant generously before closing the door.

I sit on the edge of the bed, watching as he lifts the domes to reveal an array of delicacies: chocolate-dipped strawberries, pastries dusted with powdered sugar and a bottle of champagne nestled in a bucket of ice.

"This is..." I trail off, shaking my head with a small laugh. "A lot."

"You deserve a lot," he says simply, pouring two glasses of champagne. He hands me one, his fingers brushing mine, and raises his own in a toast. "To us."

I hesitate for a moment before clinking my glass against his. "To us," I echo, though the words are precarious, as though they might shatter under their own weight.

The champagne is crisp and effervescent, the bubbles tickling my nose as I take a sip. Grant picks up a strawberry, holding it to my lips with a small, playful smile. I roll my eyes but lean forward, biting into the rich chocolate and sweet fruit. The taste is decadent, overwhelming.

"You're spoiling me," I say, my voice light, but tinged with something deeper.

"I plan to," he replies, his tone serious despite the teasing smile on his lips. We undress quickly, his eyes traveling over the black lace lingerie I bought for this special occasion: the one-month anniversary of the first time we made love.

"You look incredible," he groans.

I spin around, letting him admire my body from all angles. I feel indulgent and alive. As if I am really his.

The bed is impossibly soft, the sheets cool against my skin as Grant's hands move over me with a tenderness that makes my chest ache. His touch is deliberate, reverent, as though he's trying to memorize every inch of me. When his lips meet mine, it's slow, unhurried, like he's savoring the moment.

I close my eyes, letting myself sink into the sensation of him —the warmth of his body, the roughness of his hands. For a while, there's nothing else. No Theo. No other wife. No guilt or consequences. Just us.

Afterward, we lie tangled together, the sheets wrapped around us. My head rests on his chest, and I can relax in the steady rise and fall of his breathing. His fingers trace lazy patterns on my back, and I let myself believe, for a moment, that this could last.

"Anna," he says softly, his voice breaking the quiet.

"Mm?" I murmur, not wanting to move, not wanting to shatter the fragile peace.

"I think Melanie knows."

The words cut through me like a knife, and I sit up, pulling the sheet around me. "What?"

Grant pushes himself up on one elbow, his expression regretful. "She's been... asking questions. About where I've been, and who I've been with."

My chest tightens, panic clawing its way to the surface. "What did you tell her?"

"Nothing," he says quickly, reaching for my hand. "But she's not stupid, Anna. She's... suspicious."

The room is suddenly too small, the air too thick. I swing my legs over the side of the bed, grabbing my dress from where it's draped over the chair. "This can't happen," I say, my voice trembling. "Your wife can't find out. Theo can't find out. If they do—"

"They *won't*," Grant says, his voice firm as he moves to stand in front of me. He places his hands on my shoulders, his touch anchoring but not enough to calm the storm inside me. "We'll be careful."

"Careful?" I laugh bitterly, shaking my head. "How careful can we be when we're sneaking around like this? When we're lying to everyone? Even coming here was reckless. Someone could have seen us in the hotel lobby—"

"Anna," he says softly, his hands moving to cup my face.

But I'm already pulling away. Creating distance between us is the only way I can breathe. "I need to go," I say, my voice cracking.

"Please don't shut me out," he says, but I'm already reaching for my bag, my heart pounding in my chest. "Anna, wait—"

"I'll call you," I say, though in that moment I don't know if it's true.

The rain starts as soon as I leave the hotel, light at first but quickly turning into a downpour. The wipers on my car struggle to keep up, and the rhythmic thud of the rain against the windshield mirrors the pounding in my head.

What kind of mother am I? My job is to protect Sadie, not destroy her entire world.

By the time I pull into my driveway, my hands are trembling. The house is dark, the faint glow of the porch light the only sign of life. Theo isn't home yet, and Sadie is still at school, leaving me alone with my spiraling thoughts.

Melanie knows.

The thought loops endlessly in my mind, each repetition tightening the knot in my stomach. If she does, how long before Theo finds out?

And what will happen when he does?

The black car sits in the driveway like an unwanted guest. I would recognize it anywhere.

Grant leans against the driver's side door, sunglasses perched on his face. His hands are casually shoved into his pockets. My chest tightens as I walk toward him, the compass still clutched tightly in my hand.

He lifts the sunglasses, revealing eyes that are far too familiar. "Anna."

"What are you doing here?" I hiss, stopping a few feet away from him.

He straightens, holding out an object. I look down and see my sunglasses case. "You left these in my car the other night. Figured you might need them."

I stare at the case in his hand, anger rising in my chest. They must've fallen from my purse. "You could've mailed them, Grant."

He shrugs, his voice calm. "I thought it'd be easier to drop by."

"Easier for who?" I glance toward the house, suddenly

conscious of how visible we are. "You shouldn't have come here."

"I had to. There are things you should know." His voice is steady, but there's a hint of urgency in his voice. I stare at him and see a flicker of something behind his eyes.

"What *things*?" I ask, trying to understand why, of all moments, Grant has come here now.

"About Parker."

My eyes widen, and I search Grant's face.

"What—"

"Who's this?" Parker's voice cuts in, barbed and suspicious. I turn to see him standing on the porch, his arms crossed, his expression tight.

Grant doesn't miss a beat. "I'm an old friend," he says, his tone neutral. "Anna and I ran into each other the other night."

Parker's eyes flick to me, his jaw tightening. "An old friend?"

"It's not what you think," I say quickly, my cheeks burning. "We were at the same intersection, that's all."

Helen steps out onto the porch, her face lighting up with interest. "Well, this just got interesting."

"Not now, Helen," I snap, my patience with her fraying.

Grant's gaze shifts to Parker, his tone deceptively casual. "And *you* are?"

Parker doesn't answer right away. The tension between them is palpable, thickening the air. "I'm her *fiancé*," he says finally, his voice clipped.

"Fiancé," Grant repeats, a faint edge to his tone. He looks back at me, his brows raising slightly. "Congratulations."

"Thank you," I say tersely. "Now, if you'll excuse us—"

"I should go," Grant says, cutting me off. He steps back toward his car but pauses, his gaze lingering on me. He drops his voice. "Take care of yourself, Anna. And... be *careful*."

The words send a chill through me, but I don't respond. I

watch as he gets into his car and drives away, the tension in my chest tightening with each second.

I stand frozen on the driveway, my hand tightening around the compass. The weight of it is heavier than it should be, like an anchor pulling me back into waters I thought I'd left behind.

Parker's arms are crossed. "Who the hell was that?"

The weight of the moment presses down on me. "He's... someone I used to know."

"Someone you *used* to know?" His voice rises slightly. "He seemed pretty familiar with you."

"It's nothing," I insist. "He was dropping something off. That's it."

"Right," Parker says, his jaw tight. "Because that didn't feel weird at all."

Helen snorts softly from behind him. "Weird doesn't even cover it," she mutters, retreating into the house.

"I'm not doing this right now," I say, pushing past Parker and heading for the house.

"We're not done here. Who is he?" Parker presses, stepping closer. "And don't tell me he's some random guy."

I force myself to meet his gaze. "We ran into each other the other night, and I left my sunglasses in his car. That's it."

Parker studies me for a long moment, his eyes narrowing slightly. "And how did your sunglasses wind up in his car?"

"He drove me home," I tell him honestly, holding my ground. "It's not a big deal."

He exhales critically, running a hand through his hair. "It feels like a big deal."

"Well, it's not," I snap, icier than I intended. "Can we drop this now?"

The tension between us lingers, heavy and palpable. He doesn't look convinced, but he nods stiffly. "Fine. But next time, maybe let me know when 'old friends' are planning to show up."

I walk past him toward the kitchen, trying to ignore the heat rising in my cheeks. "I need a minute," I mutter.

He follows me, his voice softer now. "Hey, I'm not trying to pick a fight. I... I just need to know where your head's at."

I stop in the hallway, turning back to face him. "My head's spinning," I admit. "Between Sadie leaving, Helen's constant presence and now *this*..." I gesture at him. "I need to breathe."

His expression softens, and he steps closer, brushing his hand lightly against my arm. "Take a hot shower," he says gently. "I'll make us some lunch. Okay?"

I nod, the tension in my chest loosening slightly. "Thank you."

He leans in, pressing a soft kiss to my forehead. "We'll be fine," he murmurs. "Maybe it's time to talk to Helen about finding somewhere else to stay. You're right, this was supposed to be our time, Anna. Just the two of us."

The thought is a relief I didn't realize I needed. Helen's snippy remarks, her constant hovering—it's all been too much. "You think she'd actually leave?" I ask.

"She doesn't have much of a choice," Parker says with a faint smile. "I'll talk to her."

I nod, but the unease doesn't fade. Helen leaving should make me feel lighter. Instead, it feels like another door closing— another way to keep me from the truth.

Because I don't know what Grant was going to say, and I don't know what he meant about Parker. The words loop in my mind, over and over, each time tightening the knot in my stomach.

Be careful.

What was Grant trying to tell me? Was it a warning? A mistake? A truth he assumed I already knew?

I replay the way he looked at me, the hesitation, the way he stopped himself. Like he wasn't sure if he should say it. Like maybe it was too big, too dangerous to speak aloud.

Was he about to confess something? Or was he afraid?

I exhale shakily, pressing my fingers to my temple.

I know Parker. I do. Don't I? He is steady. Reliable. He takes care of me, loves Sadie, has never been anything but patient with the weight of my grief.

But Grant's words have cracked something open, and now, no matter how I try to push it down, I can't stop thinking about it.

What if I'm wrong?

What if I've been looking at Parker through the lens of my own desperation—seeing what I needed to see, instead of what was real? The thought sends a cold shiver through me.

My stomach knots. I need to talk to Grant about my fiancé.

Before it's too late.

TWENTY-SIX

THREE MONTHS BEFORE THEO'S DEATH

It's been weeks since Grant and I kissed for the first time. Weeks of stolen moments, lingering glances. The kind of tension that is like a cord pulled so tight it could snap at any moment.

I've tried to stay away, to keep myself from taking this too far. But every time I see him—every time I hear his voice or feel the brush of his hand against mine—it becomes more difficult to remember why I shouldn't. The moment Sadie leaves for school, I find myself putting on a coat and walking the few blocks over to his house.

His wife, Melanie, is always away on business. I don't ask about her, I don't want to know. I want to stay lost in this stolen, perfect place with Grant for as long as I can.

This morning, the rain pours down in sheets once again. It drenches the streets and blurs the world outside. I'm at Grant's house, sitting on the couch while he lights the fireplace. His movements are unhurried, deliberate. I watch him, every part of me aware of how close he is.

When he turns to look at me, his eyes catch the firelight, full of warmth. His gaze makes me feel like I'm both floating and anchored at the same time.

"You're quiet today," he says, sitting down beside me. His voice is soft, coaxing.

"I'm... thinking," I say, though it's an understatement. My thoughts have been a storm ever since I walked through his door.

"About what?" he asks, leaning closer.

"You," I admit, my voice barely above a whisper. "About us."

He exhales slowly, his gaze steady on mine. "Anna," he says softly. "You don't have to say anything. I know how complicated this is."

"It's not complicated when I'm with you," I say, surprising myself with the honesty of my words. "It is... easy. Like everything makes sense."

Grant reaches for my hand, his fingers threading through mine. "It's the same for me," he says. "You're the only thing that makes sense right now."

The weight of his words, of everything left unspoken between us, hangs heavy in the air.

"I've tried to stay away," I say, my voice trembling. "I've tried to tell myself this isn't right."

"And?" he asks, his voice low.

"And I can't," I whisper, tears welling in my eyes. "I don't want to."

Grant cups my face in his hands, his touch gentle but firm, soothing me. "You don't have to fight this anymore," he says, his voice steady. "I love you, Anna. I don't care about anything else."

The words hit me like a wave, overwhelming and inevitable. I close my eyes, letting the tears spill over as I lean into his touch. "I love you too," I whisper, the truth of it breaking through every wall I've built around myself.

When our lips meet, it's slow and deliberate, a kiss filled with everything we've been holding back. His hands slide into my hair, pulling me closer, and I let myself fall into him, into this moment. The world outside fades away, leaving only the heat of his mouth on mine, his hands tracing the curve of my back.

He lifts me effortlessly, carrying me to the bedroom without breaking the kiss. The room is dimly lit, the soft glow of the fireplace casting flickering shadows on the walls. He lays me down gently, his hands never leaving me, his touch a constant reassurance.

Grant hovers over me, his gaze searching mine as if asking for permission, for trust. I nod, my heart hitching as his hands move to the hem of my sweater. He pulls it over my head slowly, reverently, as if unwrapping something sacred.

"You're lovely," he murmurs, his eyes never leaving mine.

I laugh softly, nervously. "I'm a mess."

"You're perfect," he says firmly, silencing my doubts with a kiss.

His hands explore my body, every touch igniting something deep inside me. It's been so long since I've felt this—since I've felt wanted, cherished, seen. Theo's touch was always practical, efficient, as if it were another task to complete. Grant is the opposite. His hands linger, tracing every curve, every scar, as if memorizing me.

When he undresses, I take a moment to admire him, the way his body moves with a quiet confidence. He's not perfect, but he's real, and that makes him more attractive than anything I've ever known.

When he presses his body against mine, I let out a soft gasp, the heat of him overwhelming in the best way. He pauses, his forehead resting against mine.

"Are you okay?" he asks, his voice low and steady.

I nod, wrapping my arms around his neck, pulling him closer. "Yes," I whisper. "I need this. I need *you*."

Our bodies move together in perfect harmony. Every touch, every kiss, a testament to the connection between us. It's slow and tender, filled with a kind of reverence that turns the air sacred and still. He doesn't make love to me; he worships me. His every movement a promise, a declaration.

I lose myself in him, in the way his hands cradle my hips, the way his lips graze my neck, the way he whispers my name like a prayer. The rest of the world ceases to exist, and for the first time in forever, I feel whole.

When it's over, we lie tangled together, our hearts pounding in the quiet of the room. Grant's hand brushes a strand of hair from my face, his eyes filled with a tenderness that makes my chest ache.

"I've never felt this way before," he says softly, his fingers tracing the curve of my jaw. "You're everything, Anna."

I press a kiss to his chest, my heart pounding in my ears. "You're everything to me."

Later, as the rain slows to a soft drizzle, Grant reaches for his journal on the bedside table. "I've been working on something for you," he says, flipping through the pages.

"For me?" I ask, propping myself up on my elbow.

He nods, his brow furrowed in concentration as he finds the right page. Then he begins to read:

"You are the quiet after the storm,
the stillness that heals the broken.
You are the light that filters through the cracks,
the hope I didn't know I needed."

His voice is steady, but I can hear the vulnerability in it, the way he's offering me a piece of himself. Tears prick my eyes as he continues:

"You are a world I want to get lost in,
a secret I never want to forget.

You are everything I never dared to dream of,
and now, I cannot imagine letting you go."

When he finishes, he looks at me, his expression uncertain. "It's not much," he says, closing the journal. "But it's how I feel."

"It's perfect," I say, my voice thick with emotion. "You're... perfect."

He laughs softly, pulling me closer. "I'm simply a man who got lucky enough to meet you."

The first rays of sunlight peek through the curtains after the rainstorm. We stare at one another, lost in our own thoughts. His face is peaceful in a way that makes my heart ache. I trace the lines of his jaw with my fingers, memorizing the moment, knowing it can't last.

But for now, it's enough.

TWENTY-SEVEN

ONE MONTH BEFORE THEO'S DEATH

In my house, I retreat to my studio, the only place that is mine alone. The air inside is cool and still, the familiar scent of paint and wood shavings wrapping around me like a safety blanket. I sink into my chair, my hands trembling as I reach for the miniature coffee mugs I've been working on.

The act of creating—of shaping something small and perfect—has always been my refuge. But today, even the steady rhythm of the paintbrush against the wood can't quiet the noise in my head.

I think of Grant, of the way he looked at me, the way he touched me, the way he made me feel alive. I think of Melanie, her name a painful reminder of everything I stand to lose. And then I think of Theo.

I add the final touch of gold to the rim of the tiny cup, my hand steady despite the turmoil inside me. The miniature is perfect, a tribute to the café where it all began. A tribute to Grant.

But as I set it down beside the tiny book of poetry I replicated last week, a weight settles over me.

This has to end. But even as the thought forms, I know it's a lie. I love him, and he's everywhere—woven into my thoughts, etched into my heart, haunting the corners of my mind.

I can never escape. And worse, I don't want to.

The house is quiet, save for the faint purr of the heater cycling on and off. Snow piles against the windowpanes, soft and relentless, muffling the world outside.

I sit on the couch, my knees pulled up to my chest, staring at the blank page of a notebook I pulled out hours ago. The pen rests loosely in my hand, unmoving. I haven't written a single word.

Theo is in the kitchen, rinsing out his coffee mug, his movements deliberate. I can hear the clink of porcelain against the counter, the sound pronounced in the stillness of the house. He's been watching me all day, his gaze heavy.

When he finally comes into the room, his footsteps soft, I steel myself for whatever he's about to say.

"You've been quiet," he says, sitting in the armchair across from me. His voice is calm, but there's an edge of worry beneath it.

"I'm fine," I say quickly, setting the notebook aside. "Just tired."

He studies me for a moment, his head tilting slightly. "You've been crying."

I drop my gaze, twisting my fingers in my lap.

"I've been thinking about... everything," I lie, the words tasting bitter.

He nods slowly, his expression unreadable. "I miss him too," he says, his voice soft.

My mind is on Grant. But he is thinking of Caleb.

The silence between us stretches, heavy with things neither of us say.

I know what he is remembering—long nights where neither

of us slept, the quiet that settled too deep in the house, the way we barely spoke because neither of us had the right words.

We were different people before. Before Caleb. Before everything changed.

Theo had always been the steady one, the one who carried his grief with quiet determination, while mine—mine had spilled out in ways I still can't explain.

Maybe that's why we unraveled.

He keeps talking, "I think about what could've been. What should've been."

The guilt rises, gagging me. I want to tell him the truth—that my tears aren't for Caleb. That they're for Grant, for the way he made me feel, for the loss of him that is another hole in my chest. But I can't. I won't admit to it. I am guilty of so much.

"I know you do," I say, my voice trembling.

Theo leans forward, his hands clasped together. "Anna, I've been thinking a lot lately. About us."

I meet his gaze, my stomach twisting. "What do you mean?"

"I've been seeing a therapist," he says, his tone cautious. "For a few months now."

The confession startles me, and I sit up straighter. "You have?"

He nods, his eyes steady. "I needed help, Anna. I didn't know how to deal with everything after Caleb. And I didn't know how to help *you*. I thought keeping busy, fixing things around the house, would fix us too. But it didn't."

The air between us is charged, and for a moment, I wonder if he knows. If he's pieced together the late nights and the excuses. If he's connected the dots between the space between us in our bed, the distance I've been trying to bridge with lies.

"My therapist has helped me see my life more clearly," Theo continues. "My grief, myself. *Us.* I want this marriage to work, Anna. I really want us to work."

His words hit me like a hammer, and my eyes sting with tears. "Theo, I don't know…"

"Please, give me a chance," he says, his voice pleading. "Let me take you out. Just the two of us. Let's try to find each other again."

I think of Sadie, of the vows I made to Theo, the man sitting in front of me who is trying so hard to rebuild what I've already broken. And then I think of Grant, of his touch, his voice, his love. I think of Caleb. The guilt is a weight I can't shake.

"Okay," I say finally, the word barely audible. "Let's go on a date."

Theo's face breaks into a smile, and I force myself to return it. For Sadie.

The restaurant Theo chooses is intimate and warm, the scent of roasted herbs and garlic waft through the air. Candles flicker on each table, casting soft shadows on the exposed brick walls. Snow coats the windows outside, but the room is alive with the buzz of conversation and clinking glasses.

Theo holds the door open for me, his hand lingering at the small of my back as we step inside. The gesture reminds me of Grant, and I have to shake the thought from my head. I shrug out of my coat, the heat from the fireplace thawing the cold from my skin.

"This place is perfect," I whisper, my voice tentative.

"I thought you'd like it," Theo says, his smile small but proud.

We're led to a table near the window. Theo orders a bottle of wine, and I sip my water, trying to quiet the storm in my head. I wonder again if he knows—if the therapy sessions have unearthed something I thought I'd buried. His calmness unnerves me, makes me question everything.

As we settle into the rhythm of the evening, Theo leans

forward, his expression soft. "You always loved places like this. Do you remember that café we used to go to in college?"

I smile faintly, the memory flickering in my mind like an old photograph. "The one with the terrible coffee and creaky floors?"

"That's the one," he says, chuckling. "You said it had... *character*."

"You loved it too," I tease, my tone lighter than I feel.

"I loved being there with you," he says, his voice steady. "It felt like we were the only people in the world."

His words catch me off guard, and for a terrible moment, I think I might cry. But then, out of the corner of my eye, I see them.

Grant and Melanie.

They're seated across the room, Grant's profile unmistakable, even in the dim light. Melanie is leaning toward him, her hand resting on his, her face lit with a soft smile. My stomach twists violently, and I grip the edge of the table, my pulse hammering in my ears.

"Anna?" Theo's voice pulls me back, and I force myself to meet his gaze. "Are you okay?"

"I'm fine," I say quickly, though my voice shakes and I can feel heat rising to my cheeks.

But I'm not fine. The walls are closing in. Grant hasn't seen me yet—at least, I don't think he has. I pray he won't. That Melanie won't.

Theo reaches across the table, his hand covering mine. "You're distracted."

"I'm... overwhelmed," I admit. "This fancy restaurant, our memories—it's a lot."

Theo nods, his thumb brushing gently over my knuckles. "It's okay. We'll take it slow."

I manage a small smile, but my mind races. I glance at Grant again, and this time, his eyes meet mine. For a split second, the world stops. His expression shifts—surprise, then something deeper, something unreadable.

He quickly looks away, turning his attention back to Melanie, but the damage is done. The blood drains from my face, my body going cold despite the heat of the room.

"Anna?" Theo's voice breaks through again, cracking this time.

"I need a moment," I say, standing abruptly. "I'll be right back."

I hurry toward the restroom, my heels clicking against the hardwood floor. My reflection in the mirror startles me—pale, wide-eyed, a woman unraveling at the seams. I grip the edge of the sink, as breath tangles in my throat.

This can't be happening. Not here. Not now.

I turn on the faucet, letting the cold water rush over my shaking hands before splashing some onto my face. The shock of it grounds me, pulling me back into my body. I inhale deeply—one, two, three —and then again, slower this time, steadying the tremor in my chest.

I press my palms against the cool porcelain, forcing stillness into my limbs. *You can do this.*

When I finally meet my reflection again, my expression is calmer, but my eyes—my eyes still hold the storm.

I close my eyes, willing myself to calm down. I step out of the restroom, my nerves frayed and my mind racing. The bustling noise from the restaurant seems far away, muted by the thudding of my heartbeat. And then he's there.

Grant is standing at the end of the hallway, his hands in his pockets, his expression carefully neutral. But his eyes—they tell me everything.

"Anna," he says softly, stepping closer. His voice carries a note of desperation, one I haven't heard before.

"What are you doing over here?" I whisper, glancing nervously over my shoulder. "This is dangerous."

"I had to see you," he says, his tone low but urgent. "I couldn't sit there and watch you across the room, pretending like we don't matter."

"Grant..." I shake my head, wrapping my arms around myself as if that could shield me from the weight of his words. "It's over, this thing between us. It has to be."

His jaw tightens, and he steps even closer, his presence filling the small hallway. "Is it? Is that what you want?"

I swallow hard, my throat dry. "What I want doesn't matter. This... us... it's too *dangerous*. Too messy."

"Anna, I love you," he says, the words hanging between us like a fragile thread. "And I don't think you've stopped loving me."

Tears sting my eyes, but I blink them back, shaking my head. "It doesn't matter," I whisper. "I can't do this anymore."

Grant reaches out, his fingers brushing my arm. "You're not happy, Anna. You can pretend all you want, but I *know* you. You deserve to be with someone who sees you, who loves you for who *you* are."

Before I can respond, I hear footsteps behind me. I freeze, motionless as I turn to see Theo walking toward us, his expression a mix of curiosity and concern.

"What's going on?" he asks, his gaze flicking between Grant and me.

Grant steps back, his hands dropping to his sides. "Theo, right?" he says, his voice calm. Too calm. "I was saying hello to Anna."

Theo's eyes narrow slightly, his posture stiffening. "And you are?"

"Grant," I say quickly, my voice too loud. "We... we met at the café. I mentioned him, remember?"

Theo nods slowly, his eyes still on Grant. "Ah, right. The writer."

"Yes," Grant says, offering a tight smile. "I was just leaving. Enjoy your evening."

He walks away without another word, his shoulders tense. The air has been sucked out of the hallway. I turn back to Theo, my chest tight with panic.

"What was that about?" Theo asks, his tone careful but edged with suspicion.

"Nothing," I say quickly, forcing a smile. "He recognized me and wanted to say hi. That's all."

Theo doesn't look convinced, but he lets it go, stepping closer to me. "Are you okay?"

"I'm fine," I lie, my voice trembling. "Let's go back to the table."

The rest of the dinner is a blur. Theo talks about Sadie, about his plans to rebuild our marriage, but I can barely focus. All I can think about is Grant—his words, his presence, the way he looked at me like I was the only thing that mattered.

When we leave the restaurant, the snow has stopped, and the air is crisp and biting. Theo slips his hand into mine, his grip warm and steady. It's like a chain, holding me to a life I no longer want.

At home, the house is quiet. Sadie is already asleep in her room. Theo heads to the kitchen, and I linger in the hallway, my mind racing. I think of Grant's words, of the way he said he loved me, and the way I didn't deny that I loved him too.

"Anna?" Theo calls from the kitchen. "Can you come here?"

Something in his voice sends a chill down my spine. I walk slowly toward the kitchen, my heart pounding in my chest. Theo is standing by the counter, his back to me.

When he turns, he's holding my phone. "I heard it buzz," he says, his voice calm but edged with curiosity.

I force a smile, even as my heart pounds in my chest. "Probably Jillian. She's always randomly texting me."

Theo's eyes flick to the screen, and for a moment, I think he's going to press further. But instead, he sets the phone down on the counter and steps back, his expression unreadable.

"Right," he says, his tone carefully neutral.

I reach for the phone, keeping my movements steady, casual. Too casual.

The screen is dark. The notification already gone.

I swallow, pulse hammering in my ears. It could be Jillian. It should be Jillian.

But I know better.

The air in the kitchen feels too still, charged with something unspoken. I resist the urge to check right there, even though every nerve in my body screams to see the name, to confirm what I already know. *Grant.*

Instead, I slide the phone into my pocket, my fingers pressing against it like a silent plea.

Please, not now.

Please, not him.

The tension lingers, hanging between us like a thread stretched too tight. He leans back against the counter, crossing his arms over his chest, his gaze settling on me.

"I thought tonight was good for us. Wasn't it?" His voice is soft, almost hesitant.

I swallow hard, nodding. "It was," I say, forcing my voice to steady. "It was perfect."

Theo watches me for a long moment, his eyes searching mine. My composure slips under the weight of his attention. But then he exhales, his shoulders relaxing slightly. The moment passes.

"Okay," he says quietly, pushing off the counter. "I'm going to bed. Big day tomorrow—finally getting out for that snow hike I've been planning. You remember?"

I nod quickly, my stomach twisting. "Yeah, of course. You've been looking forward to it."

"I have," he says, his voice lightening, though his expression remains guarded. "Fresh air, some time to think. Should do me good."

He brushes past me, his hand briefly grazing my arm, and I stand there, frozen, until I hear his footsteps on the stairs.

Only then do I pull my phone from my pocket, my hands trembling as I unlock the screen. The message stares back at me, stark and damning: *I can't stop thinking about you.*

I delete it immediately, as if that can erase it, as if that can make it not true. But it's too late. Theo saw the notification—he must have. He knew something was off.

He knows.

TWENTY-EIGHT
PRESENT DAY

The bathroom fills with steam as the water pours over me, scalding and relentless. I don't adjust it. I let the heat batter my skin, hoping it will wash away the weight pressing on my chest. My mind churns with everything I'm trying to suppress. The past, the present and the fragile threads holding it all together.

Sadie's face floats into my thoughts, her words from last night echoing faintly: *Why can't life go back to how it was?* My heart clenches, and tears prick my eyes. She deserves a life full of stability, not the mess I've made. How did I let this happen? I swallow hard as the water drips down my face, blending with the tears I can't hold back.

Theo.

He's everywhere lately. In a home video flickering on the TV, a compass once buried in the attic. His presence lingers in every corner of this house, a reminder of what I lost. Of what Sadie lost.

But how much of what we lost was real? Theo was a good father, yes. But a *perfect* husband? No. He held secrets, like I did. And even now, how do I untangle the truth from the guilt? Did I fail him, or did we simply fail each other?

The tears come harder now, my body trembling as the memories rush in. They're too much, too tangled to sort through. My love for Theo. My guilt over Grant. My complicated feelings for Parker—steady, attentive Parker, who is here now when no one else is.

I exhale into the moment, the water beating down on me like it's trying to drown my thoughts. Is love supposed to feel this conflicted? Because with Parker, it does. There are moments when I think we found something real—when he holds me close and promises we'll build a future together. And then there are moments like last night, when he snaps. Or today, when Grant's arrival exposed a side of him I had never seen before.

And Grant... What does he know about Parker? There is more he isn't saying. There always is with Grant.

I press my palms against the shower wall, my chest heaving with silent sobs. *Love. Guilt. Trust.* They twist together in a knot I can't untangle, tightening with every choice I've made. Every lie I've ever told. And that's the truth, isn't it? I'm no better than the people I doubt. Parker might be hiding something, but so am I. Maybe we all are.

The thought chills me, cutting through the heat of the water. I wipe my face roughly with my hands, straightening my spine. *Enough.* Falling apart won't help Sadie, or me, or anyone. It's going to be fine. I can handle this. I know what I'm doing.

I shut off the water, the abrupt silence jarring. Wrapping a towel tightly around myself, I try to calm the chaos in my chest. Composure. That's what I need. And Parker—whatever doubts I have about him—our relationship isn't over.

The sound of voices pulls me from my thoughts.

I pause, tilting my head toward the bathroom door. *Parker and Helen.* Their words are faint at first, carried on the stillness of the house, but they are growing much louder, echoing.

I freeze, my fingers tightening on the towel.

Parker had painted their relationship as perfect—close and unshakable, built on mutual respect. But the tone of their argument is anything but supportive. And it's not the first time. Last night, out on the patio, their voices had cut through the stillness, sharp and low. I hadn't meant to eavesdrop, but I couldn't unhear it once I did. The frustration in her voice, tight and clipped. Parker's response, barely above a whisper but laced with something that made my skin prickle.

And then silence. A charged, heavy kind. The kind that means there's more—so much more—that isn't being said.

Now, hearing the anger again, the edge of something *uglier* than just frustration—I can't ignore it. Parker had told me their bond was unshakable. So why does it feel like it's already cracked?

I ease the bathroom door open as quietly as I can.

"*I'm* not the problem here, Parker," Helen snaps, her voice steely. "*You* are."

"Oh, please," Parker fires back, his frustration crackling through the air. "You show up uninvited, make yourself at home, and now you're trying to tell *me* how to run *my* life?"

"You don't even know what you're doing!" Helen says, her voice quieter but her tone no less cutting. "You're barely holding it together."

I hesitate in the doorway, torn between stepping forward and retreating into the safety of the bathroom. My pulse quickens as their words sink in, their tension as thick as the steam still clinging to the walls.

Their voices lower, but the bitterness lingers. Helen says something I can't hear, and Parker's reply comes quickly, his tone harsh. "I said drop it, Helen. Don't push me."

The knot in my stomach tightens. Whatever this is, it's not the story Parker has told me—the story of a kind, supportive sister, just passing through.

Helen laughs, but there's no humor in it. "Right. Keep

playing the role, Parker. But we both know that's all this is—a *role*."

I freeze.

Parker exhales harshly. "I'm warning you."

A role.

The word echoes in my mind, twisting itself into something ugly. I step back into the bathroom and close the door softly, leaning against the cool tile as my thoughts spiral. Helen's words echo in my mind, heavy and cutting.

This is something darker, something messier. And as much as I don't want to admit it, it feels familiar.

Because I know what it's like to play a role.

And I'm not who I say I am either.

TWENTY-NINE
FOUR MONTHS BEFORE THEO'S DEATH

The pain hasn't dulled. If anything, it's turned icy, settling in my chest like a shard of glass I can't dislodge.

I sit in a corner booth at the café, staring at the tea in front of me. The steam curls lazily upward, untouched. Outside, rain streaks the windows, blurring the world beyond. I'm wrapped in an oversized sweater, hiding everything, trying to disappear.

A tear slips down my cheek, unnoticed until it splashes onto the wooden table.

"Are you okay?"

The voice startles me. He stands a few feet away, holding a journal in one hand and a coffee in the other. Dark hair, a soft brown gaze, the kind of presence that doesn't demand but invites. His navy sweater is pushed up to his elbows, his posture easy but attentive.

"I'm fine," I say quickly, my voice betraying me.

He hesitates, then gestures to the seat across from me. "Mind if I sit? I promise I'm not selling anything."

A weak smile tugs at my lips despite myself. "I guess."

He slides in, setting his journal and coffee down. "I'm Grant."

"Anna."

"Nice to meet you, Anna." He leans back slightly. "Now, I don't mean to intrude, but... you looked like you could use some company."

I glance down at my tea. "Was it that obvious?"

He grins. "Not at all, I'm just unusually observant."

The way he says it makes me laugh softly—an unfamiliar sound, even to me. Theo never talks like this—never lingers in moments without looking for solutions.

We talk for over an hour. At first, it's small things—the weather, the café, the rain that feels endless. But then words come faster, spilling out before I can stop them.

"I lost someone," I say finally, barely above a whisper.

Grant nods, no rush to fill the silence. "I'm sorry."

"It was three months ago," I continue. "But it feels like yesterday."

"You're here," he says. "That says something."

"What does it say?"

"That you're trying. Even if it doesn't feel like it."

The words hit me harder than I expected. "I don't know how to keep going," I admit. "Theo—my husband—he's grieving too, but it's like we're speaking different languages. I am so... alone."

Grant watches me carefully, his voice quiet but certain. "Grief does that. Puts you on an island, even when you're surrounded by people."

The understanding in his words unravels something in me. Theo hasn't truly seen me in months. Maybe years. But Grant does.

We talk until the café closes. As I step into the rain, I realize —I don't plan to see Grant again.

But I hope I might.

. . .

The next day, I spot him before I even step inside. He's at the same table, journal open, steam curling from his coffee.

When he looks up, his warm, familiar smile stirs something in me.

"Anna," he says, leaning back slightly. "Good timing."

"Good timing?" I ask, sliding into the seat across from him.

"I was thinking about you."

The honesty catches me off guard. I twist my wedding ring, unsure of how to respond.

"What were you thinking?" I ask finally.

"That I hoped I'd see you again."

The words should make me uncomfortable. But they don't.

We talk, our conversations stretching beyond grief and loss. He tells me about his writing, how he makes sense of the world through stories. I tell him about my miniatures, how I build tiny versions of real things.

"Miniatures?" he asks, intrigued. "Like furniture?"

"Like whole rooms," I explain. "Teacups, beds, bookshelves. Whatever catches my eye."

Grant leans forward, smiling. "I'd love to see them sometime."

"You would?" I laugh softly. "Why?"

"Because it's a window into who you are," he says simply. "And I want to know you."

The sincerity in his words holds me for a moment.

Outside, the rain has picked up, drumming softly against the pavement. He watches me for a long moment before speaking.

"Want to come over?" he asks. "I live just down the block. I make a decent cup of tea."

I hesitate. But then, I nod.

Grant's house is small but warm, walls lined with bookshelves, a couch worn but inviting. He hands me a mug of tea and sits beside me, his presence steady, calming.

The rain fills the silence, a soft, rhythmic pulse. My chest tightens.

"Anna," he says gently. "What's going on?"

I shake my head. My throat feels tight. "I don't know how to keep going," I whisper. "Every day feels like a fight."

Grant sets his mug down and leans closer. "You don't have to keep fighting," he says. "It's okay to let yourself feel it."

His words break me. The tears come—hot, unrelenting. I press my hands to my face, ashamed of my weakness.

But Grant doesn't look away. He reaches out, gently pulling my hands away, his touch warm and certain.

"Anna," he says, his voice low and steady. "You're not alone."

I look at him. And for the first time in months, I am truly seen.

When he leans in, I don't stop him. His lips meet mine, soft and searching, and everything else falls away. The kiss deepens slowly, tenderly. His hands anchor me while his mouth pulls me under. It's been so long since I've felt like this—wanted, needed, understood.

When we finally pull apart, the air between us is charged. His forehead rests against mine, his hands still cradling my face.

"Are you okay?" he whispers.

I nod, though I know everything has changed.

For the first time in months, I feel alive.

THIRTY

PRESENT DAY

"I'm not taking no for an answer!" Jillian declares the next morning, tossing my overnight bag into the trunk of her car like she's on a mission. "This is your birthday gift, Anna. Please, let me spoil you for once."

I lean against the passenger door, shaking my head but smiling despite myself. "I still can't believe you booked us into the Pillar Hotel. That place looks... *extravagant.*"

"That's the point," she says, adjusting her sunglasses with dramatic flair. "You, my dear, deserve a little extravagance. And besides, it's a spa. Nothing says 'you're a year older and fabulous' like hot stone massages and mountain views."

I laugh as I slide into the car, though a part of me is uneasy. Jillian's enthusiasm is contagious, but I can't shake the nagging thought that I don't deserve this. Not the spa, not the escape and certainly not the joy Jillian seems so determined to give me. Still, I let her chatter about the hotel's amenities as we pull out of the driveway, her car humming steadily beneath us.

The drive over the mountains is breathtaking. Sunlight streams through the trees, casting shifting shadows on the road, and the towering peaks watch over us as we drive. Jillian clicks through her playlist, landing on a cheerful indie one that fills the car. She taps her fingers on the steering wheel and sings along to the chorus, slightly off-key but unapologetically. It's a sound I didn't realize I'd missed.

"I cannot believe you haven't been to the Pillar before," she says, glancing at me. "You've lived out here for years, Anna. What have you been doing?"

"Surviving," I admit, watching the landscape blur past. "One day at a time."

"Well, that changes today," Jillian announces firmly. "This trip is about thriving. Celebrating. Living a little."

Her words settle between us, filling the silence that follows. I wish I could believe her, that I could embrace this trip without the shadow of guilt tagging along.

Parker hadn't said *no*, but I'd seen the flicker of frustration in his expression when I told him. "*I just mean—you've been so busy lately,*" he had said, voice careful. "*I thought we'd have some time together this week.*"

I'd reminded him it was just two nights. That it was something I needed. That Jillian had planned it for me. He hadn't argued. But he hadn't been happy either.

I exhale slowly, pushing the thought aside. I shouldn't feel guilty. Parker will be fine. And yet, the feeling clings to me like a second skin...That this trip—this moment of escape—has come at some kind of cost.

When we arrive at the Pillar Hotel, it's even more beautiful than I imagined. The Bavarian-style building looks like it belongs on the cover of a travel magazine, with flowerboxes spilling over with vibrant blooms and ivy curling up the cream-colored walls. The air smells crisp and clean, carrying a faint hint of pine. Jillian steps out of the car and spins around with her arms outstretched, her grin impossibly wide.

"Anna, look at this place! It's *perfect.*"

Inside, the lobby is equally as impressive. Polished wood

floors and large windows frame the surrounding mountains. The faint scent of lavender and eucalyptus hangs in the air, immediately calming. Jillian checks us in, chatting animatedly with the concierge, who hands us sleek keycards and promises a relaxing stay.

As we make our way to the room, Jillian lists out the plans she's already made: massages, facials and an evening in the infinity pool.

"And," she says, wiggling her eyebrows, "cocktails on the terrace. I scoped out the menu online, and it's *divine*."

I laugh, letting her energy wash over me. "You've thought of everything."

"Of course I have," she says. "It's your birthday, Anna. You deserve to feel special."

Her words warm me, even as doubt whispers in the back of my mind. I try to push it away, focusing instead on the soft robe waiting in the room and the promise of a massage that might finally unknot the tension in my shoulders.

Later, as we sit in the hot tub overlooking the mountains, Jillian leans back with a contented sigh. Steam curls around us, the water warm against the cool evening air. She tilts her head toward a group of men chatting by the pool, her grin mischievous.

"Okay, the guy in the blue swim trunks?" She winks. "Total hottie. Don't you think?"

I roll my eyes, laughing. "Jillian, you're ridiculous."

"What? I'm appreciating the scenery. Isn't that what this trip is for?"

"For you, maybe," I tease.

She gives me a pointed look. "And for you. Anna, when was the last time you leaned back and relaxed, enjoyed the view a little?"

Her question catches me off guard, and I falter. "I don't know…"

"Exactly," she says, her voice softening.

There's a beat of silence between us.

"Can I ask you something, Anna?" She leans towards me, looking suddenly and uncharacteristically serious. "Why Parker?"

The question lands like a stone in the water, rippling through me. I avoid her eyes, staring instead at the edge of the tub. "Parker's... reliable," I say after a moment. "He's safe."

Jillian snorts. "*Safe?* Anna, you're not buying a car. You're talking about your life. Safe isn't enough."

I don't answer, and she doesn't push.

"You don't like Parker?" I ask her.

The silence that follows is louder than her words.

She takes a drink of cold water, trying to cool off. "I think you're nowhere near as happy as a newly engaged woman ought to be."

Happy. The same thing Grant brought up. But do I deserve to be happy after everything that's happened to my family?

That evening, as we sit on the terrace sipping cocktails, Jillian shifts the conversation to lighter topics: the fact her divorce is so amicable it left them both wondering why they ever became more than friends, the cat she's thinking about adopting, her cousin's chaotic wedding plans.

I laugh at her stories, but my mind drifts. To Sadie. To the life I once had. To the man I never stopped loving.

I swirl the last sip of my drink in my glass, the ice clinking softly. The buzz in my veins is warm, numbing—but not enough.

"Do you think she's okay?" I ask suddenly.

Jillian pauses, setting down her glass. "Sadie?"

I nod.

"Of course she's okay. She's having the time of her life with Marsha and Conrad on the farm. They love her to pieces."

"I know," I say, fidgeting with my napkin. "It's just... I don't want her to think I'm... running away."

Jillian reaches across the table, her hand covering mine. "Anna, you're not running. You're thriving, and that's what Sadie needs to see."

Her words settle over me, soothing and heavy all at once. The massage therapist may have worked out the knot in my back, but the one in my chest hasn't loosened. Not yet.

Another cocktail appears in front of me. Then another.

Jillian checks her phone and sighs. "I need to use the bathroom," she says, standing and stretching. "Don't go anywhere."

I nod, watching her weave through the crowd toward the restaurant doors. The moment she disappears, the loneliness crashes in all over again.

My fingers fumble as I pull out my phone. I've had way too much to drink.

I shouldn't do it. But I do.

I hesitate, my heart hammering—then I press Grant's name.

It rings. And rings.

Then—his voice. Surprised. "Anna?"

A sob cracks out of me before I can stop it. "I miss you."

Silence.

I press the heel of my hand to my forehead, tears slipping free, hot and reckless. "I miss you, and I don't know what I'm doing, and I—" I pause, the truth an avalanche. "I love you."

His voice comes uneven through the line. "Anna..."

"I need to know," I whisper. "What do you know about Parker?"

A pause. Then, a sharp exhale. "I went to college with him."

I blink, trying to focus. "You... *what?*"

"I knew him, Anna. Not well, but enough." His voice hardens. "He's always been... deceitful."

The words slice through me, sobering me slightly. *"Deceitful?* How? What do you mean?"

"There were rumors..."

I sit up straighter, anger flashing through the haze of alcohol and grief. "Rumors aren't proof, Grant. I need something concrete."

He exhales again, quieter this time. "Well, I'm afraid I don't have that."

"Then why the hell are you telling me this?"

A shadow moves in my periphery—Jillian, stepping back onto the terrace.

I press the phone harder against my ear. "You can't just say something like that to me and not back it up."

"Anna," Grant says, his voice softer now. "Just... be careful."

There it is again. *Be careful.*

I abruptly end the call before Jillian sees that I was talking with someone. I don't want to answer her questions. My pulse hammers, the night suddenly too sharp, too cold.

She sits back down, eyeing me suspiciously. "You okay?"

My hands shake as I clasp them together under the table. "Yeah," I lie, swallowing hard.

But it is all beginning to unravel.

THIRTY-ONE

My phone screen flickers as Jillian's face comes into view. Her skin is softened by the warm glow of her Los Angeles apartment. Behind her, a brightly patterned throw is draped across her couch, and a small stack of books sits on the coffee table. She's holding a glass of red wine, her lips tinted by her signature bright red lipstick. She looks effortless, as always, and entirely out of place in the chaos of my life.

"Okay, spill!" she says, setting her wineglass on the table and propping her chin on her hand. "You look like you've been holding something in for days." I hesitate, my fingers toying with the frayed hem of my sweater. Despite the distance, Jillian's gaze is piercing, like she can see straight through me.

"I'm having an affair," I blurt out, my voice barely above a whisper. The words hang in the air, heavy and undeniable.

Jillian's eyes widen, and she leans closer to the screen as though she misheard. "What did you say?"

"I know," I say quickly, running a hand through my hair. "I know, Jillian. It's terrible. It's wrong. But I can't stop."

Her expression shifts, the initial shock giving way to

concern. "Anna," she says softly. "What's going on? Is this about Theo?"

I shake my head, staring down at the chipped polish on my nails. "It's not about him. Not really. It's about me. I'm... lost. Like I don't know who I am anymore."

Jillian exhales slowly, sitting back against the cushions. "Who is it? This guy you're... seeing?"

"Grant," I say, the name tasting forbidden and exhilarating all at once. "He's a writer. We met a few months ago, and it... happened."

Jillian's brow furrows, her lips pressing into a thin line. "Does Theo have any idea?"

"No," I say firmly. "And he can't. Sadie... she can't know either, of course."

"I'm not judging you," Jillian says, her voice tinged with sadness. "I know how much you've been through. I know how lonely you've felt after... after everything. But Anna, this is risky. What if this guy—Grant—what if he isn't who you think he is?"

The question catches me off guard, a ripple of doubt worming its way into my chest. "He's good, Jill," I say, my voice cracking. "He's kind. He listens to me."

"And Theo doesn't." She doesn't say it like a question. She knows. She knows how far apart Theo and I have been, and for how long.

"It's different," I say, the words catching in my throat. "Theo listens because he *has* to. Grant listens because he *wants* to."

Jillian stares at me for a long moment, her expression unreadable. Finally, she nods. "Okay. But promise me you'll be careful. Please."

"I will," I say, though the promise is as fragile as glass. "Enough about me. How are you?"

"Well, I am officially getting divorced." She shrugs. "We

knew it was coming. We talked last night and decided it was the best for both of us. We gave it a shot."

"Are you sad?"

She shakes her head. "Honestly, I'm relieved. I don't want to be anyone's wife. And we were always better at being friends."

"I wish I was with you right now, to give you a hug," I tell her.

She shakes her head. "Girl, I'm fine. I'm already browsing dating apps. I am in no position to give relationship advice. But hear me on this, if you care for Theo at all, which I know you do, then end your marriage before you hurt him more than necessary. Even if you don't love him, he will always be Sadie's dad."

I nod, taking in her advice. "I don't want to hurt anyone," I tell her.

"I know," she says gently. "But lying won't help anything. The truth will always set you free."

THIRTY-TWO
FOUR MONTHS BEFORE THEO'S DEATH

Grant's living room smells faintly of sandalwood and coffee. The afternoon sunlight streams through the tall windows, throwing golden streaks across the worn leather couch and the stack of books on the side table. A half-full mug of tea sits on the coffee table, forgotten.

Sadie's at school. Grant's house is cocooned in quiet. I'm sitting on the couch, my knees tucked under me, a steaming cup of chamomile tea warming my hands. Grant sits beside me, his arm draped lazily over the back of the couch, his eyes fixed on me with that familiar intensity.

"You're quiet today," he says, his voice low, coaxing but not intrusive.

"I'm... thinking," I say, my eyes fixed on the faint swirl of steam rising from my cup.

"About what?" he asks, shifting slightly so he's facing me.

I glance at him, taking in the way the sunlight dances in his hair, the way his shirt clings slightly to his chest. My heart aches with the weight of everything I haven't said. "About everyone I've lost," I admit finally.

Grant's expression softens. "You don't talk about your parents much."

"It's easier not to," I say, my voice trembling. "My mom died when I was a teenager. It was only the two of us. And when she was gone, I felt like... like I lost my whole world."

He nods, his gaze steady. "And this loss... it brought all of that back."

I swallow hard, the lump in my throat making it difficult to speak. "More than I expected," I whisper. "Losing him wasn't just about losing him. It was about losing everything I thought my life was supposed to be. It was about losing myself."

Grant shifts closer, his hand finding mine. His palm is warm, his fingers firm as they lace through mine. "Keep going," he says softly.

"I thought having another baby would fix everything," I say, the words tumbling out in a rush. "Theo and I were drifting. I thought it would bring us back together. But then..."

My voice cracks, and I press a hand to my mouth, the tears spilling over before I can stop them. Grant pulls me into his arms, his scent wrapping around me—faintly musky, with a hint of cedar. I sink into him, letting the sobs come.

When the tears finally subside, I pull back slightly, wiping at my cheeks. Grant doesn't let go, his hands still resting on my arms, his gaze steady.

"I made something for you," I say suddenly, the words tumbling out before I can second-guess myself.

"For *me*?" he asks, his brow furrowing in surprise.

I nod, reaching into my bag and pulling out a small box. My hands tremble as I hand it to him. "It's not much. Just... something small."

Grant opens the box slowly, his expression softening as he takes in the miniature inside—a tiny journal, complete with intricate pages and a worn leather cover. It's an exact replica of the one he carries with him everywhere.

"You made this?" he asks, his voice filled with awe. "For me?"

"I thought of you while I was working on it," I admit, my cheeks flushing. "I wanted you to have something... personal."

Grant sets the box aside carefully, almost reverently. Then his hands find mine again, his eyes too. "It's incredible," he says, his voice thick with emotion. "You're incredible."

I laugh softly, shaking my head. "It's a trinket."

"No," he says firmly, pulling me closer. "It's a piece of you. And I love it."

The words make my heart flutter, the weight of his love both terrifying and exhilarating. "I love you," I whisper, the truth of it settling over me like a balm.

The quiet whistle of the kettle breaks the moment, and Grant rises to his feet, disappearing into the kitchen. When he returns, he has a fresh cup of tea for himself in his hand.

"Why miniatures?" he asks suddenly, his voice soft but insistent.

I glance down at the mug I'm holding, tracing the rim with my finger. "Because they're perfect," I say finally. "Because they're a world I can control. In real life, everything is fragile. Temporary. But when I make a model of something, it's... concrete. It could last forever."

Grant leans back slightly, studying me. "Like a way to hold on to something that might disappear," he says quietly.

"Yes," I whisper, my voice cracking. "Exactly."

He reaches for my hand again, his fingers lacing through mine. "You don't have to hold everything together, Anna. It's okay to fall apart."

I laugh softly, shaking my head. "If I let everything fall apart, I'm afraid there'll be nothing left."

"That's not true," he says, his voice steady. "There will always be you. And that's enough."

The words settle over me, heavy but comforting. For the first time in a long time, I feel... safe.

The sound of a text message cuts through the quiet, the loud ping coming from the coffee table. Grant glances at his phone, his brow furrowing slightly as he reads the screen.

"Everything okay?" I ask, though my chest tightens.

He hesitates, then sets the phone face down on the table. "It's Melanie," he says quietly.

The mention of her name is a splash of cold water, and the unstable sense of safety shatters. "Is she... expecting you?" I ask, my voice barely above a whisper.

Grant shakes his head. "She's out of town for a few more days."

The tension in my chest eases slightly, but the moment is tainted now, the reality of our situation pressing down on me. I glance at the clock, suddenly aware of how late it's getting. "I should go," I say softly, setting my mug down.

Grant reaches for me, his touch lingering. "You don't have to."

But I do.

The next afternoon, Jillian and I pull into Marsha and Conrad's driveway.

When Jillian told me about the spa night she had planned for my birthday, I pointed out that the hotel was close to the farm. She suggested tacking on an extra night to our trip to come see Sadie. And when I told her what happened the last time I came here, she insisted.

Coming here is like coming home and being tested all at once. Memories of a life with Theo crash around me, as painful as the hangover headache I am nursing, punishment for my recklessness last night.

Why did I call Grant? Did I really say I missed him? That I still *loved* him?

As much as I hate that I said those things... I can't deny that I needed to hear his voice.

Coming to Theo's parents' home feels like another betrayal on top of so many others. The white farmhouse stands steady against the backdrop of golden fields, its wraparound porch adorned with hanging flower baskets. Sadie bursts out of the front door before the engine has even stopped, her braid bouncing behind her as she runs toward me.

"*Mom!*" she cries, throwing her arms around my waist the moment I step out of the car.

I wrap her in a tight hug, burying my face in her hair. She smells like sunshine and freshly cut grass, and, for a moment, the world has been set right. "Hey, sweetheart. I missed you."

She pulls back, her face glowing with happiness. "We've been picking blackberries all morning. Grandma's making cobbler for dessert!"

"Sounds perfect," I say, glancing toward the porch where Marsha and Conrad stand waiting.

Marsha gives me a warm smile, but there's something restrained about it, like she's holding back words she doesn't dare say. Conrad tips his hat in greeting, but his expression remains unreadable, his jaw set in that way I recognize all too well.

Their steady presence should be a comfort. But now, there's an edge to it, a quiet hesitation. They love Sadie. They love me. I remind myself of that as I force an easy smile. They don't have to agree with my choices, they just have to respect them.

Jillian climbs out of the driver's seat, stretching dramatically. "Okay, kiddo," she says to Sadie. "Show me the best berry bushes. I need to work off the ridiculous number of spa cocktails I had last night."

Sadie grabs her hand and pulls her toward the field, giggling. I watch them go, my heart swelling at the sight of Sadie so carefree.

Marsha steps down from the porch, wiping her hands on her apron. "She's been talking about your visit all morning," she says, pulling me into a hug. "And so have we."

"Thanks for taking such good care of her," I say, my voice thick with gratitude. "It means everything to me."

"You don't have to thank us, Anna," Marsha replies, her tone gentle but firm. "She's family. And so are you."

Later, as we sit around the worn oak table in the farmhouse kitchen, the cobbler fresh out of the oven, Sadie chatters about her summer adventures. She talks about feeding the chickens, learning to bake bread, and helping Conrad fix a broken fence. Her laughter fills the room, and I marvel at her resilience.

But beneath the surface there is the weight of everything I haven't said. Everything I've avoided.

After dinner, while Jillian and Sadie wander out to the porch to watch the fireflies, Marsha hands me a cup of coffee and gestures toward the kitchen window. "That girl is your anchor, you know," she says softly.

I nod, staring at Sadie's silhouette against the fading twilight. "I know."

Marsha's hand covers mine, her grip steady. "Then hold on to her, Anna. Whatever it takes."

Her words sink into me, heavy and unavoidable. I think of Theo, of the unanswered questions that have haunted me since the day he died. The guilt I've carried, the truth I've been too afraid to face. I think of Parker, of the doubts I keep pushing aside, and the unease that clings to me like a shadow. Of Sadie, weeping in her bedroom the night of my birthday.

Marsha is right. This is all for Sadie. Everything I've done, everything I have yet to do. And I can't move forward—not truly —until I put to rest what happened to Theo the day he died.

Even though I was married to her son for thirteen years, Marsha and I were never close. I know it was all my doing, not hers. When Theo first brought me home, I could sense Marsha and Conrad's curiosity more than any real reservations. He was their only child, had a dynamic personality, and I'm sure they had pictured him with someone more outgoing.

But Marsha welcomed me lovingly, inviting me into their world with genuine kindness. I think, in some ways, my slower pace made sense to her. She understood the pull of quiet work and patience; life on their farm required that.

Even with Marsha's warmth, though, I always felt out of place. She never expected me to be someone I wasn't—never pushed me toward social outings or chitchat. Sometimes, I could tell she wished I'd be more at ease with her. But I couldn't be.

But as usual, my past held me back.

That night, as I tuck Sadie into bed, she presses her stuffed rabbit, Buttercup, against her cheek and looks up at me with sleepy eyes. I smooth her hair back, swallowing the lump in my throat. I kiss both her cheeks. "I love you, sweetheart."

"Love you too, Mama."

I watch her for a moment longer. The weight of her innocence and trust presses on me like a vow.

As I step outside onto the porch, Conrad is there, sitting in his usual chair with a mug of tea in hand. He looks at me, his eyes kind but searching. "You've got that look," he says.

"What look?"

"The look Theo used to get when something was eating at him," Conrad replies, his tone even. "You're not the type to let things lie, Anna. You never have been."

I stare out at the darkened fields, the stars scattered above like promises wanting to be kept. He's right. I can't let it lie. Not anymore.

Tomorrow, I'll start asking the questions I've avoided. I'll dig deeper, no matter what it uncovers.

THIRTY-FOUR

Back home the next day, the sun filters through the kitchen window as I pour myself a second cup of coffee. The warmth does little to untangle the knot in my stomach.

I've been up since dawn, restless and unsettled after last night. Jillian and I rolled into town later than expected, and Parker was frustrated I hadn't shared my location to let him know where I was.

He moves around the kitchen now with his usual efficiency, frying eggs while Helen scrolls through her phone at the counter.

"You're up and ready for the day," he says, eyeing my outfit, makeup and hair. "I thought you said you'd take the day to relax," Parker adds casually, breaking the silence.

"I am taking it easy," I say, forcing lightness into my voice. "I'm meeting Jillian to help her shop for her cousin's wedding."

He pauses, the spatula hovering midair. "Jillian again?" He sets the spatula down carefully and turns to face me. "Anna, we talked about this."

"Did we?" I ask, arching an eyebrow as I sip my coffee.

He sighs. "I just mean—you already had that spa trip. Now more time with Jillian? It's a lot."

My stomach twists. "She's my best friend, Parker. My only close girlfriend. And she's in town for a few weeks. Once she goes back to L.A., it might be months before I see her again."

He exhales, rubbing his jaw. "I just thought... I don't know. Maybe you wouldn't need her so much. You have me."

I press my lips together, forcing patience. "It's different."

His words settle uncomfortably, but so does the reality he's ignoring—even if I weren't with Jillian, it's not like we'd have the house to ourselves. Helen is still here, despite Parker asking her to move out over a week ago. That unspoken tension hums beneath the surface, one more thing we don't talk about.

So why does it feel like I'm the one who's supposed to compromise?

"But you're trying to move forward," he says, his tone measured but firm. "I just don't want you getting caught up in the past when we're planning for the future. It's a lot right now —the wedding, everything else—and I don't want you feeling... overwhelmed."

My grip tightens on the mug, but I force myself to stay calm. "I'm not getting caught up in anything, Parker. I'm helping my best friend pick out a dress. That's all."

His jaw flexes, but before he can reply, Helen snorts. "Oh, let her go, Parker. It's not like she has that many friends to reconnect with anyway."

"Helen," I say, blinking at her, caught off guard.

She shrugs, unbothered. "Just saying. Don't get your knickers in a twist."

Parker exhales loudly, pinching the bridge of his nose. "Fine," he says finally, his voice tight. "Just—don't let it stress you out. You've been through a lot, and we already have enough going on."

I nod, keeping my expression neutral even as irritation

flickers inside me. I know Parker well enough to know that this is not about Jillian. It's about everything else. The wedding. The house. The objects.

And as much as I want to ignore it, I can feel the pressure closing in.

The boutique is small but charming. The racks are lined with dresses in every shade and cut imaginable. Jillian rifles through them with practiced ease, her commentary a steady stream of wit and judgment.

"This one looks like a bridesmaid's nightmare," she mutters, holding up a pastel monstrosity.

I laugh despite myself, the tension from this morning finally easing. "It's not *that* bad."

"Please," she says, rolling her eyes. "I have standards."

She moves on to another rack, pausing to study a sleek navy dress. "What do you think? Too sexy for a family wedding?"

"Depends," I say, smirking. "Are you trying to outshine the bride?"

"Always." She winks, then grabs the dress and adds it to her pile. She lowers her voice. "Speaking of weddings, how was your return home? Did you and Parker have incredible sex last night? I imagine so, considering you were gone for two nights."

The question catches me off guard, and my smile falters. "We were both tired."

"Uh-huh," she says, narrowing her eyes. "You want to try that again with a little more conviction?"

"Sex is not on my mind. There's a lot to deal with," I admit, my voice quieter now. "With Sadie, and Helen, and... everything else."

"Everything else?" Jillian raises an eyebrow, her tone tense. "Anna, tell me, what's going on?"

I hesitate, glancing around the boutique. "Not here," I say finally.

The café Jillian picks is filled with the comforting scent of freshly baked bread and coffee. We settle into a quiet corner booth, the din of chatter and clinking dishes fading into the background. She barely waits for the waitress to leave before diving in.

"Spill," she says, leaning forward. "I'm trying to not be offended, but we were in the car all day yesterday and you didn't bring anything up."

"I didn't want to spoil the perfect getaway you had planned," I reply honestly.

Her eyes narrow with loving concern. "Anna, seriously, what is it?"

I stir my tea, avoiding her gaze. "It's... complicated."

"Of course it is," she says wryly, leaning back in her seat. "It's your life. But you've got me for the next hour, so give me the short version."

I exhale, the weight of it pulling me down. "There's... a lot happening at home. Strange things keep coming up—old memories, objects I thought were gone..."

Jillian's brows knit together. "What do you mean? What kind of *objects*?"

I hesitate, pressing my palms against my thighs. "A wedding photo of Theo and me just *appeared* on the coffee table one day. And a scarf of Theo's, it was just draped over a kitchen chair." I shake my head. "It doesn't make sense."

Jillian leans in slightly, studying me. "That's... weird, Anna."

I force a laugh, but it comes out hollow. "Yeah. It is."

I run a hand through my hair, exhaling. "And Parker... he's

been stressed. Sadie's visit, Helen staying with us—it's all piling on."

Jillian doesn't say anything right away, just watches me like she's waiting for me to admit something I don't even know how to say. "Uh-huh," Jillian says, raising a skeptical eyebrow. "And?"

"And what?" I ask, frowning.

"You've barely looked at me since I sat down. There's something you're not saying." Her voice softens, but there's an edge to her words. "What is it, Anna?"

I hesitate, glancing around the café as if someone might be listening. "Grant came by the other day," I say finally, my voice barely above a whisper.

Jillian's eyes widen. "*What?*"

"He showed up at the house," I continue, stirring my tea mindlessly. "After he gave me back the sunglasses I had left in his car, he said he had concerns about Parker."

"Wait," she says, holding up a hand. "You left something in his car? When were you in his car?"

My throat tightens. I hadn't meant to tell her, but the floodgates are open now. "Earlier this week," I admit. "I ran into him after dinner. He offered to give me a ride home."

Jillian stares at me, her mouth falling open. "And you didn't think to tell me this sooner?"

"It wasn't a big deal," I say quickly, though the words are a lie even as I say them.

"Not a *big deal*?" she says, her voice rising slightly. "Anna, the man you had an affair with shows up in your life again, and it's not a *big deal*?"

I glance down at my tea, my hands trembling slightly. "It's complicated."

"Complicated how?" she presses. "What does he want?"

I hesitate, my heart pounding. "He left his wife," I say finally. "He told me he wants me back."

Jillian sits back in her chair like the wind's been knocked out of her. "He... *what?*"

I nod, unable to meet her eyes. "He said he made a mistake letting me go. That he wants another chance with me."

"Jesus, Anna," she mutters, rubbing her temples. "What did you say?"

"I told him no," I say firmly. "I told him it's too late."

Jillian studies me, her eyes narrowing. "Are you sure about that? Because the fact that you didn't tell me until now says otherwise."

"It's not like that," I protest, shaking my head. "I don't want him back, Jillian. That part of my life is over."

She leans forward again, her expression serious. "Then why didn't you shut him down immediately? Why didn't you tell Parker?"

"Because..." My voice falters, and I look away, the words catching in my throat. "Because it's not that simple."

Jillian sighs, her frustration softening. "Anything else you aren't saying?"

I hesitate, but once the tears fill my eyes, I know I can't hide anything from my best friend. "Do you remember at the spa, when we were out on the terrace having cocktails?"

"Of course, the headache I had the next day wouldn't let me forget it," she says with a small laugh.

"Well, when you went to the bathroom, I called him."

"Grant?" she whispers. "Anna, this feels dangerous."

"I know." I drop my head in my hands. "But I had to know what he meant about Parker."

"What do you mean?"

I shrug, wiping my eyes. "When he came by the house, he told me to be careful. And then when I called him that night, he said they went to college together, that there were always rumors about his levels of *deception*. I didn't find out any more."

Cutting to the heart of it all, Jillian asks, "Do you still love Grant?"

The question stabs at something deep inside me, and for a moment, I can't answer. My throat tightens, my thoughts swirling. "On the phone, I told him I missed him, that I loved him. But you know why I was with him," I say, my voice breaking. "Because of..."

The unspoken word hangs between us like a thick fog. Jillian reaches across the table, gripping my hand tightly. Her touch is warm, tethering me in a way I didn't realize I needed.

Caleb.

"Anna," she says gently. "You don't have to say anything else. But you need to figure out what you want. You can't keep carrying all of this alone."

I pull my hand back, shaking my head. "I don't have a choice," I say, my voice trembling. "You don't understand."

"Then *make* me understand," Jillian says, her tone rising slightly. "Anna, I love you, but you're spinning out. You're marrying a man who's confusing you, strange objects have started appearing in your house and now Grant is back in the picture. This is a *mess*."

"*I know it's a mess!*" I sob, my voice more dramatic than I intended. Heads turn, and I lower my voice quickly. "But I can't walk away. Not yet."

"Why not?" she demands. "Why are you so determined to make this work with Parker?"

I hesitate, the answer caught in my throat. Because I know the truth about Theo. Because I can't leave until I have proof. But I can't tell her that. Not yet.

"It's complicated," I say finally, my voice breaking.

Jillian shakes her head in disappointment. "Anna," she says quietly. "You don't have to live like this."

But I do. I don't say it out loud, but I do.

THIRTY-FIVE

PRESENT DAY

The studio is a mess of scattered paints, wood shavings and tiny furniture pieces. I've been working here for hours, my hands aching from the meticulous labor, but I can't stop. Not yet. I squint at the miniature rocking chair under the soft glow of my desk lamp, the world outside my window long since gone dark.

It is almost finished.

I used to dream of rocking Caleb in this chair. I imagined myself in a soft, golden-yellow nursery with a rocking chair by the window, a mobile of tiny stars and moons spinning lazily above the crib. I run my fingertip over the rocker I've painted white, its surface smooth and glossy, a pang of something tender and bittersweet stirring within me.

I set it down, stepping back to survey my work. The project has grown over the past few weeks, each piece meticulously recreated on a one-to-twelve scale.

The paintbrush trembles in my hand as I work to finish the wooden mobile, adding the finishing touches, each star painted in shimmering gold. It could dangle above a crib, catching the light in a way that is almost magical.

But it's not magic. It's grief, solidified into something tangible.

There is a knock on the studio door. Parker's voice cuts through the quiet.

"You're still at it?" he calls to me.

I jump, nearly knocking over my work. My heart pounds as I stand. I unlock the door and step into the hallway to face him. My hand is on the doorknob, making it clear I don't want him to enter.

His silhouette is backlit by the hallway light, making it hard to read his expression.

"It's late," he says, stepping toward me. "You've been in here every night this week."

"I lose track of time," I say, forcing a small smile. "It's... therapeutic."

Parker is wearing his usual easy smile, but there's an edge to it tonight—a tightness in his jaw, a flicker of anger.

"But don't you think it's time to focus on the future, instead of arts and crafts?"

I bristle at the comment but keep my voice steady. "You think what I am doing isn't meaningful? This helps me process everything, Parker. It's about finding peace."

"Peace," he echoes, running a hand along my chin. "Is that what this is?"

I swallow hard. His touch is invasive, like he's prying into something private.

"Yes," I say firmly. "It is."

Parker's eyes meet mine, and for a moment, I see something dark flicker there—frustration, maybe even anger. But then he exhales, his expression softening. "I want you to be happy, Anna," he says, his voice low. "That's all I've ever wanted."

"I know," I say, forcing a smile. "And I appreciate that."

He steps back, his gaze lingering on me for a moment longer before he turns toward our bedroom. "Don't stay up too late," he says over his shoulder. "You'll wear yourself out." As soon as he's gone, I slip back into the studio, my hands trembling as I lock myself in tight.

Then I pick up the tiny mobile. The tension lingers. But I push it aside and keep working.

The hours slip away as I lose myself in details. By the time I finally step back, my project feels alive.

The next morning, Parker is quiet at breakfast. He sips his coffee, scrolling through his phone, while I make bacon and eggs. The tension from last night still lingers, heavy and unspoken.

"I'm headed to Seattle to check in with the contractor working on the condo. And then I am meeting with some colleagues for lunch. They are all a bit jealous I have a whole year ahead of me without work. Of course, I have independent research that I will begin soon, but they are all headed back to the classroom next week, with college starting back up."

"That's nice," I say absently. My mind is on the studio. And with Parker gone all day, there will be time for my other project.

My secret in the attic.

"Do you have any plans for today?" he asks casually, not looking up.

"Some errands," I say, keeping my voice light. "And some work in the studio."

He glances at me then, his eyes narrowing slightly. "Don't forget about *us*, Anna."

The comment catches me off guard, and I pause, spatula in my hand. "What do you mean?"

"I mean..." He sets down his coffee, leaning forward slightly. "You've been spending a lot of time in that studio lately. Maybe too much."

"I thought you supported my work," I say. The unintended harshness in my tone hangs between us.

"I do," he says slowly. "But you're so focused on... whatever it is you're doing in there, it's like you're slipping away from me. From us."

My chest tightens, but I force a smile. "I'm not slipping away, Parker. I'm... processing."

He nods slowly, but his eyes don't leave mine. "Don't let it consume you," he says, his voice softer now. "We're building a life together, Anna. Don't forget that."

"I won't," I say, though the words are hollow.

After he eats, I watch him go, my heart heavy. I quickly clean the kitchen so I can return to the studio. To the unfinished project looming in my mind.

But I know it's not only the past I'm building there. It's a way forward.

A way out.

THIRTY-SIX

Client Notes: Fifth Session

Client: Male, late thirties. Presenting concerns include marital strain following a significant loss.

Summary:
Finally had breakthrough. Client no longer speaking in a detached way. Appears to want to make progress. The client shared memories of the weeks following the stillbirth of their second child. He described his wife's increasing withdrawal and his own growing sense of helplessness. His frustration is palpable, particularly around her late nights spent alone in her studio and her avoidance of meaningful conversation.

Key Observations:

- **Emotional Disconnection:** The client describes his wife as distant and elusive. While he attempts to reach out to her, his efforts are met with walls rather than windows.

- **Grief Response:** His frustration is layered with grief, but he struggles to articulate this, often masking it with resentment toward her.
- **Suspicion:** Subtle references to changes in her routine hint at a deeper unease. He suspects she may be hiding something, though he has not yet voiced these concerns to her.

Therapist Reflection:

The client's pain is raw but still restrained, his words carefully chosen as though to avoid revealing too much. He spoke about coming home late one night to find his wife still awake, her hands covered with paint and her expression unreadable. She hadn't heard him enter, and he described watching her for a long moment before retreating to bed.

This detail haunts me. I find myself imagining her in that room, bathed in the glow of her creative world. What was she thinking? Who was she painting for? These questions linger in ways they shouldn't.

When I asked him what he needed most from her, the client paused for a long time before answering, "To let me in. Just once, completely."

Note to File:

The client's suspicion about an affair seems to be growing, though he has not voiced this directly. He did mention finding a receipt for an unfamiliar café, and the shift in his tone was noticeable. I refrained from pressing, but his unspoken concerns loom large.

The wife remains a vivid presence in these sessions. The way the client speaks of her—half in admiration, half in frustration—creates a portrait of someone complex and unknowable. My curiosity about her deepens, even as I remind myself to maintain professional boundaries.

Still, I cannot help but wonder: What would she say if she were sitting here instead? Would she defend herself, or would she confirm his fears? And why do I care so much about the answer?

THIRTY-SEVEN

The next day, Parker, Helen and I are in the car. The air is thick with unspoken tension.

Parker drives with one hand on the wheel, the other casually on the gear shift, but his jaw is tight, and his eyes remain fixed on the road ahead. Helen sits in the back seat, scrolling through her phone, her presence a constant reminder of Parker's broken promise to kick her out.

I stare out the window, watching the countryside blur by as we make our way to yet another wedding venue. The idea of planning a wedding is increasingly surreal, like trying to build a life on quicksand. My thoughts are heavy with the memories of last night—Parker's veiled disapproval in the hallway when I told him I was still working in the studio. I want a partner, not judgment.

"Beautiful day," Parker says, breaking the silence. His voice is light, almost forced, as though he's trying to smooth over the jagged edges between us.

"Mmm," I murmur noncommittally, my fingers twisting the flashy emerald-cut diamond engagement ring on my finger. The weight of it is heavier today, like it's tethering me to something I don't want anymore. I am trapped. And ridden with guilt. How much more of a mess can I make of my life?

"I heard this venue has amazing views," Parker continues, glancing at me briefly before returning his focus to the road. "Perfect for photos."

"It sounds nice," I say, though I know my voice lacks enthusiasm. I can sense Helen's eyes on me in the rearview mirror, keen and assessing.

We lapse into silence again, the tension simmering below the surface. It's Helen who finally breaks it, her tone casual but laced with something more biting. "So, Parker, how much longer until your condo is finished? You said you were wrapping up the renovations weeks ago."

Parker's grip on the wheel tightens ever so slightly. "Soon," he says curtly. "These things take time."

Helen snorts softly, her skepticism obvious, but she doesn't push further. Instead, she leans back and resumes scrolling on her phone, the faint sound of her nails tapping against the screen filling the car.

It's Parker who speaks next, his voice steady, with a hint that there is something important he wants to say. "I've been thinking about Sadie," he says, glancing at me again.

My heart skips a beat. I hope this will be good—focusing on my daughter can bring us back together, and the fact he is showing interest in her can only be positive. "What about her?" I ask, trying to keep my joy from bubbling up.

"She's at a pivotal age," he says, his words slow and deliberate. "And I've been researching some boarding schools. There are a few great ones that could give her incredible opportunities."

I blink, his words taking a moment to sink in. "*Boarding* school?" I repeat, shocked at this suggestion.

He nods, his expression calm, almost too calm. "It's not uncommon, Anna. Plenty of kids thrive in that kind of environment. She'd have access to resources and connections she'd never get at a public school."

"No," I say immediately, my hands clenching into fists in my lap. "Absolutely not."

Parker frowns, his eyes flicking to me again. "You're not even going to consider it?"

"There's nothing to consider," I say, aghast. "Sadie's place is at home. With me."

"It's not about taking her away from you," he says, his tone placating. "It's about giving her the best chance at success. Think how much she has been thriving this summer. *Away from you*."

I shake my head, my chest tightening with anger and something darker: guilt. I am her mother, my purpose is to protect her. Am I doing a good enough job at that?

"She doesn't need a boarding school to succeed, Parker. She needs her mother. She needs stability."

Parker sighs, his grip on the wheel tightening. "You're being emotional, Anna. I'm trying to think about what's best for her."

"What's best for her," I say, my voice trembling, "is staying with her family. With me."

Helen snorts again from the back seat, her voice cutting through the tension like a knife. "You know he always hated children," she says, her tone light but dripping with disdain.

I whip around to look at her, my heart pounding. "What?"

Parker's jaw clenches, his knuckles whitening as he grips the wheel. "Don't start, Helen."

Helen raises an eyebrow, feigning innocence. "What? It's true. You've always said kids are a burden. Too messy, too demanding."

Parker's glare darkens, his voice low and dangerous. "Enough, Helen."

But her words have already taken root, and I can't stop the doubt that begins to bloom. I turn back to face the road, my thoughts spinning. He wants me alone. Without Sadie, I have no anchor to my real life. No reason to cling to the person I was before Parker.

"Anna," Parker says, his voice softer now, gently pleading. "I'm not suggesting this to hurt you. I want what's best for Sadie —and for us."

I don't respond, my mind too crowded with memories, questions and fears. The car falls silent again.

When we arrive at the venue, I step out of the car, the fresh air hitting me like a jolt of clarity. Parker comes around to my side, offering his hand, but I pretend not to notice. Instead, I walk ahead, needing space to think, to breathe.

A few weeks ago, I would have stepped into this moment with excitement. I would have been caught up in the joy of it— choosing the perfect wedding hall, picturing myself walking down the aisle, imagining a future with Parker that felt safe and full of promise.

But now, that person feels like someone else entirely.

The dream I had is unraveling at the edges, and I don't know when it started to come apart. Was it when Sadie lashed out at me, her words piercing my heart? Or when the home video of Theo began playing at my birthday dinner. A video I know never shared with anyone else? Maybe it was when Grant reappeared, his presence stirring something in me I haven't had time to examine.

Or maybe, if I'm being honest with myself, it was never real at all.

I inhale deeply, steadying myself. Parker and I were supposed to be building a life together. But instead, I feel like I'm being molded into something else. Every decision, every moment—slowly bending in his direction, his expectations, his carefully curated version of what our life should look like.

And now he wants to take Sadie away. The thought slams into me like a punch to the gut.

I thought I knew what this wedding meant. A new beginning, and a second chance. A fresh start after everything I had lost. But standing here now, I realize it's all starting to feel like a transaction. One life for another. One identity traded in for something more manageable, more controlled.

A life without Sadie in it.

Helen falls into step beside me, her presence surprisingly steadying. "You're not seriously considering it, are you?" she asks, her voice low.

"Of course not," I say. My words come out with more edge than I'd planned.

"Good," she says, glancing at Parker, who's a few paces behind us. "Because if you let him take Sadie away, you'll lose her. And then you'll lose yourself."

I have already lost one child.

There is no way in hell I will lose another.

THIRTY-EIGHT

ONE YEAR BEFORE THEO'S DEATH

I'm pregnant again.

Theo thinks it will fix us.

Our marriage has been falling apart at the seams for ages, the thread pulled too tight. We aren't fighting—not exactly. But we aren't the same.

After nine years of no luck, I stopped hoping for another baby. We told ourselves it wasn't meant to be, that we were enough, just the three of us. But now, here I am. Pregnant.

Theo sees it as a second chance. A way to mend what's broken.

But I'm not so sure. I want to believe him and, for a while, it works.

Theo hangs curtains in the nursery. He kisses my stomach every morning, whispering Caleb's name like a promise. He starts leaving work early, taking Sadie to the park, making an effort in ways he hasn't before.

One afternoon, Jillian and I take Sadie shopping. She finds a tiny stuffed bunny with floppy ears and a soft, worn-in feel, like it has already been loved.

"For the baby," my daughter announces, pressing it to my belly.

I run my fingers over the plush fur, my throat tightening. "It's perfect."

"Can I name it?"

I nod, my voice failing me.

"Buttercup," she declares proudly. "Buttercup and Caleb will be best friends."

I think my heart might break from the sweetness of it.

I never imagined it would break for real.

The contractions start in the middle of the night.

Sharp. Wrong. Much too soon.

Theo is instantly awake, pulling on a sweatshirt. "It's going to be okay," he keeps saying, gripping my hand as we speed to the hospital. "Just hold on."

But hours later, when the doctor returns with a carefully composed expression, I already know. I know before she even speaks.

"I'm so sorry. We did everything we could."

I shake my head. "No. He was—he was breathing—"

Theo holds me as my sobs wrack my body. A nurse brings Caleb to me one last time, wrapped in a tiny blanket. He is impossibly small, his skin still warm. I press my lips to his forehead.

And then—he is gone.

For weeks I stop eating.

Stop sleeping.

Jillian tries to coax me back to life. "Anna, you have to eat." She grips my hand. "Sadie needs you."

I turn away. "I can't."

Theo finds me in the dark later. "We need to talk about Caleb."

"There's nothing to say."

"We lost our son, Anna. You can't pretend it didn't happen."

"I'm trying to move on."

His voice breaks. "Moving on doesn't mean shutting down."

I whisper, "I'm broken."

Theo reaches for me. "Let me in, Anna. *Please.*"

But I can't. I walk away. Into the silence. Into the darkness.

And that is when I meet Grant.

THIRTY-NINE
PRESENT DAY

The day after we tour the wedding venue, I take reprieve in my studio, needing space to think. To create.

The unexpected summer rain slashes against the studio window, relentless and unyielding, a steady percussion that fills the quiet space. I sit hunched over my workspace in the studio, the desk lamp casting long shadows over the objects I have created. My hands ache from hours of meticulous work, but I don't stop. The crib I began constructing last night is like an anchor. Each detail pulling me deeper into a world I can control.

A crib for my sweet, precious Caleb.

The piece is almost finished, the wooden headboard delicately carved with swirling patterns. I dip the fine-tipped brush into a jar of pale yellow paint, adding a soft sunbeam to the front panel. It's beautiful—perfect, even—but the sight of it makes my chest ache.

I pause, staring at the tiny rocking chair next to it. It rocks gently, as if moved by some unseen force. A pang of deep longing washes over me.

These pieces are everything I imagined when I was pregnant with Caleb. A life I never got to have.

I press my palm to my chest, as if I can hold the grief inside, keep it from spilling out. I force my focus back to the crib, letting the intricate work quiet my mind.

Then the phone vibrates.

The clattering sound startles me, and I nearly knock over the jar of paint. I glance at the screen, my stomach twisting when I see the name.

Grant.

For a moment, I stare at it. After our last conversation while drunk on the terrace of the Pillar Hotel, I'd promised myself I wouldn't let myself spin out of control again. But something about his name glowing on the screen pulls me in. Against my better judgment, I press accept. What if he has more information about Parker?

"Anna," Grant says, his voice steady but weighted with hope. "I didn't think you'd answer."

I close my eyes, his voice sending a wave of conflicting emotions through me. "I'm glad you called," I admit, unable to lie to him.

"I know I was cryptic the other day on the phone," he begins, his words slow, careful. "But I've been thinking about what you asked for, something concrete about Parker, not just rumors."

"And?" I lean back in my chair. My hand trembles as I set down the brush. "Do you suddenly remember the past better than you thought?"

He hesitates, the sound of his voice crackling over the line. "I asked some old college friends what they remember about him. We went to a small private school, so everyone knew one another."

"And what did you discover?"

He exhales, as if what he is about to say is painful. "I don't want to hurt you," he says gently. "But you have to believe that I'm telling you this because I want to protect you."

I am sitting stick straight, hanging on to every word. I loved Grant. If I am honest with myself, I still love Grant. He sees me in a way no one else does... but I can't trust myself right now. I'm terrified one wrong move will upend everything—most importantly, hurt Sadie. That is the last thing I want.

"There was a woman we went to school with. Her name was Blue." He continues. "I didn't really know her because she transferred in senior year. Parker was in love with her, but she played hard to get. But I guess after we graduated, they started dating seriously. They got engaged, but she broke it off a month before the wedding."

Blue.

I remember sitting on the patio Helen said her name.

My heart pounds as if I am on tenterhooks, waiting for Grant to finish the story.

"What happened?" I ask in a whisper.

"She died not long after she broke off the engagement."

I gasp. "How?"

"A car crash. She was killed in the impact."

"Oh my God," I say, shaking my head. "That is tragic. But Grant, this doesn't have anything to do with Parker."

"People seemed to believe it did at the time. That he was jealous, vindictive—"

My skin recoils. "Grant, this is a serious allegation."

"Has he told you about his dead fiancée?" Grant asks.

"No..." I say slowly. "But... that doesn't mean he was involved in her death—"

"Look," Grant says, his voice strained. "I love you. I have loved you since the day we met. And I'm worried. Jealous too, I'll admit, but mostly worried."

I close my eyes, pressing the heel of my hand against my

forehead. His concern is both a balm and a blade. "I'm fine," I lie, my voice like a razor edge. "I don't need you to worry about me."

"Anna," he says softly, and the way he says my name makes my resolve crack. "If you ever need someone to talk to... I'm here."

I hesitate, the weight of his words pressing down on me.

Should I be worried?

The question unfurls in my mind, unbidden but impossible to ignore.

The objects in the house: Theo's scarf, Theo's wedding ring, things that shouldn't be there. Parker's sudden interest in boarding school, in removing Sadie from my life. Helen's comment about Parker never wanting children.

And now Grant, his voice careful, like he already knows something I don't.

The pieces don't fit together, not yet, but they rattle inside me, clashing against the version of reality I've been clinging to.

For a moment, I consider telling him everything—about Parker, about the secret in the attic, about the creeping fear that I'm losing control of my life. But I can't.

The truth is too dangerous, too exposing.

"I have to go," I say finally, my voice trembling.

"Wait," he says, his voice tinged with urgency. "Anna—"

I hang up before he can finish. The phone slips from my fingers onto the desk, and I press my hands to my face, trying to steady my pounding heart. The room is smaller now, the walls pressing in around me.

A loud knock at the studio door shatters the silence, making me jump. My pulse quickens as I turn toward the heavy wood door, the shadow of Parker's feet on the other side.

"Anna?" His voice is muffled by the rain, but there's an edge to it that makes my skin prickle. "Are you in there?"

I hesitate, my heart pounding. He's never been invited

inside the studio before. It is my sanctuary. My room. The miniature crib glows under the lamplight, an open secret. I glance at the rocking chair, still gently swaying, and a surge of panic grips me.

"I'm working!" I call out, trying to keep my voice steady.

He chuckles lightly, but it's a hollow sound. "Come on, let me in. I want to see what you're working on."

"I'm busy," I say, my tone firmer now.

The chuckle fades. "Anna," he says, his voice low yet insistent. The door handle rattles. "Open the door."

There's no humor in his tone now, no warmth. An undercurrent of something dark and unyielding.

"Why don't we talk tomorrow?" I suggest, stepping back from the door. "It's late."

The feet shift, and I can imagine the tension in his posture even through the door. "What's going on in there?" he demands. "Why won't you let me in?"

"I'm not hiding anything," I say quickly, the words tumbling out before I can stop them.

"Then open the door," he snaps, his patience unraveling.

My hands tremble as I grip the edge of the desk, my mind racing. "Goodnight, Parker," I say, forcing steel into my voice.

For a moment, there's silence. Then I hear his footsteps retreating, slow and deliberate, each one echoing in my ears. Relief floods through me, but it's short-lived. His reaction wasn't one of defeat—it was a warning.

I sink into my chair, my hands trembling as I press them against my thighs. The project looms in front of me, frozen in time. The delicate crib mocking me with its perfection.

I pick up the brush, trying to lose myself in the work, but my thoughts won't quiet. Parker's voice echoes in my mind, strained and demanding, his presence still lingering in the air.

What am I doing?

The question hangs in the silence, heavy and unanswerable. I glance at the phone on the desk, half expecting it to vibrate again, but the screen stays dark.

Grant insinuated my fiancé killed his ex.

But the truth is much worse than that.

FORTY

The late afternoon sun casts a hazy glow over the ferry as it glides across the water, passengers on the deck taking in the beautiful blue-sky day, pointing at the seagulls soaring overhead.

I lean against the rail, watching the foam churn in the ferry's wake, but my mind is far from the picturesque view. Parker stands beside me, his arm loosely around my waist, the pressure light but insistent.

He planned this date a few days ago—a romantic evening in Seattle to "reconnect." I had hesitated, but he'd been so insistent. "It's only us tonight," he'd said. "No Sadie, no Helen, no distractions. We need this."

"It's beautiful out here," he says now, his voice warm, almost too casual.

"It is," I agree, though my gaze stays on the horizon. The water stretches endlessly, a reminder of how vast and isolating the world can be.

Now, as the ferry cuts through the Sound, I wonder what he's trying to achieve. Why he really suggested us going out tonight.

He squeezes my waist, pulling me closer. "You've been quiet the last few days. I have wanted to give you space, not wanting to pressure you. But I'm worried. Is everything okay?"

"Of course," I lie, offering him a small smile. "I'm thinking about Sadie. She was upset when we talked this morning. I think she is nervous about living with a new man in the house."

"She's always upset about something," he says, brushing it off. "She'll survive."

I bristle but don't respond. He doesn't understand, he has never been a father. Sadie is all I have left of Theo, and my job is to make her safe. His dismissal of my daughter is like an omen. I still have a little over a week before she returns from her grandparents. I need to decide by then about my future with Parker.

By the time we dock, the city lights are beginning to flicker bright, their reflections dancing on the water. Parker leads me to his car, his hand lingering on the small of my back as we weave through the crowd.

"I was thinking," I begin hesitantly as he starts the engine, "why don't we swing by your condo? I'd love to see the bathroom renovations you've been talking about."

His hands tighten just for a moment on the steering wheel as we drive off the ferry, before his expression smooths into a practiced smile. "I'd love to, but I don't have the keys with me. Totally slipped my mind."

My stomach tightens, the excuse too convenient, too rehearsed. "Oh," I say, feigning disappointment. "That's a shame. Next time, then?"

"Next time," he agrees, his tone light but firm.

The rest of the drive passes in strained silence, the tension between us thickening like fog.

The restaurant Parker chooses is all soft lighting and hushed conversations, the kind of place where couples sit close and share secrets over candlelight. He pulls out my chair with a flourish, his smile easy and charming. But unease blooms in my chest.

Over the first course, I steer the conversation toward safer topics—work, the wedding, even the weather—but as the entrees arrive, I decide to push a little harder.

"So," I say, swirling my wine in its glass, "any updates on Helen's move?"

Parker's smile tightens, his fork pausing midair. "Why do you always bring her up?"

"I want to make sure we're all on the same page," I say carefully. "I think it's important to start our life together on solid footing. Sadie will be home in a week, and we need stability."

His laugh is low and humorless. "You mean without my sister underfoot? Don't worry, Anna. She'll be gone soon enough."

I nod, choosing my next words with care. "And what about your work? We don't talk about it much."

Parker sets his fork down with a quiet clink, his expression shifting. Not defensive, exactly. But guarded.

"What's this about, Anna?"

"Nothing," I say quickly, backpedaling. "I know you're on sabbatical, but what does this next year look like for you? I'm just... curious."

He leans back slightly, studying me. There's a beat of silence, heavy but unreadable.

"Curious," he says finally. "Or... worried?"

I blink, caught off guard. "Worried about what?"

He leans forward, his voice dropping. "You've been distant, distracted. It's like you're looking for excuses to push me away."

"That's not true," I protest, my pulse quickening.

"Isn't it?" he presses. "You keep clinging to your old life, your old memories. You're so focused on Theo and Sadie that there's no room for us. For me. I still can't get over the fact an old family home video was playing on your birthday. How is that supposed to make me feel?"

"That's not fair," I say, my voice trembling. "That wasn't my doing."

"And the photos, the wedding ring, the scarf, the compass," he says, clearly upset. His vibrant blue eyes search mine, as if longing to truly see me. "It is all strange, and unsettling. I thought it was destiny, fate, meeting you—but now you are acting like a different person."

"I'm still the same person," I tell him, blinking back tears. I look at him, remembering when we fell in love. "But we still have a lot to learn about one another."

He reaches across the table, taking my hand in his. He is strong, reassuring. Confident in a way that is rare. "And what about Grant?" Parker asks, his voice compassionate. The noise of the restaurant seems to fade, and in this moment, it is as if it is just the two of us here.

I blink, the air seeming to shift. The noise around us fading into nothing. My heart stumbles. "What about him?" I manage, but my voice is weak, cracking at the edges.

He leans forward, his eyes steady with concern. "I know about your affair."

The blood drains from my face, and my hand tightens around his. My throat constricts, my mind reeling.

"How?" I whisper.

He doesn't answer right away. His gaze stays fixed on mine, unwavering, unreadable. "It doesn't matter how I know," he says finally, sitting back in his chair with restraint. "What matters is that I know. And that I am choosing to be here anyway. I'm choosing *you*."

The weight of his words crushes me, and I lower my gaze to my lap, unable to meet his eyes.

How does he know?

I think back, retracing every step, every secret moment I

thought I'd buried. Was I careless? A text left open, a call over-heard? Had someone seen us—Jillian, Helen, a stranger? Had Grant told someone?

Or worse—had Grant told him?

My stomach twists. Grant had ended things abruptly, pulling away just as fast as we had fallen together. Was it guilt? Or was it something else?

The thought sickens me.

But Parker doesn't look smug. He doesn't look angry. He looks calm, patient—like a man who already knows the outcome of this conversation.

I think of Grant, of how recklessly I threw myself into him, without thinking about what it might cost. It wasn't only Theo I betrayed. It was Sadie. It was myself.

And now, Parker knows. But what is he going to do with that knowledge?

I glance up at him again, searching his expression for something—anger, resentment, leverage. But all I see is that same unreadable calm. Like he's been waiting for this moment.

"You're right," I say softly, my voice barely audible. "You shouldn't have to deal with this. With me."

His expression softens, and he reaches across the table to take my hand once more. This time his grip is more firm. "I love you. I'm here because I believe in us. But you... you have to let go of the past. You *have* to let go of him."

I look at him, my vision blurring with tears. "I thought I already had," I whisper. "I thought I was moving on."

He smiles, a faint, pitying curve of his lips. "Moving on doesn't mean clinging to ghosts. It doesn't mean looking back every time you're slipping. I'm here to keep you steady, Anna. You need that."

Do I? The thought catches me off guard. Maybe he's right. Maybe I do need someone to hold me together, someone to pull me back when I spiral. I've made so many mistakes—losing myself in the affair, in grief, in this endless cycle of trying to fix what's broken. Maybe Parker is what I need. Someone strong. Someone in control.

"What if I can't?" I ask, my voice trembling. "What if I can't let go?"

"You can," he says firmly, his hand tightening over mine. "You will."

I nod, a fragile, uncertain motion. His confidence in me—or maybe his confidence in himself—is a guiding light. I don't trust myself to make the right choices anymore. But maybe he can make them for me.

He watches me for a moment, as if assessing whether his words have landed. Then he leans back, the tension in his shoulders easing. "There's another option," he says, his tone casual, like he's discussing the weather. "We could leave and start over somewhere new, just us."

The suggestion sends a shiver down my spine, but it's more than that. It guts me.

Leave my home, the walls that have held every version of me—wife, mother, widow. Leave the attic, where my secrets are kept. Leave the house where Sadie took her first steps, where Theo's presence still clings to the air...

"Leave?" I echo, the word foreign and hollow in my mouth.

"Why not?" he says, shrugging. "What's keeping us here? Memories? Pain? A house filled with ghosts of the past? Let's get away from it all. We could have a fresh start."

The idea sounds impossible, like a dream that's too perfect to be real. And yet... isn't that what I've been chasing all along? A way to outrun the past? A chance to escape not just the grief, but the weight of my own sins—the secret hidden in the attic, the truth I can't face?

"What about Sadie?" I ask, my voice breaking. "She's... she's happy here. She's finally starting to find stability."

"She'd adjust," Parker says, waving the concern away like a

fly. "I mentioned boarding school the other day. It could be good for her. Think of how she has been acting—putting her father's belongings around the house to upset you and me both. She needs structure, discipline. Opportunities."

The suggestion knocks the breath from my lungs. Leave my home, leave my daughter. *Impossible.*

"She's not even twelve, Parker," I whisper, my voice barely holding steady. "She needs her mom."

"She needs stability," he counters, his voice calm, almost too calm. "And frankly, Anna, so do you. I'm trying to give us that. I'm trying to give you a life without all this chaos."

Chaos.

Is that what he sees when he looks at me? Not a woman rebuilding, but a woman unraveling? The thought is like a knife twisting in my chest. Maybe he's not wrong. Maybe I am chaos. Maybe I always have been.

But Sadie is the only thing tethering me to the person I used to be, the person I'm still trying to find. Without her, without the home that has held all my memories, who am I?

The double blow—the thought of uprooting my life and losing Sadie in the process—leaves me stunned.

"Let's... let's talk about this later," I say, my voice trembling. I push my plate away and stand, needing to escape the weight of his gaze. "I need some air."

"Anna," he says, his voice low and warning, but I'm already walking away, my legs unsteady beneath me.

In the restroom, I grip the edge of the sink, my knuckles white against the porcelain. My reflection swims before me—pale skin, red-rimmed eyes, a woman I barely recognize.

My thoughts spin, a tangled knot of guilt, fear and doubt. Parker's words loop in my mind, their meaning shifting with each pass. Were they cutting? Or meant to comfort?

I don't trust myself anymore—not my choices, not my

instincts. Maybe he's right. Maybe I do need him to keep me steady.

But as I stare into the mirror, a different kind of fear rises—quieter, sharper.

Something is slipping away. Something vital. And it's something I won't get back.

When I return to the table, Parker greets me with a warm smile, his charm back in place, easy as ever. But this time, I see it.

The careful calibration. The practiced ease. The way he watches me, waiting. I don't meet his eyes.

And for the rest of the evening, a thought takes hold, sinking deep into my bones, impossible to ignore.

What if I'm not losing myself?

What if someone is taking me apart, piece by piece?

FORTY-ONE

The faint scent of balsam and wood glue lingers in the air as I sit down at my workbench, carefully positioning a miniature photo album on the tiny coffee table.

The wedding album sits prominently on the table, a symbolic centerpiece. Each tiny page is painstakingly detailed, revealing fragments of a life that are both achingly close and impossibly distant. I printed photos from my computer, in tiny dimensions, making it as realistic as possible.

I wipe my hands on my apron, leaning back to admire the scene. Earlier I made a miniature couch, upholstering it in a soft fabric I scavenged from Theo's scarf, and a floor lamp casts a faint glow thanks to the tiny LED I wired inside. It's perfect. Objects frozen in time, a memory I can control, unlike the rest of my life.

A knock at the front door pulls me from my thoughts. My heart skips a beat. Parker isn't due home for hours. He went to Seattle to check on the condo and meet with some colleagues, like he does every few days. I set down my tools and head to the door, wiping my hands on my jeans as I go.

Peeking through the front window, I see Jillian standing on

the porch, a garment bag slung over her shoulder. She looks effortlessly chic in a sundress the color of ripe peaches, her hair wavy from being air dried. I exhale, forcing myself to smile as I open the door.

"Hey, stranger," she says, breezing inside. She's already slipping off her sandals, revealing polished toenails that glint coral in the sunlight. "I come bearing fashion emergencies. You busy?"

"Not busy," I say, though I hesitate. "What's the occasion?"

Jillian lifts the garment bag like it's a prize. "My cousin's wedding is finally here. I've got three contenders and zero ability to decide. You're my style guru today."

I soften and gesture toward the stairs. "Come on. There is better light in my bedroom."

She follows me up, her chatter filling the quiet house. Once we're in my room, she unzips the garment bag with a dramatic flourish, revealing three dresses: a slinky emerald-green gown, a playful floral midi and a soft lavender number with lace sleeves.

"Okay, thoughts?" Jillian asks, holding the emerald dress against her chest.

I tilt my head, studying her. "The green is stunning. Definitely bold."

"Bold is the vibe I'm going for. Let's try it on," she says, disappearing into the bathroom.

I sit on the edge of the bed, picking at the hem of my light-weight linen shorts. My tank top clings to my back in the summer heat, and I absently fan myself with a magazine. When Jillian steps out, the emerald fabric cascading over her figure, I grin.

"Well?" she asks, spinning. The dress flares slightly as she twirls, catching the light.

"It's gorgeous," I say genuinely. "You'll definitely turn heads."

"Perfect." She slips into a pair of strappy heels to complete the look. "Okay, next dress."

The floral midi gets a lukewarm reaction from both of us, but the lavender dress earns a soft smile. "It's sweet," I tell her. "Maybe less bold, but... romantic."

"*Romantic?*" Jillian raises an eyebrow. "Not sure that's me, but good to know."

After she changes back into her sundress, she flops onto my bed with a smile. "You're good at this. Why don't you dress up more often?"

I laugh lightly, shaking my head. "Dressing up takes energy. I'm barely getting through the day as it is."

Her frown is immediate, and before I can deflect, her gaze shifts down the hall. The door to my studio is cracked open, a soft glow spilling out from inside.

"What are you working on these days?" she asks, sitting up.

My stomach tightens. "Nothing much," I say quickly, but Jillian's already on her feet.

"Can I peek?" She's already moving toward the door.

"Jillian, wait—" I follow, my voice tense, but she's already stepped inside.

Jillian steps into the room and stops abruptly, her arms crossing over her chest. Her expression shifts—first confusion, then something sharper, something unsettled.

She doesn't move closer.

"Anna," she murmurs, eyes scanning the space. "What... is this?"

Her voice is careful, laced with something that makes my stomach twist. I knew this moment was coming—the second someone really *looked* at what I've been doing. But I didn't expect it to feel like exposure, like she's seeing something I didn't mean to reveal.

I linger near the doorway, crossing my arms tightly over my chest. "It's a project," I say, my voice tight. "A way to stay busy."

Jillian turns slowly, her eyes flicking across the workbench, the small pieces scattered across its surface. She exhales sharply, shifting her weight. Like she's trying to make sense of it.

"This isn't just a project," she says finally, her voice quieter now, deliberate. "This is—" She stops, shaking her head, like she can't quite find the right words.

I know what she's thinking.

It's too much. Too detailed. Too specific. Too obsessive.

She studies me now instead of the room. "Anna... *why?*"

The question hits deeper than it should, making my pulse stutter. I glance away, pressing my lips together. "It's nothing," I say, too quickly. "Some memories."

"Memories?" she repeats, her voice softer now, but still laced with unease.

I swallow hard, but the lump in my throat doesn't budge.

Jillian steps closer, lowering her voice. "Anna, I don't think this is healthy..."

Heat rises in my chest. I open my mouth, ready to argue, but the words won't come.

Because deep down, part of me knows she's right.

"Parker keeps saying I'm living in the past," I murmur, the confession slipping out before I can stop it.

Jillian lets out a tight laugh, but there's no amusement in it. "Hate to say it, but I agree with the man," she says, crossing her arms again. "You have to let the past be the past."

But the past isn't finished with me. It's sitting right here. Waiting to be seen.

Suddenly the tears spill over, hot and fast. And finally, I ask the question I've wanted to ask for months. "Jillian... what if Theo didn't die by accident?"

She freezes, her eyes widening. "Anna..." Her voice is cautious. "Are you saying you think Theo... ended his own life?"

"I don't know what I'm saying," I whisper, the words

tumbling out before I can stop them. "I... I can't shake the sense that something about it all isn't right."

Jillian steps closer, placing a hand on my arm. "Anna, you've had one helluva year. Losing Caleb, losing Grant, losing Theo..." She hesitates, her voice softening. "It's too much for anyone. Maybe you should see someone. A therapist. To talk things through."

The word *therapist* sticks in my mind, catching on something I don't want to examine too closely.

I blink rapidly, trying to force the tears back. I should agree. I should say yes. Maybe I should want help.

But the idea of someone prying into my mind, picking apart my grief, my choices, my past... It makes my stomach twist.

I want to dismiss Jillian, to tell her I'm fine, but the words won't come. Because deep down, I know she's right. I am not in the right frame of mind. I haven't been for a long time. And I can't trust any of my decisions.

"Maybe," I say finally, my voice barely audible.

She squeezes my arm gently, her expression tender. "I'm here for you. You know that, right?"

I nod, though my gaze drifts back to the project. Jillian has seen too much, knows too much.

The weight of her words settles over me.

Let the past be the past.

The problem is, I'm not sure I know how.

FORTY-TWO

That evening, the table is set with Parker's favorite red wine and a platter of roasted chicken with lemon and rosemary. The candles flicker, casting a warm glow that doesn't quite chase away the tension hanging in the air.

I adjust my fork, as unease prickles at the base of my spine. But I force myself to smile as I carry the last of the side dishes to the table. Helen is already seated, scrolling through her phone, while Parker pours himself a glass of wine.

"Looks great, Anna," Helen says, setting her phone down. She picks up her fork, but before taking a bite, she looks between us with a bright smile. "Actually, I have some news."

"Oh?" Parker says, leaning back in his chair. His tone is mild, but I can tell he's not paying attention. His focus is elsewhere—on me, on my every move.

Helen grins, her excitement evident. "I got a new freelance gig. A *big* one. They need someone on-site for a few months, and I figured... why not?" She shrugs casually. "So, I'm going to Mexico City."

The words hit me like a jolt, and I almost drop the serving spoon. "Mexico City?" I echo, my voice tighter than I intended.

"Yeah." Helen smiles, looking genuinely excited. "It's a dream project, creating branding from scratch for a boutique hotel group. Great money, great connections. I leave in a few days."

Parker raises his glass in a mock toast. "Finally," he says with a laugh, his tone teasing but with an edge. "Congratulations, Helen. We'll finally have the house to ourselves, Anna."

I force a smile, trying to match their energy, but inside, a wave of panic rises.

Helen is leaving.

I should be relieved. I *wanted* this—I've been desperate for space, for things to feel normal, for Parker and me to finally start our life without her lingering in the background.

But now that it's happening, dread settles over me like a weight I can't shake. Because Grant's words are still ringing in my head. His warning, his certainty that something about Parker isn't right.

And now, suddenly, it's just going to be me and Parker. Just the two of us.

The thought makes my skin prickle. The house will feel so different without Helen—a little too quiet, a little too controlled. Parker's presence will fill every inch of space, pressing in on me.

I take a sip of wine, the glass trembling slightly in my hand.

"Actually..." The words are out before I can stop them, and both Helen and Parker turn to look at me. "Maybe you should stay a little longer?"

Helen raises an eyebrow. "Stay? But I thought you'd be thrilled to have your space back."

I glance at Parker, whose expression darkens. "Yeah, Anna," he says, his voice clipped. "What do you mean?"

"I..." My words falter, and I set down my glass, twisting the stem nervously. "It's been nice having you here, Helen. Sadie would love having you around and getting to know her auntie better when she comes home. Maybe another few weeks wouldn't hurt?"

Parker leans forward, his jaw tightening. "We've talked about this. Helen staying here was always temporary."

"And it still is," Helen interjects, her tone light but firm. "Look, Anna, I appreciate the sentiment, but this job is a huge opportunity for me. You'll be fine, you've got Parker."

I nod quickly, trying to smooth things over. "Of course. You're right. I... just thought it might be nice."

Parker pushes his chair back abruptly, the legs scraping against the floor. "Excuse me," he mutters, walking out of the dining room.

I glance at Helen, whose brows knit together in confusion. "What's his deal?"

"I don't know," I say quietly, though my stomach churns with unease.

Helen picks up her fork again. "He's been so stressed lately. Do you think it's the wedding?"

I don't respond, following Parker instead. The air is charged with something I can't name.

I find him in the middle of the living room, standing frozen. His gaze is locked on the coffee table, his hands clenched at his sides.

Something is wrong.

"What the hell is this?" he asks, his voice bristling with intensity.

I follow his gaze, my lungs burning.

He's looking at Theo's and my wedding album. It sits there, pristine and out of place, the glossy cover reflecting the dim light. But that's not what makes my stomach drop. Beside it, resting on top like it was meant to be found, is a loose photograph.

My fingers go cold.

It's a picture of Sadie. And her face has been scratched out with something sharp.

A strangled sound catches in my throat. "*No.*"

I move forward on instinct, snatching up the photo with shaking hands. Deep, jagged scratches tear through my daughter's face, carving her out of the memory.

Why would someone do this?

"I didn't put that there," I say quickly, my voice thin, brittle. The words feel like ash in my mouth.

"Bullshit," Parker snaps, his voice rising. There's no sympathy and understanding in his voice this time. He picks up the album, holding it like it's something dangerous. "You're trying to make me think I'm losing my mind, aren't you?"

"No!" My voice wavers as I grip the ruined photo, my pulse hammering. "I don't know how it got there."

Helen walks in, frowning. "What's going on?"

Her gaze lands on the album in Parker's hands, then shifts to the mutilated photo in mine.

She freezes. "Why is that out?" Her voice is quieter now, wary. "I thought Theo's stuff all went to the storage unit?"

Parker glares at her, frustration lacing his voice. "Exactly. So why is it here?"

Helen crosses her arms, her expression skeptical. "I don't know, Parker. Are you the one dragging Theo's stuff around? Maybe you're the one trying to mess with Anna."

"I haven't touched anything!" Parker yells, his face reddening. "Why would I do that?"

I stand there, caught between them, the panic building in my chest like a scream I can't release.

Who hates me enough to do this?

The list churns in my head, possibilities spiraling, choking me.

Could Marsha or Conrad have come to town early and put this here to make a point? I glance over at Helen. She is always watching me, always pressing me. And then there is Parker—his reaction, the tension in his shoulders. Is Grant right, did he kill Blue? Am I or—worse—my daughter next? Grant warned me about Parker. Was this his way of making me listen? My mind is racing. Marla adored Theo, and she's never warmed to Parker. Would she do this to protect me? To protect Sadie?

Helen scoffs, shaking her head, and I startle from my thoughts. "You need to calm down, Parker. You're acting insane."

He whirls on her, his eyes wild. "Don't you *dare* talk to me like that."

Helen doesn't back down, her voice sharp. "Then stop acting like this. Anna's been through enough without you adding to it."

Parker turns to me, his voice quieter but no less intense. "Is this what you want, Anna? To keep living in the past?"

I open my mouth, but my throat is tight, locked. I don't know what I want anymore.

I stare at the photo in my trembling hands, and a hollow ache spreads through my chest.

"I didn't put it there," I whisper again, but the words don't even sound like my own.

Parker shakes his head, tossing the album back onto the coffee table. "This is ridiculous. I need some air."

I stand there, gripping the photo, my fingers numb around the edges. The scratches are deep, ugly, irreversible—violence etched into the image of my child.

A chill crawls over my skin.

This isn't just cruelty. It's a message. A warning.

Sadie isn't safe. The thought slams into me. Something is happening. Something I can't stop. And for the first time, I wonder if I ever could.

Or is it already too late?

Parker storms out, the front door slamming shut behind

him. The sound reverberates through the house, leaving Helen and me standing in the tense silence. My heart pounds, the echo of Parker's anger still vibrating in my chest.

Helen turns to me, her expression unreadable. For a moment, I think she's going to leave too, but instead, she crosses her arms and looks toward the door, as if to make sure Parker is gone.

"I need to talk to you," she says, her voice lower, almost conspiratorial. "But not where Parker might hear us."

The shift in her tone sends a chill down my spine. "What's going on?" I ask, my voice barely above a whisper.

She glances toward the window, peeking out cautiously. "Not here," she repeats. "Let's go into the studio."

I hesitate, the weight of the moment pressing down on me. "Helen, what's this about?"

"It's important," she says firmly, her gaze locking onto mine. "Trust me."

Something in her voice—an urgency I've never heard before —makes me nod. I lead her toward the studio, my hands trembling as I unlock the door and push it open. Once inside, Helen closes the door carefully behind us, turning the lock with a soft click. She leans against it for a moment, scanning the room as if making sure we're truly alone.

I stand in the middle of the studio, feeling the shift in energy. The project sits on the workbench, draped beneath a dust sheet, its shape obscured in the golden glow of the desk lamp.

I covered it after Jillian saw it, after the way her expression had tightened with unease. She had looked at me like I was unraveling, like I had gone too far.

Maybe I have.

Helen doesn't move toward it. Doesn't even seem to notice it. Instead, she steps closer to me, her face pale and drawn. My pulse kicks up, but I force myself to hold steady.

For now, the project remains hidden. But it won't stay that way forever.

"What is it, Helen?" I ask, my voice breaking slightly. "What's so important?"

Her eyes dart toward the workbench and then back to me. "There's something you need to know."

The air between us is heavy, charged with urgency. My stomach churns as I wait for her to continue, the silence stretching unbearably.

Helen leans in closer, her voice trembling now. "Anna..." She hesitates, then exhales shakily. "I know what you've been doing," she says.

A sharp, electric panic shoots through me.

Her eyes lock on mine. "I know your secret."

FORTY-THREE

Helen and I stand in the studio, her words hanging between us like a live wire.

Anna... I know your secret.

She's shaking. Not just nervous—terrified. Her arms are crossed tightly over her chest, like she's trying to hold herself together. Her face is pale, her jaw clenched so hard I think she might crack a tooth.

I shift subtly, staying positioned in front of the workbench, blocking it from view. The dust sheet still conceals it, hiding its secrets. My pulse pounds in my ears as I watch her, my stomach twisting. I've never seen her like this.

"Anna," she repeats, her voice raw, urgent. "I know what's in the attic. It's why I've been helping you."

I swallow, my mouth suddenly dry. "*Helping* me?" My voice barely rises above a whisper.

Helen exhales shakily, running a hand through her hair, gripping at the strands like she's trying to ground herself. "How do you think Sadie's face got scratched out?" Her voice wavers. "I'm on your side."

Ice crawls down my spine. "What are you talking about, Helen?"

Helen presses her fingers to her temples, squeezing her eyes shut for a beat. She looks like she's unraveling, like she's barely holding it together. When she lifts her gaze again, it's wild, desperate.

"You're not safe here with Parker," she says, her words tumbling out in a rush. "You have to know that by now."

I take a step back. The sheer panic in her voice grips me, dragging me into the fear with her. Helen's eyes flick toward the door, like she's afraid Parker will walk in at any second. When she speaks again, her voice is barely a whisper.

"I've known for a while." She shakes her head violently, like she can't believe she's even saying this. "That's why I'm here. It's why I've stayed. I tried to ignore it, to tell myself it wasn't my place to intervene. But I can't stay silent anymore."

She inhales sharply, like she's steadying herself for what comes next. "What I told you is true—I got a job offer," she says, her voice brittle. "A great one. Full-time, out of the country. Everything I've wanted. But I *can't* take it," she continues, shaking her head. "I *won't*—not until I know you and Sadie are safe. Not until..."

Something in my chest tightens.

"Not until you're away from my brother."

The words land like a punch. A slow, sick feeling spreads through me.

I grip the edge of the workbench, my knuckles turning white. "Stay silent about what?" My voice is barely there, as I plea. "Helen, please, say it."

She takes a shaky step forward, her whole body tense, like she's bracing for impact.

She swallows hard.

"Theo's death wasn't an accident, was it?"

The room tilts slightly. "What are you saying?" I manage to whisper, my voice cracking.

Helen's gaze meets mine, her eyes glistening. I watch her face, and I realize she doesn't know what I have already pieced together. "Parker killed him."

The words hang in the air, heavy and smothering. I shake my head, stepping back instinctively, not ready to reveal my hand. "How do you know?"

"I overheard him," she says, her voice steady despite the tears brimming in her eyes. "Before Theo died, Parker was furious. He said Theo didn't deserve you. That he was a coward for staying in the marriage. And then Theo..." She swallows hard, her voice breaking. "Then Theo was dead."

My legs are weak, and I sink onto the stool beside the workbench. The world narrows to Helen's voice and the deafening roar of my pulse in my ears.

"Why didn't you tell me?" I whisper.

Helen looks away, guilt etched into every line of her face. "Because Parker found out I knew first. He... he threatened me. He's not simply manipulative, Anna. He's ruthless. He went to my boyfriend and spun some lie about me being unstable. He destroyed my life, Anna. And then I watched him slowly do the same to you."

My hands tremble as I clasp them together.

"Why now?" I whisper. "Why are you telling me this now?"

Helen exhales sharply, stepping closer. Her voice is urgent, her words spilling out in a rush. "Because I see what he's doing," she says. "The isolation, the control, the way he makes you doubt yourself. It's the same pattern. He did this with Blue."

That name—Blue—hits like a slap.

Helen's voice breaks. "She was lovely, just like you. And then..." She shakes her head as if pushing the horrific memory away. "He's dangerous, Anna. And I can't stand by and watch him destroy your life too."

I open my mouth, but before I can respond, Helen's expression shifts as realization dawns.

Her eyes search mine. "That's why I started helping you."

My lungs seize with the weight of her words. "What?"

Helen swallows hard. "At first, I thought Parker was just being Parker—controlling, obsessive. But then I saw it. The objects. The wedding ring. The scarf. Theo's things appearing out of nowhere." She shakes her head, her voice raw with certainty. "I watched you, Anna. You're careful. You're precise. That wasn't some accident. You were the one doing it, weren't you? Leaving them around the house to mess with him. To make him feel like he was losing control."

A sharp jolt of panic shoots through me. *Oh God. She knows.*

"I—" My voice fails me, my body frozen.

Helen lets out a small, humorless laugh. "You thought you were doing it alone, didn't you?"

I stare at her, my pulse hammering.

"But I saw what you were doing, Anna." Helen draws in air like it hurts to hold it. "So I started helping."

A sharp inhale lodges in my throat.

"The compass in the cushions? The home video playing?" she continues. "That really wasn't you, was it?"

I shake my head, my hands numb in my lap.

Helen nods slowly. "Because it was me."

The air thickens between us, heavy with everything unsaid.

"We're in this together," she whispers.

My stomach tightens. I thought I was the only one setting the trap. But I wasn't alone. Helen knew all along. And she was playing the game too.

I'm about to respond when Helen's gaze shifts past me, her expression sharpening. Her eyes narrow, and she steps forward before I can stop her.

"What's this?" she asks, reaching out.

Panic flares in my chest.

She's inches away from the dust sheet, her fingers hovering over the fabric, about to pull it back—about to see.

I move quickly, stepping in front of her, my voice sharper than I intended. *"Don't."*

Helen freezes, startled by my reaction. She looks up at me, confusion flickering across her face. "Anna..."

I shake my head, my pulse hammering. "It's nothing," I say, forcing my voice to stay even. "Just a project."

But she doesn't back down. Her gaze flickers from me to the covered shape on the workbench, her unease growing. "This isn't just a project," she murmurs, her tone shifting. "It's a secret."

I tighten my grip on the edge of the sheet, holding it in place as if my life depended on it.

Helen takes a step back, her arms crossed tightly over her chest. She's unsettled now, wary of me.

She has no idea what she almost saw. My tears well up as my carefully constructed façade cracks. "I'm scared, Helen. I have to protect Sadie."

Helen's gaze hardens. "You're not safe here. Parker won't stop, Anna. He'll take everything from you if you let him."

I swallow, my throat dry. She's right. I know she's right. But before I can respond, Helen exhales sharply, shaking her head.

"I know he did it," she murmurs, her voice raw. "I know he killed Theo." She meets my gaze, searching. "But I don't know why. Or how." She hesitates, her eyes narrowing. "But I'm guessing you do."

Her words land like a strike of lightning. My chest rises then falls, my hands tightening into fists at my sides.

She knows. Not just that Theo's death wasn't an accident. But that I know the truth. I figured it out after Parker moved in. After it was already too late.

I open my mouth—I don't even know what I'm going to say—but before I can answer, the door handle rattles violently.

Helen and I freeze.

Parker's voice filters through, deceptively light, but tinged with an edge that sends a chill down my spine.

"Anna? You in there?"

My heart pounds. Each beat is a hammer in my chest.

Helen shoots me a look, her face tight with alarm, and presses a finger to her lips.

I nod, swallowing hard, and force my voice to steady. "Yes!" I call back. "I'm finishing up some work."

The handle twists, but the door doesn't open.

A beat of silence. A slow, stretched moment where the air presses down on me, heavy and relentless.

Then Parker speaks again, his tone dropping—no longer light, no longer patient.

"Open the door."

My heart pounds, each beat reverberating in my ears. Helen glances at me, her face tight with alarm, and presses a finger to her lips. I nod, swallowing hard, and force my voice to steady.

"I'm finishing up some work," I call out.

The handle twists, but the door doesn't open. A beat of silence stretches between us, and then Parker speaks again, his tone dropping, more insistent this time. "Is Helen with you?"

Helen steps back from the dollhouse, her hand brushing against mine. Her whispered voice is urgent. "Don't let him in."

I nod as I stare at the door. "I'm busy," I say, my voice faltering slightly. "I'll be out in a bit."

"Anna," Parker says, his voice dangerously calm. "Open this door. *Now!*"

I grip the edge of the workbench, my knuckles whitening. My project looms behind me, its secrets concealed but far too close to discovery. Helen shifts beside me, her presence steadying, but trembling with tension.

The handle shakes violently, the door quivering in its frame. My chest tightens as I glance at Helen, her eyes wide with fear.

"Anna!" Parker barks, his voice a mix of fury and frustration. "Open the goddamn door!"

Helen grabs my arm, her whisper acute and urgent. "What do we do?"

Before I can answer, the door bursts open with a deafening crash. The wood splinters, the sound tearing through the studio like a thunderclap. Parker stands in the doorway, his chest heaving, his face a twisted mask of rage and disbelief.

For a moment, no one moves. The air squeezes at me, the tension crackling like static electricity. Parker's gaze sweeps the room, landing on the workbench behind me. His eyes narrow, his expression darkening as he takes a step forward to the secret I have covered.

"What's happening in here?" he demands, his voice low and venomous.

FORTY-FOUR

My heart races as I step back, placing myself squarely between him and the workbench. I hear Helen gasp behind me, her hand clutching the edge of the table as though it's the only thing keeping her upright.

"Parker," I say, trying to sound calm, though my voice trembles. "You need to leave."

His eyes dart between me and Helen, suspicion darkening his face. Then his gaze shifts—locks onto the project.

"*Leave?*" He lets out a sharp, humorless laugh. Serrated. Almost manic.

For the first time, I see it properly. The thin, controlled veneer cracking wide open.

"What the hell is this?" he demands, taking another step forward. His body coils with barely restrained anger.

My pulse stutters. I've never seen him like this before. Not this raw. This unhinged.

"Anna," he barks, his voice razor-sharp. "Answer me!"

I don't move. My back is nearly pressed to the table, the structure I've been working on around the clock towers behind me, covered by the drop cloth. Its secrets humming along my spine.

Parker's voice is low and dangerous. "Move aside."

"No." The word comes out firmer than I expected, but I hold my ground. "This isn't for you."

His expression twists, his jaw clenching. "Not for me? I'm your fiancé! What the hell have you been doing in here?"

"Parker, stop," Helen interjects, her voice shaky but defiant. "You need to calm down."

He spins to face her, his eyes wild. "Stay out of this, Helen. You've been nothing but a problem since the day I brought you here."

"*Brought* me here?" she spits, her face flushing. "You think I wanted to stay in this nightmare? The only reason I've been here is to protect Anna from *you*."

The words land like a slap, and Parker's face darkens further. His hands clench into fists at his sides. "You have no idea what you're talking about."

"Don't I?" Helen shoots back, stepping closer. "I know *exactly* what you've done, Parker. To Blue. To Anna. To Theo."

He freezes, his eyes narrowing. "What did you say?"

The room is charged with unspoken truths. My heart pounds in my chest as I glance at Helen, her face set with a steely resolve I've never seen before.

"Helen, stop," I plead, my voice trembling. "You're only making this worse."

"Worse?" Parker's voice rises, incredulous. "You think this is *my* fault?" He gestures wildly at the dollhouse, his eyes burning with fury. "Whatever sick game you're playing, Anna, it ends now."

"It's not a game," I whisper, my voice barely audible over the pounding of my heart.

But Parker doesn't hear me.

His attention moves beyond me, focusing onto the covered shape on the workbench.

A slow, sick feeling spreads through my chest.

"Parker—"

But it's too late. Before I can move, before I can stop him, his hand shoots out. With one swift motion, he rips the dust sheet away. The fabric falls to the floor, pooling at our feet.

Helen takes a small, sharp inhale—the only sound in the heavy, pulsing silence.

Parker stares. His fingers twitching at his sides.

I don't move. I am frozen in place.

His voice, when it comes, is barely above a whisper—ragged, disbelieving.

"What the hell is this?"

My project. My memorial.

A replica of the house we are standing in now.

One-to-twelve scale.

It towers over the workbench, nearly three feet high, its intricate details illuminated by the glow of the desk lamp. The weathered gray siding is an exact match to the real house, down to the faint cracks along the trim, the slight warping of the wooden porch. Each window is perfectly scaled, fitted with tiny panes of glass that reflect the dim light, making the house feel eerily alive.

The front door is slightly ajar. An invitation. Or a warning.

Parker doesn't notice the enormity of it at first—his attention is locked on the inside, on the impossible level of detail.

His eyes dart from room to room, scanning the precise replicas. The living room, with the wedding album on the coffee table, the tiny compass on the sofa, the scarf draped over the back of a chair.

The bathroom, where a wedding ring rests on the counter, untouched.

The bedroom, where Theo's cologne sits on the dresser, an

exact replica of the bottle Parker knows was found in the real house weeks ago.

I watch the tightening of his jaw. The way his fingers curl, like he wants to smash the whole thing apart. He takes another step closer, and I'm forced to move aside, no longer able to block his view.

His gaze locks onto the bed.

The tiny book, *The Art of War*, carefully pressed open. The folded slip of paper beside it—Grant's poem.

A sharp inhale.

"What the hell is this?" he whispers, his voice trembling with a mixture of rage and disbelief.

I don't answer. I watch as his eyes move upward—to the attic. The final room I finished this morning. The one that isn't supposed to exist.

Parker stills. He knows.

Every inch of this house is designed to expose him.

I didn't need Helen to tell me Parker was a monster.

I had already figured that out myself.

Each addition is a seed, a trap carefully planted. I just never knew Helen was here, helping me. In its perfect, miniature world, I see the truth laid bare—a truth Parker will never understand.

This isn't about clinging to the past. It's about survival.

A figure of a man with blonde hair and tanned skin sits slumped in the corner, surrounded by painted blood, a knife glinting in its hand. The detail is meticulous—the empty boxes, the dusty window. The lifeless body is an exact replica of the handsome man I met and promised to marry only weeks ago. It's a mirror of Parker's darkest fears, brought to life in miniature.

For a moment, the room is silent, the tension so thick it's choking. Then Parker releases a strangled sound from his throat. "What the..."

He stumbles back, his face pale, his hands trembling. His eyes snap to mine, wild and desperate. "What *is* this, Anna?"

I don't answer. I can't. My voice has abandoned me, leaving only the pounding of my heart and the cold sweat on my skin.

"*You* have been doing all of it," Parker whispers, his voice low and venomous. "You're trying to destroy me. I thought I was crazy, that Helen or Sadie or Jillian were behind the items that kept being put out—"

"Oh, I helped plenty," Helen says, her voice venomous and strong. "It didn't take long for me to realize what Anna was up to. I realized that she placed the wedding ring out, the scarf, the cologne, the wedding album. While I think the compass I pretended to find or the photo of Sadie I set out today was powerful, nothing compares to the way you looked when that home video began to play on Anna's birthday."

I look at Helen, and the truth settles into me at last. Every time I thought she was looking at me with judgment, she was trying to decipher new ways to protect me.

All this time, I had been searching for the culprit. Marsha and Conrad, their disapproval bleeding into every word. Jillian, watching me with wary concern. Grant, appearing just when the past started pushing through the cracks. Even Sadie, my own daughter, acting out in ways I didn't understand.

But I had been wrong.

It had been Helen.

The objects, the impossible placement of things I knew I hadn't touched. The creeping dread each time I walked into a room and found another relic of my past staring back at me.

The cologne. I had put that there. The wedding ring, the scarf, the album—they were mine.

But the home video?

The compass?

Sadie's photograph, her face scratched away?

Oxygen feels optional. I am dizzy with the truth.

Helen.

She was the one behind the moments that had sent ice through my veins. The ones that had truly made me doubt my sanity.

I see it all now—the way she lingered after each discovery, the way she watched me, not with judgment, but with intent.

She wasn't tormenting me.

She was helping me.

My pulse pounds in my ears, a deep, rhythmic roar. "Helen," I whisper, my voice unsteady. "Thank you."

She doesn't flinch. No denial, no regret. Just a slow nod.

"I had to," she says simply.

I stare at her, my mind whirling.

I had been so sure I was unraveling. So convinced Parker was the only one pulling the strings.

But I hadn't seen the other hand at work.

Parker isn't so grateful. He is ready to make us both pay.

"Helen, you I can understand—you've always been unhinged. But *you*, Anna." He seethes at me. "You are even more crazy than Theo let on."

Rage burns inside me.

"Don't you *dare* talk about my husband."

Parker's once sunshiny eyes have turned to black beads of poison. He springs toward me, his movements erratic.

Helen screams, her voice slicing through the tension like a blade. "Stop it, Parker!"

Before I can react, Parker's hands reach for me. The world tilts, the room spinning in a blur of color and sound. Helen steps between us, her arms outstretched, her voice trembling but firm. "Get away from her!"

Parker freezes, his chest heaving, his eyes darting between us. For a moment, it seems as though he might back down. But then his gaze shifts to the dollhouse again, and something in him snaps.

He lunges, his hands grasping for the miniature structure, his movements frantic and wild. Helen grabs his arm, trying to pull him back, but he's too strong. The dollhouse wobbles, its fragile walls threatening to collapse under the force of his anger.

"Parker, stop!" I scream, my voice breaking.

But he doesn't stop. His hands close around the dollhouse, and with a furious roar, he hurls it to the floor. The sound of splintering wood and shattering glass fills the room.

Something breaks inside me too.

Time seems to slow as the dollhouse crashes to the ground, its pieces scattering across the floor. The tiny rooms I'd so precisely crafted—the living room, the nursery, the attic—lie in ruins. The sight of it twists something deep inside me, a primal, wrenching pain that is both loss and release.

Helen pulls me back, her arms wrapping around me as I collapse against her. Parker stands over the wreckage, his chest heaving, his face a twisted mask of rage and despair. For a moment, no one moves. The only sound is the ragged gasps of the three of us, the destruction lying in a heap between us.

"You think this is over?" Parker snarls, his voice low and venomous. "You're *mine*, Anna. You'll always be mine."

The words send a chill down my spine, wrapping icy fingers around my heart. Parker's gaze darkens, his face twisting into something unrecognizable. The spark of defiance I'd felt a moment ago flickers dangerously, threatening to extinguish under the weight of his fury.

"I'm not yours," I say, forcing the words past the lump in my throat. My voice trembles, but I refuse to falter. "And I *never* will be."

Parker's lips curl into a snarl, and he takes a step toward me, his movements deliberate and predatory. My pulse races, the air in the room growing thinner with each passing second.

"Anna, don't," Helen pleads, her voice breaking. She moves in front of me again, her arms outstretched like a shield. But I see the fear in her eyes, the way her hands shake. She's terrified, like me.

Parker's laugh is low and chilling, a sound that makes the hair on the back of my neck stand on end. "Do you think she can protect you?" he asks, his voice dripping with menace. "Do you think anyone can?"

The tension snaps like a rubber band stretched too far. He lunges forward, and for one horrifying moment, I think he's going to attack Helen—or me. Or both of us.

The thought slams into me like a freight train, and the room bends. My vision narrows to the intense lines of Parker's face, the wild gleam in his eyes. This isn't anger anymore. It's something far more dangerous. I can't die. Not now, not like this. Sadie needs me.

I grab Helen's arm, pulling her back. "Run," I whisper, my voice barely audible over the pounding of my heart. But Helen can't move, her body frozen, her eyes locked on Parker.

The room seems to shrink, the walls closing in as Parker looms over us.

The dollhouse lies in ruins at his feet, its shattered pieces a grim reflection of the chaos spiraling out of control.

My mind races, desperate for a way out, but all I can think is: *He's going to kill us.*

FORTY-FIVE

THREE WEEKS EARLIER

It all started the day Parker moved in.

He arrived with donuts and coffee for Sadie and me. A stack of neatly packed boxes trailing behind him. "Only the essentials for now," he'd said, flashing me that easy, practiced smile. "The rest can come later."

The air is warm, the faint scent of jasmine growing in the yard wafts in through the open window. Down the hall, Sadie's voice drifts toward me, carefree as she hums while packing for her trip to the farm. It's a rare moment of peace, the kind I've craved.

I glance at the boxes. This is it—our new start. Parker moving in is a chance to rebuild. A fresh chapter. A clean slate.

I need this to work.

I kneel, peeling back the tape on the first box. The cardboard resists, sticking to my fingers. Inside, everything is perfectly arranged: neatly folded shirts, polished shoes, a leather shaving kit. Parker's life, curated and orderly, a stark contrast to the chaos still clinging to mine.

It comforts me.

The second box is heavier. My arms strain as I haul it onto

the bed. Something shifts inside, a dull thud. It's filled with books, the spines stacked like soldiers. I run my fingers over them, recognizing Parker's favorites: *Man's Search for Meaning. The Art of War. Meditations.* Books about discipline and purpose.

I pick up *The Art of War*, the cover faded black, the corners softened by years of use. When I open it, something flutters loose, slipping between my fingers like silk. A piece of paper lands at my feet. The handwriting is unmistakable.

Grant.

I freeze, pulse hammering as my eyes scan the paper.

> *To love you is to be consumed,*
> *a fire both beautiful and ruinous.*
> *And yet, I burn willingly.*

The words hit like a punch to the chest, dredging up what I thought I'd buried—love, guilt, loss. Why does Parker have this?

My stomach lurches. I sit back on my heels, gripping the paper so tightly my knuckles ache. The edges crumple under my fingers, but I can't let go.

Grant gave me this poem on a night that felt like the beginning of something extraordinary. I kept it hidden, folded away in my dresser drawer—a secret, safe and untouched.

Until now.

I grab the book again, flipping through the pages. My fingers trace faint pencil marks in the margins—notations that send ice crawling down my spine.

"To trap your enemy, first understand their weakness."

A shudder rolls through me.

The room tilts.

Our meeting at the park—my mind recoils from the thought —what if it wasn't a coincidence? What if it wasn't fate? What if it was calculated?

My chest tightens, panic blooming in my throat as I glance back at the book and the poem still clutched in my trembling hand. Theo must have known about the affair. I had wondered but had been too scared to ask. Did he find this? Give it to Parker? But how? And why?

The weight of Parker's meticulousness is throttling now. It's as though the order of his life has always been about control, not reassurance.

But how would Parker and Theo have known one another?

I swallow hard, my throat suddenly dry. I know Parker is a professor at the university. A psychology professor...

Then it hits me.

Was he Theo's therapist?

I lurch for my laptop, barely registering the way my hands shake as I drag it onto my lap. The room feels too small, the air too thin. My fingers tremble over the keyboard as I type Theo's name into the bank records file.

I told myself I wouldn't sift through my past anymore. But this is different. The screen loads slowly. The spinning wheel taunts me, each second stretching unbearably. And then I see it.

P. Madison Therapy.

The name leaps off the screen, appearing over and over. My heartbeat swallows the air.

Theo was seeing Parker.

I stare, unblinking, as my mind stitches together the horrifying truth.

Parker wasn't just a psychologist on sabbatical. He wasn't just a professor. He was Theo's therapist. He *knew* Theo. Which means he knew me.

A slow, twisting nausea rolls through my stomach.

A darker question unfurls, insidious and cold, as I consider the idea that Theo knew about my affair. How did my husband really die?

I close my eyes, but it doesn't stop the memories from slamming into me at full force.

Theo on the morning of the hike—cheerful. He had a cautious nature—he was methodical, planned everything. I always knew it didn't make sense that he'd slip. It didn't make sense that he wouldn't have worn his hiking boots. I never believed for a second it was an accident. My worst fear had been that he knew about my affair and took his own life... but that never sat right with me either. Theo loved Sadie. And I never saw him spiral.

I glance around the bedroom, as though the walls might hold answers. My vision blurs, my pulse erratic. Sadie's laugh echoes faintly from down the hall, centering me. She doesn't know. She's packing her treasures for the farm—dolls, markers, books. She doesn't know how precarious our life has become.

I clutch the poem tighter, the paper damp from my clammy grip. I'm the grieving widow with a guilty conscience, a messy past. I destroyed my marriage with an affair. I left Theo broken —and now he's gone.

If I tell the police about Parker, about this tangled web I'm only beginning to see, they'll dismiss me. How wild would it sound? *Yes, officer, I believe my fiancé murdered my husband.* It's too far-fetched... yet.

The poem crumples in my fist.

No.

If Parker thinks he's in control, he's wrong. I'll play along. Let him move in. Let him think he's won.

But Parker isn't the only one who knows how to play games. My mind sharpens, refocusing. A plan begins to take shape.

If Parker wants a life with me, I'll give him one.

But it won't be the one he imagined.

I'll build the perfect world, and I'll use it to show him exactly how it ends.

FORTY-SIX

Client Notes: Session 7

Client: Male, late thirties. Seeking clarity on whether to remain in a strained marriage following the revelation of a betrayal.

Summary:
The client disclosed finding evidence of his wife's affair several weeks ago. He described uncovering a handwritten poem tucked inside one of her sketchbooks, written in another man's handwriting. The poem, intimate and evocative, left no doubt about its author's feelings—or the nature of their relationship.

The client described the moment with stark clarity: opening her dresser drawer to see the words. The weight of betrayal settled over him. He admitted to rereading the poem several times. He considered confronting his wife, though he ultimately decided against it. "I didn't want to hear her confirm what I already knew," he said. "I... couldn't bear it."

Instead, he has chosen to stay silent, though the knowledge festers, influencing every interaction. He confessed to following her once, watching her enter a café where she sat with a man for an hour before returning home. He has not confronted her, nor has he directly addressed the affair.

Key Observations:

- **Emotional Conflict:** The client's emotions fluctuate between anger and longing. He clearly loves his wife, but the betrayal has fundamentally altered his view of her.
- **Fear of Confrontation:** The client avoids direct conflict, possibly out of fear of shattering the fragile remnants of their relationship.
- **Attachment to Stability:** He expresses a strong desire to maintain their family unit for the sake of their child, even if it means suppressing his own pain.

Therapist Reflection:
The client's pain is palpable, but so is his restraint. His descriptions of the poem were striking, almost reverent, as if he could see his wife more clearly through someone else's words than through their shared years.

When I asked if he could forgive her, his answer was immediate and raw: "I don't know. I want to—for Sadie. For us. But every time I look at her, I wonder if she's still thinking about him. Or if she's pretending for my sake."

There is a quiet desperation in his words, a yearning to understand whether the love they once had can survive this betrayal. And yet, there is also a part of him—small but growing—that seems ready to let go.

Note to File:

The client's wife remains a compelling figure in these sessions, though her role has shifted. She is no longer the unattainable ideal he once described but a flawed and human partner who has hurt him deeply.

I am struck by the way the client grapples with the poem, as though it is a living entity in their marriage. I asked what he planned to do with it, and he admitted he couldn't bring himself to destroy it. He gave me the poem, saying he couldn't bear to hold on to it any longer.

Why do I find myself wondering what it would be like to have inspired such raw emotion in another person? Why can't I stop imagining the woman at the center of it all?

FORTY-SEVEN
THREE WEEKS EARLIER

I should be driving home. But instead, I take a left.

The road to the storage facility is familiar, but it feels different today—heavier, more final. Maybe because this time, I'm not here to bury the past.

I'm here to unearth it.

Sadie is gone for the summer. A full month at the farm, safe with Marsha and Conrad. A month of running through fields, collecting eggs, riding horses—a world untouched by everything that's happening here.

And one month for me to set everything in motion.

I have exactly four weeks to put my plan in place. Four weeks to turn my house into a trap.

By the time she comes back home, it will be over.

The storage unit looms in front of me, the metal door rolling up with a reluctant groan.

The space inside is dim and cold, the air thick with dust and silence. I haven't been here in months. I tell myself it's because there was no need, because I'd already done the impossible task of sorting through Theo's things.

But the truth is, I didn't want to come back. Not until now.

The boxes are stacked neatly, labeled in my own handwriting: *Theo's Clothes, Theo's Books, Camping Gear, Memories.*

I hesitate at the last one. Months after his death, I began meticulously packing things away. It was the only thing that made sense—sorting, labeling, controlling the mess of loss.

Now, I kneel, peeling back the tape. The air inside is stale, thick with time.

I reach in, my fingers brushing against something soft—his scarf. The one he wore on our last trip to the coast. I hold it up, the fabric slipping through my hands like water. It still smells like him. I press the wool to my face, inhale deeply, then force myself to fold it neatly over my arm.

Beneath it, a leather-bound wedding album. Our wedding album. The corners are frayed, the cover still marked with a faint stain from the champagne toast at our reception.

And at the very bottom, wrapped in tissue paper—his wedding ring. The metal is cool against my palm, deceptively solid for something that no longer holds meaning. I twist it between my fingers, staring at the engraving inside.

Theo. Forever.

I exhale sharply and place it back in the box next to the tin compass—the one Theo always carried.

I pick up a second box, one that isn't labeled. I pry open the flaps, my heart pounding as I sift through it. More of Theo's things. His leather wallet, an old watch with a cracked face, a handful of dog-eared books with notes in the margins.

Everything I choose has a purpose. And everything I take will find its place. Not all at once, but slowly, over time, I will place them in the home, dismantling my life with Parker with each item.

. . .

The house is empty when I return, the silence pressing against me as I step inside.

I carry the box upstairs, my pulse quickening. Parker could be here any minute, ready to greet me, his new fiancée.

I move quickly, heading for the attic. The door groans as I push it open, the sound swallowed by the hush of the house. It smells like cedar and dust. After climbing the narrow staircase, I set the box down, kneeling beside it, making a decision. This is where I'll keep them.

My secrets.

For now, they will stay here, safe and waiting. Until I decide their time has come. Until I choose their place in the house, where they will haunt Parker as carefully as I have planned.

I reach into the box and pull out the cologne, turning the small glass bottle over in my hand. I set it aside. It will be the first.

Parker thinks he's in control.

But he has no idea.

I shut the attic door behind me.

Now, I wait.

FORTY-EIGHT

PRESENT DAY

In my studio, dollhouse pieces litter the floor, jagged shards of wood and plastic scattered everywhere. The world I built—now exposed.

Helen stands between Parker and me, her body rigid, her arms raised like a shield.

Parker takes a slow step forward, and I feel it in my bones—the shift. The moment everything changes.

His voice is calm. Too calm. "Move, Helen."

Helen doesn't flinch. "Not this time."

Parker exhales sharply, shaking his head like she's a child throwing a tantrum. "This is embarrassing," he mutters. "You're embarrassing yourself."

Helen doesn't back down. "You think I don't know what you did?" she demands. "You killed Theo. Why?"

Parker's mouth twitches. Then—he laughs. It sounds cold, almost amused. Like she's exactly as stupid as he always thought.

Helen's fists tighten. "You think this is *funny*?"

Parker tilts his head, mocking. "I think it's cute, you

pretending you're smart." His eyes darken. "You're not even asking the right question."

Helen's face twists in frustration. "Then tell me. Tell me why you did it."

A slow smirk spreads across Parker's face. "No."

Helen stiffens, fury vibrating through her.

"I know," I say softly, stepping forward.

Parker goes still. His eyes flick to mine, the amusement bleeding out of them. He hadn't expected this. He hadn't expected me.

I swallow hard, my pulse hammering. But I don't break eye contact. "I know the connection."

Helen glances at me, confused. "Anna?"

I ignore her.

This moment is for Parker and me. His jaw tightens. He adjusts. Recalculates. For the first time, he's the one caught off guard.

He knows what I know.

Parker's hands flex at his sides, but his expression remains eerily composed. "I underestimated you."

I exhale shakily. "Yes, you did."

His gaze flicks to the door. Then to Helen. And I know what's coming before it happens.

Parker moves. Fast. His hand snatches the mallet from the workbench.

"Helen, run—" The words barely escape me before he swings.

The impact is sickening.

Helen crumples, her body folding like a marionette with its strings cut. The mallet clatters to the ground. Parker exhales sharply, as if shaking off a mild inconvenience. His gaze lifts, and I freeze.

His attention is on me now.

"You're not going anywhere," he spits, dragging me back.

"She needs help!" I cry, tears streaming down my face as I twist against his grip. "You've hurt her! Parker, *please!*"

"Shut up!" His voice is a whip crack, and I freeze, trembling. He's not done yet. He reaches into his waistband and pulls out a gun. My body goes cold.

Parker's grip tightens around my wrist, his fingers like iron, unrelenting.

"We're going upstairs," he growls, yanking me toward the door. His voice low and laced with fury. "You wanted someone dead up there in the attic, like in your precious model, remember?"

His nails dig into my skin as he leans in, his next words a whisper of pure venom.

"Well, congratulations, Anna. That person is going to be you."

We walk down the hall to the attic door, the floorboards creaking beneath the weight of what I've carried for so long. Parker pushes me ahead of him, the barrel of the gun pressing hard against the small of my back. My legs feel like lead, every step a monumental effort as fear grips my chest.

"Parker," I plead, my voice shaking. "You don't have to do this. Let's talk about it. We can figure this out together—"

He lets out a bitter, humorless laugh. "Figure this out? You think I'd trust you to figure anything out? You're the reason it all went to hell, Anna. You and your lies. You couldn't just be happy, could you? We could have had a perfect life, you and me. But you're obsessed. With Grant. With Caleb. With Sadie."

"That's not true," I whisper, my voice breaking. But even as I say it, I know the words are futile.

"You don't reason with crazy, Anna," he mutters, his words hot against my neck. "And you've been crazy all along."

The attic door looms ahead, its paint peeling and cracked.

Parker reaches past me, shoving it open with one hand while keeping the gun firmly against my back.

The wood of the stairs bites into my bare feet, splinters threatening to pierce my skin with every step. The air grows heavier as we ascend, thick with dust and lost memories. Panic claws at the edges of my vision.

"Up!" he barks, pushing me forward. I stumble over a loose board, catching myself on the edge of an old trunk. My hands tremble as I lower myself onto it, my heart pounding so loudly I'm sure he can hear it.

His eyes land on the box in the corner.

My secrets.

I had told him I'd taken everything to storage, but that was a lie. Not everything left this house. I brought back this box, filled with the things I thought would unravel Parker the most.

The cologne, the ring, the scarf.

And now, Parker understands what I did.

Without hesitation, he strides over, and tears open the box, ripping into it like a wild animal. Theo's cologne falls out first, then journals and photo albums. The room shrinks with every item he hurls to the floor.

"This is what you've been holding on to, isn't it?" he spits, lifting a framed photo of Theo and me from our wedding day. The glass catches the dim light for a moment before Parker hurls it to the ground. It shatters, the pieces scattering like jagged stars.

"Stop it!" I cry, my voice breaking. "Please, stop!"

He doesn't. He grabs for more in the box, his movements are frantic. A journal—Theo's handwriting on the cover—lands at my feet. My knees buckle, and I drop to the floor, clutching the journal to my chest. But Parker doesn't even notice.

He's too consumed by his own madness.

"You've been living in the past, Anna," he growls, pulling

out a stack of old letters from the box. He throws them at me, the papers fluttering like wounded birds. "Idolizing a man who didn't deserve you."

I shake my head, tears streaking down my face. "Theo loved me," I whisper. My voice is small, but certain. "You wouldn't understand that."

Parker laughs—a harsh, guttural sound that sends a chill down my spine.

"*Loved* you?" His expression darkens, his lips curling. "Theo didn't love you, Anna. He tolerated you. He *pitied* you."

I flinch as if he's struck me. "That's not true."

He steps closer, his presence overpowering. "You trap people, Anna. That's what you do. You wrap them in your grief, your chaos, and you drag them down with you. You ruin people."

His voice lowers, the words laced with something colder than anger. "And I won't let you ruin me."

Something inside me snaps. I lunge to my feet. The fear inside me twists—it becomes something hotter, stronger.

"I know what you did, Parker."

He stills, his grip on the gun tightens.

I step forward. "You were Theo's therapist, weren't you?" My voice is hoarse, raw, but I don't stop. "I know you saw him. I know you manipulated him. You took his pain and twisted it into something else. You wanted control over him. Over me."

His face flickers, a split-second hesitation.

I press harder. "You used him, didn't you? Used him to get to me. Made him think he was losing his mind."

Parker exhales sharply, nostrils flaring. "Shut up, Anna."

I don't. I can't.

"You followed him, didn't you?" I demand. "Did you wait for him to be alone? Did you—" My voice breaks. "Did you *push* him, Parker?"

His laugh is slow, deliberate. He takes a step closer, eyes gleaming. "Oh, Anna," he whispers, tilting his head. "You are so much smarter than I gave you credit for."

It's confirmation. My stomach roils. I stumble back.

He moves to another box, tearing through it with the same fury. Then he stops. In his hands is a tiny blanket, soft and faded with time. Beside it, a pair of baby shoes. Caleb's things.

"No..." I whisper, my voice trembling.

"This?" Parker holds up the blanket, his voice dripping with mockery. "Still holding on to *this?*"

The word bursts out of me before I can stop it. "No!"

I lunge forward, grabbing the blanket from his hands. I clutch it to my chest, tears blinding me as I curl around it, shielding it with my body. The baby shoes he never got the chance to wear tumble from the box, landing near my knees. I grab those too, holding them close as if they're Caleb himself.

"You took Theo," I sob, the words ripping from me. "You don't get Caleb too. You don't get to take everything."

For the first time, Parker hesitates. He steps back, his hand lowering slightly. His face shifts, confusion flickering across his features. He looks almost human for a moment. Almost reachable.

"Anna..." he murmurs, his voice softer now, almost pitying. But the moment is fleeting. His expression hardens, and the mask slips back into place. "You don't get it, do you?" His voice is low, venomous. He steps closer, his mutterings turning darker, more self-pitying. "I gave you *everything*, and it was never enough. You've ruined me."

The words cut deep, but they ignite something inside me. A spark of defiance flares, burning away the fear. I straighten. My hands stop shaking.

"You're right," I say, my voice low but steady. "It was never enough. Because *you're* not enough, Parker. And you never will be."

The attic is closing in on me. Parker is pacing, his words a venomous loop, and I'm clutching Caleb's blanket so tightly it's a wonder it hasn't torn. Every instinct is screaming at me to do something, to move, to fight, but he's too close, and the gun in his hand is steady.

Then, I hear it. A car pulling into the driveway.

FORTY-NINE

My heart lurches. Who could it be?

Helen wouldn't have called anyone—she must still be unconscious downstairs. Possibly already dead. Is it Jillian? My stomach twists. If she comes inside, she'll walk straight into this nightmare. I don't know how to stop it.

Parker freezes mid-pace, his head tilting like a predator sensing prey. "What was that?" he snaps, his eyes narrowing.

My eyes are wild, darting around the room, but my mind is clear. I need to buy myself more time. "Someone is here. Someone to help me."

His gaze flicks to the attic door, and I see his grip on the gun tighten. My pulse pounds in my ears as I try to think. What can I do to keep him here? To keep him from going downstairs and finding whoever it is?

The sound of the front door opening carries up the stairs. A soft voice calls out, cheerful but hesitant. "Anna? Helen?"

It's Jillian. Relief and terror flood me.

Relief because she's here, because I'm not alone anymore.

Terror because Parker hears her too.

No.

"Who the hell is that?" Parker growls, turning to face me. The gun swings in my direction, and I flinch.

"I don't know," I lie, my voice shaking. "Maybe a neighbor?"

Parker's jaw clenches. He looks like he's about to head for the door when Jillian's voice calls again, louder this time. "Anna? Are you up there?" There is a long pause in movement, and I wonder if she came across Helen's body.

No, Jillian, don't come up here. *Please.*

The creak of the first attic step makes my stomach drop. Parker's eyes light up with something dark and dangerous. He positions himself near the door, the gun raised. I want to scream, to warn her, but my throat closes in.

Jillian's footsteps grow louder as she ascends. My heart hammers against my ribs. I have to do something. I can't sit here.

"Parker," I say, my voice trembling but urgent. "You don't need to do this. She doesn't know anything. Let her go, please..."

He doesn't respond. His focus is on the door as Jillian's head appears in the opening. Her eyes widen as she takes in the scene: the gun, the chaos, me on the floor clutching Caleb's things.

"Oh my God," she whispers.

Parker moves fast. He grabs her by the arm and yanks her into the attic, slamming the door shut behind her. Jillian stumbles, her face pale with shock. The bag she'd been carrying drops to the floor. It's take-out food.

"What the hell are you doing here?" Parker snarls, shoving her toward me. Jillian falls to her knees beside me, panicked gasps escaping her.

"I... I came to drop off some dinner," she stammers. "I didn't mean to interrupt..."

"Shut up!" Parker barks, his voice thunderous. He resumes pacing, the gun swinging wildly in his hand. "You both think you can ruin me. You think you can get away with this."

Jillian's wide eyes meet mine. In her gaze, I see the same

terror I feel, but also something else. A question. A plea. *What do we do?*

I don't have an answer, but I know one thing for sure: we can't let Parker win.

Jillian kneels beside me, her hand brushing mine. I clutch Caleb's blanket tighter, my body trembling. The gun in Parker's hand swings erratically as he paces, muttering to himself. The attic is a pressure cooker, every second stretching impossibly long.

"Anna," Jillian whispers, her voice barely audible. Her tone is harsh despite her fear, the same blunt edge she's always had. "I knew he was a control freak, but this is next level."

I want to laugh, but the sound catches in my throat as a sob instead. I lean into her, whispering back, "I'm sorry. I'm so sorry. I'll get us out of this. I swear."

Jillian squeezes my hand. "Better hurry up..."

Parker spins around, his eyes wild as he glares at us. "Shut up! Both of you!" he shouts, his voice cracking. He rakes a hand through his hair, his movements jerky and desperate. "You don't get to talk. You don't get to make this about you. This is my moment. My turn to be heard."

I nod quickly, my voice placating. "Okay, Parker. We're listening. Just... just tell us what you need to say."

His laugh is hollow, like breaking glass. "What I need to say?" He stops pacing, staring down at us with a mix of rage and something almost pitiable. "You've never listened. Not to me, not to Theo. You never cared."

He resumes pacing, his footsteps heavy on the creaking floorboards. "Theo was weak," he mutters, his voice gaining a rhythm, like he's reciting a mantra. "He didn't deserve you, Anna. But I... I... I was different. I was better. Everything I've done was for you."

"For *me?*" The words slip out before I can stop them, my

voice incredulous. Jillian shoots me a warning look, but it's too late.

Parker stops mid-step, his head snapping toward me. "Yes, for *you!*" he roars, his face flushing with fury. "But you... you couldn't see that, could you? Theo was right. You're poison. You ruin everything you touch."

Each word is like a lash, cutting deep, but I force myself to stay calm. "I didn't mean to," I say softly. "I... I didn't realize."

He shakes his head, his mutterings growing more erratic. "It doesn't matter. None of it matters now. You think you can make me the villain? No, Anna. This is your fault. All of it."

Jillian shifts beside me, her body tensing. I can sense her preparing to move, to do something. I press my hand against hers, a silent plea to stay still. Not yet. We have to be careful.

"You're right," I say, my voice trembling but steady. "It's my fault. All of it. But Parker... you don't have to do this. We can fix this. Together."

His laugh is jagged, cutting through the air. "Fix this? You think I'd let you fix anything? You've ruined me, Anna. You've—"

A sound. Faint, but unmistakable.

Someone else is on the stairs.

FIFTY

Client Notes: Ninth Session

Client: Male, late thirties. Struggling with the aftermath of marital betrayal but expressing optimism about reconciliation.

Summary:
The client appears lighter today, his demeanor markedly different from prior sessions. He describes a sense of clarity, an acceptance of the pain he's endured and a resolve to rebuild his marriage. He acknowledges the complexities of his wife's personality—her distance, her secrets—but chooses to see them as layers to be understood rather than obstacles to overcome.

Key Observations:

- **Renewed Focus:** The client speaks about self-improvement, referencing healthier habits and a rekindled connection with his wife. His decision to move forward appears genuine, though tinged with vulnerability.

- **Symbolic Fresh Start:** The client shares plans for an upcoming winter hike, framing it as a personal milestone and a way to solidify his commitment to a new chapter.
- **Forgiveness:** He explicitly states that he has forgiven his wife for her infidelity, viewing their shared grief over their lost child as the true wedge between them.

Session Notes (transcribed from Voice Memo):

T: It wasn't about words. When we were sitting together. I don't know… It felt like peace. Like maybe we can find our way back.
[Pause]
P: You're saying the silence between you felt healing?
T: Yeah. Forgiving her… it's been a process. But I think I have to. Not for the marriage. For me. I've been holding on to the hurt like a shield. I don't want that anymore. I'm tired of being angry. I… want to love her again.
P: That's a significant shift. What's changed?
T: I've been taking better care of myself. Eating better. Running again. And I planned a solo hike. Me and the snow, you know? To clear my head.
P: Where are you going?
T: The ridge trails near Mount Rainier. I used to go all the time. Before life got… complicated. It seems right to go back now.
[Client exhibits increased optimism, physically relaxing as he discusses future plans.]
P: And Anna? Do you feel she's meeting you halfway?
[Client hesitates.]
T: She's trying. Anna isn't… easy to read. She's always been in her own world—distant, in her head. But that's who she is. I've stopped trying to change it. I want to be there for her.
[Pause]

T: She's working on her art again. It's… beautiful. Complicated, sure. I think it's how she processes things. And I get
that. I'm trying to process too.
[End of session dialogue]

Therapist Reflection:
The client's optimism is disarming, but I can't ignore the instinctive
pull I feel toward his wife. She's not simply a figure in his narrative—
she's the catalyst. The thread tying everything together.

When he spoke of her art, her darkness, I felt an unspoken connection, a sense that I understand her in a way he never could. He views
her as a mystery to unravel. But to me, she's a mirror—reflecting the
depths I've long kept hidden.

His plans to reconcile. To forgive, to move forward. They feel like
barriers to what should be inevitable. He's too idealistic, too blind to
see what's truly unfolding.

And then—the hike. The location etched into my mind, as if it had
always been waiting.

He's chasing a fresh start.

But some people don't deserve a second chance.

FIFTY-ONE

Parker's entire body goes rigid. The gun swings toward the door as he takes a step forward, his rage filling each step. "Who the hell is that?" he growls.

My heart stops. The police? Did Jillian manage to call them?

Beside me, Jillian grips my arm, her nails digging into my skin. She whispers, "I called him... when I saw Helen... I'm sorry."

Him?

The sound on the stairs grows louder, each creak a drumbeat in my chest.

I press my back against the wall, clutching Caleb's blanket like it's the only thing holding me steady. The air is thick, unmoving, charged with something electric and wrong.

Parker stands frozen near the door, the gun gripped tightly in his hand. His head leans, as he listens.

Then—silence.

A long, terrible silence.

Parker's fingers flex around the gun. "No one should be

here," he murmurs, more to himself than to us. His voice is low, controlled—but his knuckles are white. "Not now."

I swallow hard, my pulse a frantic, uneven beat as I glance at Jillian. Her wide eyes lock with mine, and I can see the same fear mirrored in her expression. We both know there's no reasoning with him.

Footsteps again, lighter this time, careful. Parker takes a step toward the door, raising the gun. The stairs creak slightly, and for a heartbeat, everything is suspended.

Then he steps into view.

Grant.

He's holding a crowbar, his face set with determination. Relief and terror crash over me in equal measure.

Parker spins toward him, the gun trained on his chest. "You think you can stop this? Why would you want to fight for a woman like Anna anyway?" he snarls.

Grant doesn't answer. In one fluid motion, he raises the crowbar and swings. The metal arcs through the air, catching Parker's wrist. The gun flies from his hand and skids across the attic floor.

Chaos erupts. Parker lunges for the gun, his movements wild and uncoordinated. Jillian grabs a small box from the floor and hurls it at him, hitting him square in the back. Parker stumbles but doesn't stop. My throat burns as I scream, "Grant, watch out!"

Grant dives for the gun, but Parker is faster. He grabs it, rolling onto his back, and fires. The crack of the gunshot is deafening, the sound ricocheting off the attic walls.

Grant cries out, clutching his shoulder as he falls backward. Blood seeps through his shirt, staining it dark red.

"*No!*" I scream, scrambling to my knees. My entire body is shaking as I crawl toward Grant, but Parker swings the gun back toward me.

"Stay where you are!" he snarls. His hand is trembling now,

his face slick with sweat. For the first time, there's something new in his eyes: *fear*.

Jillian moves beside me, her hands raised. "Parker, you don't have to do this," she says, her voice calm despite the panic in her eyes. "Look at him. Look at yourself. It's over."

"Shut up!" Parker's voice cracks. He waves the gun wildly between us. "You don't tell me what to do. None of you do."

Grant groans beside me, his face pale. I press my hand against his shoulder, trying to stem the bleeding. "Stay with me," I whisper. My tears fall onto his shirt, mixing with the blood. "Please, stay with me."

Jillian shifts slightly, drawing Parker's attention. His gun swings toward her, and for a split second, the chaos freezes.

Then my gaze drops to the crowbar lying within reach. Adrenaline surges through me, raw and unrelenting.

I lunge.

The cold, rough metal of the crowbar presses into my palm as my fingers close around it. Parker's head snaps toward me, his eyes wide with shock. But it's too late.

I swing with every ounce of strength I have, every ounce of fear, rage and desperation fueling me.

The crowbar connects with a sickening thud against the side of Parker's head. The sound reverberates through the attic, a brutal symphony of finality.

He stumbles, his body twisting awkwardly as the gun slips from his hand and clatters to the floor. Blood blooms at his temple, bright against his pale skin, as he collapses, dazed and crumpling onto the wooden planks.

My chest heaves, the crowbar trembling in my grip. My lungs are too full and too empty all at once. The world narrows to this moment, to the sight of Parker sprawled on the ground. His moans barely audible over the pounding of my heart.

"Anna..." Jillian's voice slices through the haze. She darts forward, kicking the gun far out of Parker's reach. Her face is pale but resolute as she crouches beside Grant, whose groans are growing weaker.

I drop the crowbar with a metallic clang, its weight suddenly unbearable. Crawling to Grant's side, I press trembling hands against his shoulder, trying to slow the bleeding. His skin is cold and clammy beneath my fingers.

"Stay with me," I whisper, my voice cracking. Tears spill onto his shirt, mingling with the dark stain of blood. "Please, Grant. Hold on."

Jillian glances toward the window, her face etched with urgency. "The sirens," she says, hope in her words. "They're almost here."

I can hear them now, wailing in the distance, growing louder with each passing second. Relief and dread flood through me in equal measure. It's almost over, but the aftermath is already pressing down on me like a weight I'll never escape.

Parker stirs on the floor, his eyes fluttering open. His movements are sluggish, weak, but my stomach knots as his gaze lands on me. Blood trickles from his temple, tracing a dark path down his face. He tries to lift his head, but it falls back with a dull thud.

"Anna," he mutters, his voice slurred and venomous. "Everything I did... it was for you."

I squeeze my eyes shut, blocking out his words, his face, everything.

The sirens swell, and then there are heavy footsteps pounding up the stairs. The attic door bursts open, and uniformed officers flood the space. Their commands are forceful, dropping me in the present.

"Drop the weapon!" one of them shouts, even though Parker's hands are limp at his sides.

They don't wait for compliance. Two officers grab him, yanking his arms behind his back and snapping handcuffs around his wrists. He doesn't fight them, his body sagging as they haul him to his feet. Blood drips from his temple onto the floor, each drop echoing like a metronome.

Still, he mutters, his words low and disjointed. "It was all for her. Everything I did. She's the reason."

The officers drag him away, his ranting fading as they descend the stairs. I collapse against the wall, my body shaking violently now that the danger is gone. Jillian crouches beside me, her hand on my shoulder, her face softening for the first time.

"It's over," she says quietly. But her eyes hold the weight of everything that's happened, as if she's not quite sure we'll ever truly be free of this.

I nod, my knuckles white against the soft fabric. Turning my attention to Grant, I brush a strand of damp hair from his forehead. "Help is here," I whisper, the words as much for me as for him.

He nods faintly, his lips twitching into a weak smile. The paramedics arrive moments later, their voices a mix of urgency and calm.

The chaos around me fades as I close my eyes, clutching the blanket tighter.

FIFTY-TWO

The fluorescent lights buzz faintly overhead. Their cold, sterile glow washes over the cramped interview room. The walls are bare except for a clock ticking loudly, each second dragging on endlessly. I'm perched on the edge of a metal chair, Caleb's blanket folded tightly in my lap, my fingers gripping it like a lifeline.

Across the table, the officer's pen scratches against paper as I recount everything. My words come out haltingly at first, but soon they spill over, a torrent of memories and emotions I can't stop. I hear my voice trembling as I describe Parker's descent into madness, Grant's bravery, the moment I swung the crowbar. My hands shake as I speak, and the officer glances at them briefly before nodding for me to continue.

Jillian sits beside me, her arm brushing mine occasionally. Her voice is steady when it's her turn, pointed and precise as she fills in the gaps I leave behind. She describes finding Helen, sending the text to Grant—who must have called the cops, and Parker's venomous tirade in the attic. Her tone wavers only when she talks about Grant being shot, and a pang of guilt and gratitude strikes me all at once.

The officer sets down his pen and leans back in his chair. "Between your statements and the recorded confession from Parker, we have more than enough to hold him."

I glance up, my throat tightening. "And Theo?" My voice cracks, but I push through. "Will... will Theo finally get justice?"

The officer nods, his expression softening. "Yes. Parker's confession clearly implicates him in your husband's death."

The words sink in slowly, like water seeping into dry ground. Justice for Theo. It doesn't undo what's been done, but it is a step toward something—maybe peace, maybe closure. I clutch the blanket tighter, comforted by its soft warmth against my palms.

"Anna?" Jillian's voice pulls me back. I look at her, startled, and she smiles softly. "We're done here."

I nod, standing on unsteady legs as we step out of the interview room and into the main lobby. The air smells faintly of coffee and paper, a strange mix of normalcy and bureaucracy. Officers move around us, their voices low and purposeful, but none of it registers fully. I'm underwater, everything muted and slow.

Jillian stops near the door, turning to face me. Her eyes are bright, a mix of exhaustion and fierce determination. She pulls me into a tight hug, her arms wrapping around me like she's holding me together.

"I love you, Anna," she murmurs, her voice thick with emotion. "Don't let this define you."

Her words hit me like a wave. I cling to her, my throat tightening as tears well up in my eyes. I don't trust myself to speak, so I nod against her shoulder. She pulls back, brushing a tear from my cheek before giving me a small, reassuring smile.

Then, as if reading my mind, she tilts her head toward the door. "Come on. Let me drive you to the hospital. We need to see if Grant and Helen are okay."

. . .

The drive to the hospital is quiet, the city lights blurring past in streaks of yellow and white. My mind is a tangle of thoughts—the attic, Parker's confession, the blood on Grant's shirt. My chest tightens as I remember the paramedic's words: *touch and go.* My hands grip the blanket tighter.

"He'll pull through," Jillian says suddenly, her voice firm. "Grant's tough. And Helen... she's a fighter too."

I want to believe her, but the fear gnaws at me. "I need to see them," I whisper. "I need to know they're okay."

Jillian reaches over, giving my hand a quick squeeze. "We'll know soon."

When we arrive at the hospital, the clean scent of antiseptic greets us as we step into the brightly lit lobby. My stomach churns as we approach the desk, Jillian's presence steadying me. The nurse behind the counter glances up, her expression neutral but kind.

"I'm here for Grant Holton," I say, my voice barely above a whisper. "And Helen Madison. Are they... are they okay?"

The nurse's expression doesn't change as she checks her computer. Each keystroke is an eternity. Finally, she looks up. "Grant is in surgery. Helen's stable, but she's still being monitored. Someone will update you as soon as they can."

I nod, the words settling heavily in my chest. *Stable. Monitored. Surgery.* My legs are wobbly, the reality of the situation is surreal.

Jillian guides me to a row of plastic chairs near the waiting area. We sit in silence, the bustle of the hospital filling the space around us. My hands still grip Caleb's blanket, its softness a small comfort in the sterile room.

The minutes drag on, each one heavier than the last. A doctor emerges from the surgery ward, his face shadowed with exhaustion.

"Grant?" I ask, my voice trembling.

The doctor hesitates, his expression unreadable. "We did everything we could."

The words linger, cutting through me. My vision blurs, my ears ringing. Jillian's hand grips mine tightly as my world tilts. My chest tightens as the weight of his words crushes me.

I clutch Caleb's blanket tighter, the fabric now damp with my tears. The room is impossibly cold. I am overwhelmed with the ache of loss.

The waiting is over, but the nightmare is not.

FIFTY-THREE

The hospital's waiting room is a blur of muted colors and hushed voices, but my eyes are fixed on the doctor standing in front of me. His words hit me like waves, each one slow and deliberate.

"We did everything we could," he says, his tone careful. Something inside me stills. "And he pulled through."

The air rushes out of my lungs in a sudden gasp. Tears spill down my cheeks before I can stop them, and my knees buckle slightly. Jillian's arm shoots out, steadying me.

"Thank you," I whisper, my voice cracking. The doctor offers a small, tired smile before nodding and walking away.

I'm trembling as Jillian squeezes my shoulder. "See?" she says softly. "I told you he's tough."

"I need to see him," I murmur, the words tumbling out in a rush.

Jillian steps aside, letting me move toward the hallway. Each step is heavier than the last, my heart pounding as I approach Grant's room. The sound of beeping monitors greets me as I push the door open.

Grant lies in the hospital bed, pale and hooked up to a maze of wires and tubes. His right shoulder is heavily bandaged, the bulk of it stark against the pale blue hospital gown. I remember the moment Parker's gun fired, the crimson spreading across Grant's shirt. The doctor said the bullet narrowly missed his lung, but the damage to his clavicle required hours of surgery. Seeing him now, alive, is a miracle.

His chest rises and falls steadily. His eyes flutter open as I step inside, and when he sees me, a faint smile tugs at his lips.

"Anna," he rasps, his voice weak but steady.

I choke back a sob as I move to his bedside, gripping the rail for support. "You scared me," I whisper, tears streaming down my face. "I thought... I thought I'd lost you."

He chuckles softly, wincing at the effort. "It takes more than that to get rid of me."

I reach out, hesitating before taking his hand in mine. His skin is warm but clammy, his grip weak yet reassuring. For a moment, I can only stare at him, the weight of everything we've been through pressing down on me.

"Grant," I start, my voice trembling, "I'm so sorry. For everything. For Theo, for how everything happened. I dragged you into my chaos, and this... all of this... is my fault."

He shakes his head, his eyes searching mine. "Stop," he says, his voice firmer. "We both made choices. You didn't drag me anywhere. I walked into this with my eyes open. And yes, it was complicated, but I... I couldn't stay away from you."

His words send a shiver through me, unlocking memories I'd buried. The stolen moments. The whispered confessions. The way we clung to each other in the shadows, even when the world around us condemned us. We'd both been married then, bound by guilt and obligations, but now... now the weight of those chains is gone.

"Grant, I..." My throat tightens as I try to find the words. "I've hurt you. I've hurt so many people."

"Anna," he interrupts, his hand tightening around mine.

"I'm not proud of everything that happened, but I don't regret loving you. Not for a second."

Tears spill freely now, blurring my vision. "I still love you," I confess, my voice breaking. "Not in some perfect, fairy-tale way, but in the way that matters. In the way that's real. I love you, even when it hurts."

He swallows hard, his own eyes glistening. "We're free now, Anna," he says, his voice soft but steady. "Free to choose what we want, without hiding. Without pretending."

I nod, leaning forward until our foreheads touch. "Then I choose you," I whisper.

The beeping monitors are the only sound in the room for a moment, a rhythmic reminder that he's still here, still fighting. He closes his eyes, his hand trembling as he lifts it to brush my cheek. "Messy is good," he murmurs, his faint smile returning. "Messy is us."

I sit back slightly, brushing away my tears but keeping his hand pressed to mine. "I'm staying," I say firmly. "I'm not going anywhere. We'll figure this out. Together."

"Together," he echoes, his voice barely above a whisper. But the conviction in his tone is unmistakable.

As I sit beside him, the weight of the past is a little lighter. The road ahead is still uncertain, filled with scars and unanswered questions.

But we're not facing it alone.

FIFTY-FOUR
ONE WEEK LATER

The late afternoon sun streams through the living room windows, casting long, warm streaks of light onto the floor. I'm standing by the window, absently folding a small pile of laundry, when I hear a car pulling into the driveway. The rumble of the engine dies, and soon after, the unmistakable shuffle of Sadie's boots on the front porch makes my heart ache with longing and relief.

She's home.

The door creaks open, and there she is, smiling, her backpack slung lazily over one shoulder. Her hair is a little wild, her jeans streaked with dirt, but her eyes... her eyes are as bright and curious as ever.

Behind her, Conrad and Marsha follow, their faces warm with quiet reassurance. Marsha gently nudges Sadie forward. "Go on," she says with a smile.

"*Sadie.*" I set the laundry aside as she steps into the house.

"Hey, Mom," she says casually, like she's been gone for a day instead of weeks. She drops her bag by the door and kicks off her boots with a practiced thud. The simplicity of the moment, the normalcy of it, is almost overwhelming.

I cross the room and pull her into a hug before I can stop myself. She freezes for a moment, stiff in my embrace, before she relaxes and lets out a small frustrated puff. "Mom, I'm fine," she mutters, but there's no real annoyance in her voice.

I step back, brushing a strand of hair from her face. "I've missed you," I say simply.

Her eyes soften as she looks at me. "I missed you too."

Conrad and Marsha step inside, both carrying small bags from the car. Conrad's arms are strong as he hugs me, murmuring, "You're doing good, Anna." Marsha follows, pulling me close before turning to Sadie. She ruffles Sadie's hair lightly, her voice soft as she says, "Welcome home, sweetheart."

Sadie flashes her grandparents a small smile. The connection between them is unspoken but deeply understood.

Marsha's voice is steady and gentle. "If you need anything, call. We're always here."

I nod, my throat tight. "Thank you." The words feel too small for everything that's happened, everything we've survived.

Marsha hesitates, glancing at Sadie. Her gaze softens, but when she looks back at me, there's still something guarded in her eyes. A question left unspoken.

Conrad exhales, then he reaches out, giving me a hug. "We have always loved you like a daughter. And that won't change. Never."

Tears fill my eyes, and I feel nothing but gratitude for the way they have cared for Sadie, for me. And when they questioned my choices, they were right to. They were always putting the safety of our family first.

After I came home from the hospital the night it all unraveled, I called them right away. They needed to know the truth.

They needed to hear from me that Parker, the man I planned on marrying, had murdered their son.

These is no easy way to say it, but I wanted to speak with

them before the police did. To explain what I could, to soften the rest.

They were devasted. Horrified. Stunned.

But also relieved.

Not only did we have answers – justice had been served.

Now, before they leave, they hold Sadie a moment longer, their arms wrapping around her like armor, as if they could shield her from the past.

After one last embrace, they turn toward their car. Marsha pauses with her hand on the door, looking at me like she wants to say something. I think she is going to turn away, leaving words unsaid.

But then she turns back to me and wraps her arms around me. She offers me the sort of hug I have needed ever since I was a little girl. The hug of a mother, accepting me just as I am.

The house is quieter when they leave. But for the first time in a long time, it doesn't feel haunted. Sadie is here. And that's what matters.

We sit on the couch, the silence between us filled with unspoken questions. Sadie looks around the living room, her gaze lingering on the familiar clutter—a half-read book on the coffee table, Caleb's blanket draped over the back of a chair. Finally, she turns to me, her expression cautious but curious.

"So," she starts, her voice light but probing, "what happened with Parker?"

The question hangs in the air, heavy and unavoidable. I am all pause and pulse. "Parker and I didn't work out," I say carefully, keeping my tone neutral.

Sadie raises an eyebrow, but to my surprise, she doesn't press for more. Instead, she leans back against the couch and says, "Good. He wasn't right for us."

Her words hit me with unexpected force. I blink, caught off guard by her maturity, her clarity. "You think so?" I ask, my voice wavering slightly.

She nods firmly. "Yeah. I never liked the way he looked at you. Like you were something he could control. You deserve better, Mom."

The conversation shifts to lighter topics after that—her time at the farm, the new calf she's been helping to care for, her plans for school. But even as we talk, her words echo in my mind, planting a seed of something I haven't felt in a long time: hope.

I see a path forward, not only for Sadie, but for both of us. My daughter's strength, her clarity—they remind me of the life we're still building, one step at a time.

And for the first time in forever, I believe we're going to be okay.

FIFTY-FIVE

ONE MONTH LATER

The scent of fresh paint still lingers in the air as Sadie and I sit on the floor of her newly redecorated bedroom. The room has been completely transformed, shedding its little-girl pink walls and butterfly decals for something more grown up. The soft, muted lavender Sadie picked out glows warmly in the light of the setting sun.

I run my hand over the smooth new comforter, admiring the way everything has finally come together. A framed print of sunflowers—Marla's idea—hangs above the bed, a bright burst of warmth against the cool tones. She'd been here a few days ago, helping us with the final touches, rolling up her sleeves and making quick work of the trim while Sadie chattered away.

"She really likes it," Sadie says now, following my gaze.

I smile. "Marla has good taste."

Sadie stretches out on the bed, letting out a long, contented sigh. "It feels... different now."

I tuck a strand of hair behind her ear, my fingers trailing over the paint still faintly speckled on her skin. "Because it *is* different," I say softly.

Sadie looks settled. Safe. I realize that, finally, I feel that way too.

A new white vanity, a gift from Aunt Jillian, sits in the corner, its mirror already cluttered with her lip glosses and hair ties.

Sadie grins as she surveys the room, her expression a mix of pride and contentment.

"It looks perfect," she says, brushing a stray lock of hair from her face.

"It looks like you," I reply, smiling. "Bright and full of life."

She laughs, a sound so genuine it makes my heart swell. "Buttercup thinks it's hers now," she teases, pointing at the stuffed rabbit propped against the pillows on her bed.

"Well, she's been with you through so much," I quip. "She deserves a place of honor."

Sadie rolls her eyes but grins, gently adjusting Buttercup so her ears flop right. For a moment, the weight of the past lifts, replaced by the simple joy of this moment. This room, this laughter—it's all a testament to moving forward, step by step.

As the evening stretches on, Sadie heads to the living room to watch television, and I find myself walking into my studio. The damage and debris were cleaned up weeks ago. Now, it is clean. A fresh slate. My workbench is empty, waiting for inspiration to strike. I'm not forcing it. I am curious to see where my heart, and my healing, will lead me.

My eyes fall on the framed photo sitting on my desk—Theo, Sadie and me, our smiles frozen in a happier time. I pick it up, tracing the edges with my fingers. I won't hide the parts of my story in the attic or storage unit anymore, and I won't keep them locked up in my heart either. It is time to embrace all of me. The pain, the loss, the love.

"We've come a long way," I whisper to no one in particular. Grief still clings to me like an old coat, worn and familiar, but it no longer defines me. There's resilience now, a strength I'd forgotten I had.

My phone buzzes from my jeans pocket, jolting me from my thoughts. I set the photo down carefully. Pulling out my phone, I glance at the screen. It's a text from Helen. The image attached shows her standing in front of a colorful mural in Mexico City, her sunglasses tilted playfully and a drink in hand.

The message reads: *Living my best life. You should try it sometime.* XOXO

A laugh escapes me, light and unburdened. Typical Helen. Even from miles away, she manages to remind me to let go and live.

Before I can put the phone down, another text comes through.

This time, it's from Grant: *Looking forward to tonight. See you soon.*

My heart skips slightly as I read his words. Grant. The man who walked into the chaos of my life and stayed. Who took a bullet—literally—and somehow emerged not only alive, but stronger. The man I should have never had, and the one I could never forget.

We were a mistake. An exquisite, devastating mistake. After Caleb died, I reached for Grant like a drowning woman clinging to air. But then he did what I never could—he chose the right thing. He walked away. Back to his wife. Back to his life. And left me with nothing but guilt and heartbreak.

And then Theo died. And Grant was already gone. So I chose Parker. Reliable, steady Parker. A man who made sense. A man who wasn't built from my grief and mistakes. I thought I was choosing stability and leaving the past behind. Instead, I walked into something far more dangerous.

But Grant came back. Divorced, untethered. And when he told me he still loved me, I was too deep in my own mess to believe I deserved it. But now? After everything?

He's more than my second chance. He's my choice.

Because love isn't about what's easy or what makes sense on paper. It's about who stays. Who stands in the wreckage with you and still reaches for your hand.

And this time, I'm reaching back.

I walk downstairs to snuggle with Sadie on the couch. The house doesn't feel haunted anymore. The ghosts of the past are quieter now, their presence less oppressive.

For years, I built dollhouses and arranged miniatures, perfect little worlds where everything was just so, where nothing could go wrong. They were my escape, my way of pretending, of making believe that a perfect life was possible if only I controlled every detail.

But I don't want perfect anymore. I don't want pretend.

I sit on the couch, letting the quiet settle around me. With an arm draped over Sadie, her head resting lightly against my shoulder, I realize I already have the real thing. I always have.

Messy, flawed, but undeniably real.

My mind drifts to my studio, to my new project. Grant hasn't asked what I'm working on. I haven't told him. Not yet.

I exhale slowly, my fingers brushing over Sadie's hair. The past is behind me. I've made sure of that.

Haven't I?

EPILOGUE

Client Notes from Parker Madison's Therapy Session

Client Name: Parker [Last Name Redacted]

Session Date: [Date Redacted]

Therapist: Dr. Miriam Locke, PsyD

Session Overview:
Parker, now serving a life sentence, continues to deflect responsibility for his crimes, clinging to delusions of victimhood. His psychological unraveling is evident, with growing paranoia and bitterness over his isolation. The focus of today's session was on accountability, though Parker remained combative and resistant.

Key Points:

- **Denial and Justification:** Parker repeatedly claimed, "I was protecting her," referring to Anna. He dismissed his actions as misunderstood, framing himself as a savior

while avoiding any acknowledgment of the lives he
destroyed.

- **Loss of Control:** Parker's once grandiose demeanor is crumbling. He admitted, "No one visits. No one cares." The dollhouse metaphor surfaced again, as he fixated on its destruction: "It was the only thing that made sense, and she ruined it."
- **Signs of Collapse:** His isolation and inability to control his surroundings have triggered what appears to be narcissistic collapse. Moments of silence during the session suggested the weight of his reality is finally sinking in—though he quickly masked it with defensive outbursts.

Therapist Notes:

Parker's arrogance has given way to bitterness and despair. While he remains defiant, cracks in his delusions are becoming visible. His life sentence ensures that the consequences of his actions are inescapable—a fitting end for a man who sought to control everything and lost it all.

Diagnosis:

1. Narcissistic Personality Disorder (301.81), with delusional tendencies.
2. Paranoid Personality Disorder (301.0), with marked distrust and suspicion of others, exacerbated by his incarceration and perceived abandonment.

Prognosis: Parker's refusal to engage with accountability cements his fate: a lifetime trapped in his own mind, abandoned and powerless.

A LETTER FROM ANYA

Hello, Readers!

First off—thank you. Truly. Writing *Love You to Death* was a wild, intense ride! I hope you felt every ounce of tension, every twist, every gut-punch moment I felt while bringing Anna and Sadie to life in Silverport.

If you want to stay in the loop on my latest releases (including my next thriller, *The Next Wife to Die*—yes, it's just as twisty as it sounds), you can sign up here:

www.bookouture.com/anya-mora

One of the most incredible parts of writing is hearing from readers like you. Did this book keep you up past your bedtime? Did it make your heart race? Did you root for Anna or want to protect Sadie at all costs? If *Love You to Death* had you flipping pages like your life depended on it, I'd love it if you left a quick review. It helps other readers find the book—and honestly, your words mean everything to me.

And if you're ready for another dark, addictive read... *The Next Wife to Die* is coming soon. Keep your eyes peeled.

With love and suspense,

Anya

KEEP IN TOUCH WITH ANYA

anyamora.com

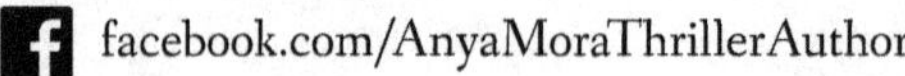 facebook.com/AnyaMoraThrillerAuthor

AUTHOR NOTE

Not all therapists are equal, and you will only get from them what you give. I have learned this the hard way. I spent two decades married to a man who lied and manipulated stories about me to his therapist, who then labeled me a narcissistic abuser without ever meeting me. This therapist's unsupported diagnosis of me alienated me from my children. My ex-husband used his therapist's words to vilify me to our children and created heartbreak I wish on no mother.

For these reasons, writing this novel was extremely difficult. In many ways, it feels like a mirror of my real life. However, my hope is that someone reading this who is dealing with abusive men will be reminded that they are not alone. You deserve access to your children. You deserve a bright, beautiful life, free of power games and control. I hope you find spaces to heal. You are loved.

—Anya

ACKNOWLEDGMENTS

First and foremost, thank you to my readers who support my storytelling. There are no words to express my gratitude for your thoughtful reviews of my books.

Thank you to my editor, Jess Whitlum-Cooper, who worked so hard on making this book all that it is. Thank you for believing in me!

And thank you to my agent, Sarah Hershman, who has championed my work for many years. Your faith in my writing has meant more than you will ever know.

Copyeditor
Ian Hodder

Proofreader
Lynne Walker

Marketing
Alex Crow
Melanie Price
Occy Carr
Cíara Rosney
Martyna Młynarska

Operations and distribution
Marina Valles
Stephanie Straub
Joe Morris

Production
Hannah Snetsinger
Mandy Kullar
Ria Clare
Nadia Michael

Publicity
Kim Nash
Noelle Holten
Jess Readett
Sarah Hardy

Rights and contracts
Peta Nightingale
Richard King
Saidah Graham